Shadows From Her Past

Melanie Robertson-King

King Park Press

Published by King Park Press

Copyright © Melanie Robertson-King, 2016

Cover design by Melanie Robertson-King

ISBN: 978-0-9921423-9-1

ACKNOWLEDGMENTS

There are a number of people I want to thank for making Shadows From Her Past a reality.

Once again, I'd like to thank the volunteers at the Aberdeen and North East Scotland History Society. Joyce Irvine provided me with information on criminal trials and sentences during the 1880s in Aberdeen.

Lynne Wilson, scotlandshistoryuncovered.com, who helped me determine which prison my criminals would have been sent to in Aberdeen. Thank you.

Thanks to Kathy Newland who recommended the book, *View from the Bedpan*, by Beverley June Richmond.

Thank you to the staff of the Aberdeen Central Library who gave me a tour of their facility, focusing on the Local Studies Department, when I visited in 2013.

Thanks to Jill Chalmers who helped me with all the references to the NHS (National Health Service).

Huge thanks to my great team of beta-readers – Sue Bowen, Berta Plaschka, Marike Harris, Laura Hone, and Julie Jordan.

I'd especially like to thank my husband, Don, who continues to support and encourage me, and provides a shoulder to cry on when things don't go well. He redesigned my website making it mobile-friendly. You've understood when meals became a bit too well done, and helped out on the domestic front so I could write.

1

Sarah groaned and tried to snuggle closer to Robert. The strong scent of disinfectant assailed her nostrils. A searing pain shot through her lower leg, raced up her thigh and settled in her hip. Her ankle hadn't bothered her since she sprained it the night she and Jenny escaped from the asylum. The sudden, burning pain surprised her.

"Look, Mum, she's awake."

That was her younger sister Rachel's voice. What was she doing in Sarah's and Robert's bedroom at Weetshill? Had she traveled back into the past, too? "Wh-where am I?" Sarah murmured. Her eyes flickered open. She raised her left arm to shield them from the bright light but was unable to hold it in that position. It dropped to the bed, limp.

Mrs. Shand rushed to her daughter's bedside. "You're in hospital. You've given us all a nasty scare."

"Where's Robert?" she asked, pushing a wayward lock of brown hair away from her face.

"Who?"

"M-my husband, we got married the other day over at Weetshill mansion," Sarah faltered.

"It's impossible, Sarah. That old place is derelict and has been for at least fifty years since they pulled the roof off it."

"No, it can't be. I was there, Mum, and it was beautiful. The granite walls were clean and sparkled in the sunlight. The windows were intact and the roof covered with slate tiles. And that's just on the outside. Inside there were huge fireplaces and the most gorgeous antique furniture. I don't think they thought of it as antique, though."

"Sarah, you've been here in hospital since August. Since the night you took my bottle of sleeping tablets and got hit by the car on the Kendonald Road."

"But ...," Sarah paused. Sleeping tablets? Hit by a car? What was her mother talking about? Those things never happened. She didn't know how she ended up in the past at Weetshill, but she did and that's what mattered to her. Sarah swallowed and continued, "You met him and the wee girl we adopted – Jenny. We saw you the day after our wedding. We had walked to the stone circle. While we were there, the farmhouse became visible again so we walked down the hill. I tell you I've been living at Weetshill," she cried out.

Sarah stared at her hand. She blinked a few times but her wedding band and her ruby and diamond engagement ring weren't there. The IV tube and the tape-covered needle where it went into the back of her hand were the only things there. "Wh-where are my rings?"

"In my bag. When they brought you in they had to cut them off you."

"Can I have them?"

"Yes." Mrs. Shand took out the small, manila envelope and gave it to her daughter.

"Not those ones," Sarah cried. "They're my birthstone and amber. I want my wedding and engagement rings." Seeing the gold gemstone reminded her of the trinket box in her room at Weetshill.

"But you're not married, Sarah," Rachel interjected.

"I am," she retorted.

A short, grey haired gentleman entered the room. Dressed in a red pinstriped dress shirt and black trousers, he wore a stethoscope around his neck. "So you've decided to join us again, young lady. I'm Doctor Compton, your consultant," he announced. The physician strode to the end of the bed and plucked her chart from the rack.

After skimming over the notes in it, he examined Sarah. He checked her pulse and blood pressure, and shone his torch in her eyes. "Hm, hm," he mumbled. "Your pulse is a wee bit quick and your blood pressure is up but otherwise, all seems to be quite in order, my dear. We'll keep close tabs on your vitals. It could be because you're awake and a touch agitated at the moment now. We'll order another CT scan to be certain," he stated, scribbling the results into her chart.

"Wh-why can't I move?"

"You've just woken up my dear girl. You've been in a coma since August. You need to build your strength up again. That's why you're unable to move," the doctor replied.

Sarah tried to prop herself up on her elbows but didn't have the strength. She stared towards the foot of her bed. "But why don't I remember any of this?" she asked.

"It would be the head injury," he stated, plunging his hands into his trouser pockets. "We've kept you in a drug-induced coma so your brain would have a chance to recover from the trauma. We've been gradually bringing you out of it hoping you would wake up. You will have a long road to a complete recovery, I'm afraid. It's going to take a lot of hard work and commitment on your part."

"My throat hurts like bloody hell."

"Sarah," her mother scolded.

"You're all right. I've heard far worse," he conceded to Mrs. Shand smiling before turning back to his patient. "You've only been off the ventilator since the day before yesterday. It's very common to have a sore throat."

Sarah cocked her head to one side. Zaphod Beeblebrox from *The Hitchhiker's Guide to the Galaxy* flashed into her mind. She giggled.

"This is no laughing matter, young lady."

"Sorry, thought of something funny. Not even sure where it came from."

Doctor Compton continued, "You were on the ventilator so it could breathe for you. When you reached a level of consciousness where you began fighting it, we took you off it. In other words, you were breathing on your own. Do you remember anything about the accident?"

"What accident? I sprained my ankle a while back and the groom at Weetshill gave me a right going over."

"Not those incidents."

"If not either of them, what then? On 30th October, I married Robert Robertson, the Laird of Weetshill."

"Oh Sarah," Mrs. Shand moaned, tightening her grip on Sarah's right hand.

"Disorientation and confusion are common for the first while after waking."

"I'm neither. Now will someone please tell me what's going on and why I'm here?"

Doctor Compton pulled up a chair and sat down. He stroked his chin and began. "When you were first brought in here on 10th August, we didn't think you would make it. Your injuries were most grave. You were struck by a car, thrown over the bonnet into the windscreen and over the top. According to police, it was travelling at least sixty miles per hour. The force of the impact broke both your legs. You landed on the road and struck your head on the tarmac. The impact fractured your skull, resulting in bleeding and severe swelling of your brain. You also had several broken ribs but luckily no internal bleeding. You arrested on us in A&E three times before we were able to get your condition stabilized."

"Arrested? You mean my heart stopped?"

"Yes."

Sarah recalled watching episodes of *Casualty* on television and seeing the defibrillator used. The vision in her mind frightened her.

"You did give us all a scare but you're a strong young lady. As I said earlier, there's no reason to think you won't make a complete recovery, but I warn you, it will take time."

"Are you sure?"

"Yes, dear; I wouldn't say it otherwise." Dr. Compton continued, "Once we got you stabilized, we took you to the orthopedic trauma unit. The specialist surgical teams there went to work to repair the damage to your legs. After surgery, we kept you under heavy sedation so your brain would have a chance to heal."

"So you're telling me I dreamt everything that happened to me at Weetshill?"

"Yes, I'm afraid so. The subconscious acts in mysterious ways we will never understand. I must go now. I'll leave word at the desk you're awake. Mr. Youssef, the head orthopedic trauma surgeon, will be in to see you in the next day or so. He'll explain your surgery to you."

"It can't be. It can't be," Sarah sighed. "I know I was at Weetshill. I've been there since August. I kept telling them I lived at Gordonsfield but when Robert took me there, the farm didn't exist. He told me the land belonged to the Christies. It's been in our family, like forever. You or dad never said any different. I went to the stone circle, too. The fields were full of gorse and long grass except for one area where Mrs. Christie had a small rose garden. Those fields aren't like that. Am I losing my mind, Mum?" Tears pricked at her eyes then rolled down her cheeks in scorching rivulets.

"No, Sarah. I don't know how the accident has affected you but you're not losing your mind. I'm going to ring your father and tell him you're awake. He's been so worried about you. If not for the farm, he would be here, too."

"What about the B&B? It's so important to you. You can't be here and at home running it, too."

"Your Gran has helped. It's taking its toll on her, Sarah. She's too old to be looking after a house that size and extra people all the time. Now you're awake, I can spend more time at the house and let her rest."

"You mean you're going to start leaving me alone here?"

4

"I'll still be here every day. I've told your Gran not to worry about evening meals. It's too much and until you're fit and well again, there won't be any. I'll be back every afternoon and stay with you until they make me leave."

"Mum, I do love you, you know. I didn't mean to put you through all this grief. Did I really take your sleeping tablets?"

"I found the empty bottle at the stone circle. No boy is worth taking your life over, Sarah. You were angry and upset over Blair cheating on you and probably even more so because it was with Niamh. Your father and I should have been more understanding and listened to you when you tried to tell us. How were we to know you were going to run off and get yourself half killed? If we had, we would have given you the attention you craved."

"Oh Mum," Sarah wailed.

"You rest now. I'm off to ring your father."

"Please tell dad to come see me. I need to see him. It's important."

After Mrs. Shand left the room, Sarah turned to Rachel. "You believe me, don't you? I'm not crazy. I don't know what happened or how but I did spend time at Weetshill and I married the Laird. You saw him. Jenny, too. You were at the house when we came and I said my goodbyes because I belonged with them and was happy there."

"And when did this take place?" Rachel mocked.

"1886 a couple of days before the opening of grouse season. Robert's grandfather died on the twelfth. We had to make alternate arrangements for the shooters who had come. One of them was an archaeology professor. We talked about ley lines, the stone circle, and mystical powers over our meal one night. Anyway, Angus arranged for them to hunt on neighboring land."

"Sarah, I think you've gone around the twist. There is no way you would end up in 1886 when you got hit by a car."

Sarah clenched the bottom sheet, frustrated no one believed her. "I know what happened to me. I was at Weetshill in 1886. It was beautiful. I married the Laird," she yelled and took a deep breath before continuing. "He's handsome and older and the kindest man I could ever meet. Nothing at all like Blair ...," her voice trailed off.

Mrs. Shand returned. "Girls, I could hear you squabbling well down the corridor. Keep it down. There *are* other patients in this unit."

"Sorry, Mum," Rachel answered first.

Sarah gawped at her sister and mother. "I can't believe you don't remember meeting Robert and Jenny. Dad will remember them. I know he will. All three of you were there. Robert swore to dad he would keep me safe. Jenny hid behind me because she was afraid of you lot."

"You're tired and confused, Sarah. Tomorrow you'll see things a lot clearer. It's getting late, Rachel. We should make a start for Gordonsfield," Mrs. Shand said leaning down to hug her daughter.

Sarah lifted her arms and returned her mother's embrace. "Can you raise the head of my bed before you leave please, Mum?"

Her mother pushed the button raising Sarah into a sitting position from which she got a good look at her legs. Her left one had a sort of cage thing around it. Worse though, it appeared embedded in her lower leg. Metal disappeared inside the bandages swathing it.

Watching her mother and sister leave, tears ran down Sarah's face. She didn't know if she was sad because they were going or because Robert and Jenny only existed in her mind. It was all too much to take in. And what of Doctor Compton's conversation with her? Had she been in a drug-induced coma all this time and just taken off a ventilator?

2

"Mary Elizabeth, John Bryce, Jenny. Why don't the three of you go outside and play?" Margaret suggested. "It's a beautiful day. You don't need to be cooped up indoors. Make sure you put your outer clothes on before you go out."

"A fine idea. Listen to your mother and your auntie," Robert reiterated. He loved his niece, nephew and daughter with all his heart. Still, three children under the age of ten stuck inside had taxed his patience to the breaking point. He worried about Sarah, too, and that added to his foul humor.

Shutting his newspaper, he tossed it onto the coffee table. Robert strode to the window that faced the direction of Gordonsfield. Only a day before he, Sarah and Jenny had walked to the stone circle and then down the hill and met her parents. He made a solemn vow to Sarah's father he would look after her and now he had failed. Sarah was gone and he had no clue to her whereabouts.

"I-I love you father," Jenny stammered, hugging him.

Hearing her refer to him that way melted the hardness in his heart and he squatted down and hugged her back. "I love you, too. Now off you go." He kissed the small girl on the forehead before dismissing her.

Jenny paused by the front door. She wanted Robert to hug her again and convince her everything would be all right and Sarah would return. Still, deep in her heart, she knew they had lost Sarah and she missed her terribly. She dashed back into the mansion before returning to her waiting cousins.

"Come on Jenny. Must you be so slow?" John Bryce asked.

"She's smaller than us," Mary Elizabeth said in Jenny's defense.

"So what," he snorted.

"I-I had to t-tell f-father I l-loved him," Jenny spluttered once she caught up with the others.

"He's not your father," John Bryce sneered.

"Is t-too."

"Stop teasing her," Mary Elizabeth demanded, slapping her brother's arm. "Let's go over to the stone circle Jenny told us about. Come on. I'll race you both. Bet I can win." And with that, she took off on the run leaving the other two to catch up.

John Bryce soon overtook his sister leaving Jenny behind.

"C-c-come on," she cried out, "W-wait for m-me."

"Aw come on, Jenny, you're such a wee baby. Stay back there on your own and Sawney Bean will come and get you." He taunted turning and running backwards.

Mary Elizabeth stopped and waited for the little girl to catch up.

"Wh-who's Sawney Bean?" Jenny asked.

"A cannibal that eats wee girls that can't keep up," John Bryce answered chuckling.

Jenny froze in her tracks. She looked around searching for the person her cousin had mentioned.

"John Bryce, you are truly incorrigible. Scaring Jenny with tales of Sawney Bean," Mary Elizabeth scolded.

"You and your big words. I'll wager you don't even know what it means."

"Come, Jenny," she coaxed, extending her hand. Turning her head and thrusting her nose in the air, she uttered a loud "Harrumph."

Jenny took the offered hand and imitated her older cousin's actions. The two continued up the laneway to the Kendonald Road, leaving John Bryce behind.

"Come on," Mary Elizabeth called to her brother. "Or perhaps I should set Sawney Bean on you."

"L-l-look, o-over th-there," Jenny stuttered and pointed to the laneway leading to the stone circle. She started across the road but stopped part way. One of the saplings on the far side a few yards closer to Kendonald looked much older. The trunk was fatter and had a funny looking scar like something had hit it. She crept closer, knowing the last time she'd seen the tree it was the size of her wrist.

When she reached out to touch it, something shiny on the ground distracted her. Jenny bent down and retrieved the item. "I-I found s-something," she called out. "I-I'm g-going t-to take it t-to f-father."

"Don't be such a baby, Jenny," John Bryce taunted.

Jenny ignored his jibes and ran back to Weetshill clutching the foreign object in her hand. "F-father," she yelled, charging through the front door. "L-look wh-what I f-found."

Mrs. MacEwen intercepted her. "Slow down child. Whatever has you in such a state?"

"I-I f-found th-this," she stuttered holding the foreign object out for the housekeeper to see.

Robert entered the great hall from the library. He knelt by Jenny and looked at what she held in her hand. Was this the thing Sarah was so upset over losing on her arrival at Weetshill? He'd never seen anything like it before. "Calm down, Jenny. Deep breaths and tell me where you found this." He took her hand and led her into the library. Sitting in Sarah's favorite chair, he lifted the child onto his lap.

Jenny nodded. "A-a t-tree. S-saw it b-bigger. F-found th-this in th-the g-grass n-near it."

"You miss Sarah, don't you? So do I," Robert assured hugging the small girl. "She'll be back, I promise." He hoped he spoke the truth. He wanted Sarah back so much it hurt. He could not imagine the pain Jenny felt because of Sarah's disappearance. There was a bond between them he would never understand, but it was there and he would do nothing to shatter it. He had to find Sarah and bring her back, not only for his sake, but for Jenny's, too. And he would do whatever it took to reunite his family. "Off you go and play with your cousins." Robert patted her head and sent her off then stood and walked to the window facing Gordonsfield. The emptiness in his heart made him feel like he had a weight crushing down on his chest. If it weren't for the wee girl, he'd crawl into his bed and stay there for the rest of his life.

As Jenny skipped out of the library, he held the futuristic object with his index finger over one end. When it vibrated he dropped it like it scorched him. Robert examined his hand but there were no burn marks. He gawked at the device on the floor. Now there were pictures on it. They weren't visible when Jenny first brought it into the house and gave it to him.

Robert picked it up and in so doing, touched one of the pictures. It changed to a single larger image. "Have you ever seen the like?" he uttered.

Margaret joined her brother and looked over his shoulder. "Never. What manner of thing is it?"

"I have no clue," Robert replied. He brushed his finger against it and the image changed again. This time, Sarah's name and a series of numbers showed on the device. It had to be the object Sarah was so worried about losing. But how did Jenny come to find it? He tucked it in his coat pocket and walked to the door.

"I'm going out for a walk, Margaret. I shan't be long."

"Would you like me to join you?"

"No, you stay and work on your needlepoint."

Robert recalled Jenny's description of the tree being different and he had to investigate. With the butler's help, he slipped into his overcoat. Putting on his hat and gloves he walked out the mansion's front door.

The laneway from the house to the Kendonald Road appeared normal. The closer he got to the main artery running through the parish, the darker it became yet it was still early in the day. By the time he arrived, it was pitch black.

Two strange glowing red, flashing lights blazed in the inky darkness. Below those, two shone solid white. Smaller orange ones blinked at the opposite end of the strange object. Despite his fear, Robert sprinted to the location and ran his hand over the shiny, smooth surface. The door on the right hand side was open but there was no one inside. Was this one of those vehicles Sarah had told him about? It had to be. There was no other explanation.

The trees lining the road were larger than he knew them to be. It was impossible for them to grow that much in such a short time. Back in the direction of the Weetshill laneway, Sarah laid on the road with someone crouched over her. He recognized her at once. She wore the same clothes she had on the night she first crashed into his life. He snapped his head around and looked at the tree then back to Sarah. Was this person responsible for Sarah's injuries?

While he stared in disbelief, the skies returned to the cloudless blue from earlier. The trees were saplings and the strange vehicle no longer rested against one of them.

The children. Were they safe? Robert charged up the track across the fields to Gleanstane and the stone circle. Reaching the road bisecting the fields, he saw three heads bobbing among the stones. Knowing they were all right, he slowed down and walked the rest of the distance.

When Jenny saw him, she called out, "F-father."

"Is it time to come home, Uncle Robert?" John Bryce asked.

At first Robert didn't hear them. He was too preoccupied with his encounter down at the Kendonald Road. When he and Margaret played at the stone circle as children, strange things appeared to him. Sarah and her grandmother had on more than one occasion. The farmhouse at the foot of the hill that he, Jenny and Sarah had visited and met Sarah's family wasn't there. Things were as they had always been. Nothing had changed.

3

Sarah flopped back on the bed and stared at the ceiling. The air in the corner shimmered and she turned her head in its direction. Was it? No, it couldn't be. It had to be her imagination. She continued staring and two figures materialized in the space. A man and a little girl, Robert and Jenny, appeared in front of her.

Seeing them confused Sarah more than she already was. Perhaps it was a hallucination brought on by all the drugs they had pumped into her. "You're here. How did you get here? How did you find me? Please help me, Robert."

"Dearest Sarah, by all that is Holy, what manner of things have they done to you? You're trussed up like a Christmas goose." His golden-brown eyes were moist with tears.

"I'm fine, Robert. Honest, I am. But I missed you." She turned to Jenny. "And I missed you, too, sweetie."

"S-Sarah hurt?" the little girl asked.

"I was but I'm all the better for seeing you," she replied and patted the bed beside her.

Jenny turned to Robert who nodded, then clambered up and cuddled to Sarah.

"I missed you."

"J-Jenny m-missed S-Sarah, t-too."

Sarah wished she could roll over and hold Jenny to her. Since she couldn't, she had to settle for letting the little girl snuggle and wrap her arms around her. It required keeping her IV tubes from becoming tangled in the web of arms.

Holding the child almost reduced Sarah to tears, she was so happy to be with Robert and Jenny again. Despite standing next to her bed, he hadn't tried to kiss her or touch her. Worried by his lack of physical contact, she looked up at him. "I won't break. You can touch me." The realization the two most important people in her life in the past were here in the present with her made her gasp. "How did you end up here – in my time?" Sarah asked.

"I don't know. Jenny found this and brought it to me," he replied reaching into his pocket. After a few seconds of fumbling, he extracted the object and held it out to her.

"My iPhone," Sarah exclaimed. "Where did you find it? How did you find it?"

"Jenny found it and brought it to me. Dear God, what of the other children? John Bryce and Mary Elizabeth – we were on our way back from the stone circle at Glea-Gordonsfield," he corrected. "And now Jenny and I are here? How could that be? And what's more important, where *is* here?"

"They tell me I'm in Aberdeen Royal Infirmary. But that doesn't explain how you both got here. It's over thirty miles away from Weetshill. Not to mention, it's almost two hundred years in your future," Sarah answered. She placed her phone on the bed beside her and reached for Robert with her left hand.

"Where are your rings?"

What could she tell him? She'd lost them? The hospital took them? "I-I'm not sure where they are. Please don't be angry. I don't remember taking them off but maybe they're in the trinket box in my room at Weetshill?"

Robert opened his mouth to speak but stopped. The sound of approaching footsteps grew louder and he gathered Jenny up into his arms in preparation of a hasty escape.

"B-but J-jenny d-doesn't w-want to l-leave S-Sarah."

Sarah looked at them. "Please stay," she pleaded.

"I thought I heard voices in here," a man stated entering the room. "But that would be impossible because there's no telly and I know your mum and sister left a short time ago."

Sarah stared at the far corner where Robert and Jenny had dematerialized. They were gone.

The man wore a sky-blue tunic and navy trousers with a stethoscope hanging out of a front shirt pocket. He stole a glimpse at the corner like he'd seen something but returned his attention to Sarah. "I'm on duty this evening so checking in on you. We've nicknamed you Sleeping Beauty. Now you're awake we'll have to come up with something else."

The next thing Sarah knew, he was next to her bed holding her wrist. She knew he was taking her pulse but his touch was gentle like Robert's. He resembled Robert, too. Not enough to say he *was* Robert, but perhaps a brother or a close cousin. He even had the same curly, dark brown Robertson hair.

"It's good to see you awake. I know this sounds crass but the staff here in intensive care have started a pool betting on when you'd wake up. Yeah, I was in on it, too; telling you up front before you hear it from one of the nurses or Sister Sutherland, the head. I think I might have hit the jackpot."

"Y-you bet on when I'd wake up?" Sarah couldn't believe what she'd heard. It was bad enough she was stuck in hospital without Robert and Jenny. Finding out people were placing bets on when or *if* she would come around? It beggared belief.

"Your mum has been here every day since they brought you in," he defended checking on both of her legs. "Wouldn't leave you despite our assurances we would ring with any developments."

"Wh-who are you?" Sarah asked. "You look so familiar."

"David. David Robb – medical student here at ARI."

"I feel like I know you from somewhere."

"Unless you've been in here before. Visited our A&E department? I do rotations there, too, then I can't think where you would have seen me before. I work. I sleep. I live this place. Sometimes I live *in* this place. Grab a few hours kip in one of the resident's lounges."

Sarah raised her arm so he could wrap the blood pressure cuff around it. As it tightened, she closed her eyes.

"Much better than when Doctor Compton took it earlier," he cited. Writing the numbers into her chart, he bent down to check something on the side of her bed. "Output is good, too."

"Output? What are you talking about? I *am* here. Talk in language I can understand."

"Sorry. I'm used to you being asleep when I'm in here. Output. Well, you have a catheter and at the end of it, is a bag collecting your urine. We check it to make sure your kidneys are still functioning as they should. And yours are doing fine."

"Oh," Sarah answered. "When will I be able to get out of bed?"

"Not for a while, yet. You've just woken from a coma. And that decision isn't up to me. It's something you need to discuss with Doctor Compton, your consultant. He'll be in to see you again tomorrow."

"Can I have some water, please?"

"Sure." David walked to the tray table to fill her glass. He picked up the jug and swirled the water in it. "Ugh, warm. Let me freshen it up for you. Back in a flash." He smiled and left the room.

Sarah shrank back into the pillows. Her worst nightmare had come true. She had returned to her own time without her beloved Robert and Jenny.

Before she could dwell on it any longer, David returned with her refilled pitcher. As he poured, the ice cubes toppled in and splashed water on the table. "Let me help you," he offered. Putting his hand behind her back, he helped her to a sitting position and held the Styrofoam cup at an angle to her lips so she could drink.

"Thank you."

David eased her back down and ensured the call button was within her reach. He dimmed the lights, winked at her and left.

In the corridor, David leaned back against the wall. He had seen something in Sarah's room, but what? He couldn't explain it. Being a medical student, he did put in many long hours so in the end passed it off to lack of sleep.

Scrubbing his face with his hands, he set out for the nurses' desk near the lifts. "Quiet on the floor tonight?" David asked.

"So far," the woman replied without looking up. "You off home now?"

"Not for a bit. Have some paperwork I have to catch up on. Then I'm off for twenty-four hours. Here are my notes on Miss Shand, if you would enter them for me."

"What am I, your secretary?" She looked up at him, her brown eyes boring into him.

"Ah come on, you love me, you know you do. I'm so knackered I'm afraid I'll make a mistake." He looked at her ID badge then added, "Jill."

David patted the back of her hand and strolled to the lift. As the doors opened, something in the darkened family room moved. He ignored the elevator and walked to the room's entrance. It was empty. Shaking his head, he returned and jabbed the button as the doors closed.

After stepping into the empty elevator, David pondered the strange occurrences. He couldn't ask anyone about them. Fearing they would think he was crazy and section him under the mental health act. He couldn't afford that. Not if he were to become a doctor. He stopped in the student lounge and sat down in front of one of the computers. A sharp tap on the space bar brought the screen to life. At least what he had to do was simple clicks of the mouse – almost impossible to bugger that up. Task finished, he stepped through the archway into the locker room. A row of benches separated two banks of lockers.

David removed his street clothes from the one bearing his surname on the door. He laid them on the bench, pulled his stethoscope from his neck and placed it on the shelf. After changing, he wadded his uniform up and dropped it in the hamper on his way out the door.

Outside the hospital, the cold, damp air cut through David's body like a knife. He zipped his leather bomber jacket up and thrust his hands in his jeans pockets. Jogging out onto the main road, he wound his way through the quiet, residential streets to Whitehall Place and his flat.

Robert stopped in his tracks. He was back on the laneway to Weetshill. How did he get back? Where had he been? Reunited with Sarah for a brief time was bliss but the events surrounding it were terrifying. He felt a tug on his arm and looked down at his side. Jenny stood there, gripping his hand. Without warning, he realized he was shaking. He'd been at the stone circle and on his way home but somehow between then and now, he went somewhere else. Not so much of a place but a time, and an unrecognizable one at that. Not even the fantastic things he experienced at the Edinburgh Exhibition compared to what he saw and heard. Beads of cold, clammy sweat formed on the nape of his neck and trickled down his back making him shiver. Jenny would ask questions about their experience and how they ended up with Sarah. What was wrong with her? Why all the tubes and wires? How could he answer the little girl when he couldn't explain the events himself?

"F-father?" Jenny asked.

"Yes," he drawled trying to prolong the inevitable.

"Wh-where w-were we? Wh-what w-was wr-wrong with S-Sarah?"

Kneeling down, Robert drew Jenny to him and hugged her. "I'm not sure. I think we were in Aberdeen in a hospital."

"H-how d-did w-we g-get th-there?"

"I don't know. One minute we were walking back to Weetshill from the stone circle and the next we were ... there." He stood. "We must get home now. Make sure John Bryce and Mary Elizabeth got back there without mishap. Margaret would never forgive me if something were to happen to them. Come along. It's not much further now."

Robert worried about his niece and nephew the rest of the trip back to the mansion. He stepped into the library and breathed a sigh of relief seeing them both there with his sister.

"Where did you and Jenny go, Uncle Robert?" John Bryce asked. "One minute you were walking ahead of us, then you were gone," he continued his eyes wide as saucers.

"He's right," Mary Elizabeth piped up. "It's hard to explain but one minute you were both there and then you faded away until you were gone. It was most frightening."

"All right, children that's enough. Why don't the three of you go play upstairs so I can talk to Robert in private."

Jenny wrapped her arms around Robert and clung to him.

"It will be fine. You go with your cousins. I'll come and find you after I'm done talking with Auntie Margaret."

A tear rolled down the little girl's cheek and Robert brushed it away. He kissed her forehead, and patted her on the backside. "Now off you go."

She stopped inside the door and looked back at him.

"Do as I say, Jenny," he snapped.

Bottom lip quivering, she turned and bolted out of the room.

"Suppose you tell me what all this is about," Margaret chirped. "My children returned terror-stricken."

Robert dropped onto the sofa and dragged his hands through his hair. He wasn't sure he could explain it any better to an adult than his young daughter.

"You look like you could use this," Margaret commented. Her skirts swished as she moved about the room.

He glanced up and saw his sister's outstretched hand holding a glass of whisky. "Thank you. I could use a dram after that experience."

Margaret sat in the armchair next to him. "I'm listening."

Taking a gulp, and plunking the glass on the coffee table, Robert began. "I'm not sure where to start, but Jenny found something – something belonging to Sarah. You saw it. I showed it to you. After she brought it to me, and I sent her to catch up with the others, I went to where she said she had found it."

"That doesn't explain the fear instilled in my children, Robert."

"I know but I have to start at the beginning." He paused and took another drink. "So I went to where Jenny told me she had found the object. She hadn't made much sense when she came in ... talking of trees being larger than they should be and other strange things. Well, when I reached the Kendonald Road, it was black as night. The trees were larger and there was a carriage, the like of, I've never seen before crashed into one of them. I turned back towards our laneway and I saw Sarah lying in the road and some other person kneeling over her."

"Oh, Robert," she lamented wringing her hands. "That is the most far-fetched thing I've ever heard of."

"You must believe me, Margaret. You must," he implored, taking her hands in his and squeezing.

"Did my children witness any of what you've just told me?"

"No. The only person who saw something strange was Jenny. She didn't see the carriage or Sarah or this other person," he answered. He then whispered almost under his breath, "until later."

"I heard that, Robert."

"After what I saw on the Kendonald Road, I was frightened for the children. Hoping they were at the stone circle, I went there. When I got close enough, I saw their heads bobbing amongst the stones so I knew they were safe." Robert picked up his glass and drained the remaining contents, stood and paced about the room.

"Will you please tell me what happened?" Margaret demanded.

Robert sat down on the sofa. "John Bryce asked if it were time to leave. I don't remember what I told him. I remember taking Jenny's hand and we started walking towards Weetshill." He sprang to his feet and strode to the window. "I don't know how to explain it. Jenny and I were on our way here, except we ended up elsewhere."

"Really," Margaret belittled.

"When Sarah was here, she and Professor Ross talked about the theory of mystical lines joining sacred places like stone circles. Sarah called them ... called them ..." Robert struggled to find the word he wanted. "Ley lines," he blurted out. "As well you know, there are no shortage of stone circles here in Aberdeenshire." Robert turned his back to the window.

Margaret twisted in her chair and stared at him. "Will you please get to the point?"

"I'm getting there. This is the part that's hardest to explain. We, Jenny and I, we ended up in what I believe to be a hospital in Aberdeen, but it was nothing like I had ever seen before. Sarah was there in a bed with transparent wires and whatnot coming out of her from everywhere, it seemed. Funny boxes with blinking lights made strange beeping noises. My poor Sarah looked like she was trussed up like a Christmas goose. But worst of all was this thing her leg was impaled on and in more than one place. It was something out of a torture chamber in Edgar Allan Poe's works."

Margaret looked down her nose at him.

"The most amazing thing though, was wee Jenny wasn't at all frightened by any of it. She climbed up onto the bed and cuddled with Sarah. It did my heart good to see them together like that."

"And you expect me to believe this malarkey?" Margaret asked before taking her brother's side by the window.

"I am telling you the truth," Robert insisted. "I'll swear it on the Bible if needs must."

"That won't be necessary. But how can you expect me to believe such a tale?" She took his hands in hers, like he had done earlier.

"I know it sounds incredible – beyond incredible, but that's what happened. It was terrifying yet fascinating in equal measure. During the time Jenny and I were there, wherever that was; with Sarah we heard voices. The next thing I knew we were back on the laneway to Weetshill. Dearest sister, I *wish* you would believe me."

Margaret hugged him then left him on his own in the library.

"Robert, come now," Margaret shrieked.

He raced out of the library following his sister's hysterical voice. He found her and her children standing in the doorway of what was once his elder brother's room. Jenny twitched and convulsed on the oak floor.

Robert charged to the child, snatched her up into his arms and held her close. She was in the midst of a seizure. He had seen it before and hoped holding Jenny in this way was the right thing to do. Her eyes rolled back showing the whites of her eyes, scaring him. He thought for sure she was dead.

When the seizure ended Jenny's eyes returned to normal. She blinked a few times then spoke. "Wh-what's wr-wrong w-with m-me?"

"My darling, wee lassie, there is nothing wrong with you. You had a bit of a fright today and this was how your body dealt with it." Robert stood up, holding Jenny in his arms. "Let's get you to your room. I think you've had enough excitement for one day."

"B-but J-Jenny is h-hungry."

Robert chuckled. The wee girl felt better and appeared to be fine despite suffering the fit. "All right. We'll see if Mrs. MacEwen can't find something for you to eat, but I still want you in bed afterwards.

You need a good night's rest. I'll get Archibald to summon Doctor Burnett to come and examine you."

"J-Jenny all right."

"I know you are but I want a professional opinion."

The housekeeper met them at the foot of the main staircase. "I heard the ruckus, sir. Is the wee lassie all right?" Mrs. MacEwen asked, wiping her hands on her apron.

"She's fine now but hungry. Can you see she gets something to eat? I want her to have an early night. Oh and, Mrs. MacEwen, can you ask Archibald if he could get word to the doctor? I'd like him to come and look at Jenny this evening, if possible."

"Aye, sir. Come wi' me, Jenny, I's sure cook has somethin' in the kitchen you can have."

Jenny hugged Robert before scrambling out of his arms and taking the housekeeper's hand. She skipped alongside the older woman as if nothing had happened.

Robert's heart warmed at the sight, but his mood darkened because Sarah wasn't there to see how happy Jenny appeared.

About an hour later, the butler announced the evening meal. Robert entered the dining room first followed a short time later by his sister and her children.

"Is wee Jenny all right?" Margaret asked as Archibald seated her.

"I think so but I've sent for Doctor Burnett to be certain."

"An excellent idea. You can never be too sure," she replied spreading her napkin over her lap.

"John Bryce would you like to say grace before we eat?" Robert asked his nephew.

"Ouch! Why did you do that, Mary Elizabeth? Why did you kick me?" the young boy yelped.

"Children, please. You know you wouldn't be acting up if your father were still here at Weetshill," Margaret scolded.

"Sorry mama," Mary Elizabeth apologized. She unfolded her napkin and laid it on her lap.

"John Bryce, Uncle Robert asked you to say grace," Margaret stated, her voice filled with authority.

Rolling his eyes, he muttered something and followed it up with a rousing 'amen'."

Once the maids brought the food in and served, they withdrew.

Robert stood and carved the roast. "Have you heard from George since he returned to the city, Margaret?"

"No. It takes time to sell a shop. He'll have to be in Edinburgh until he completes the transaction."

"The children – they should be in school. We have a fine one here in Kendonald."

"And shouldn't Jenny, too?" she retorted.

"Yes," Robert replied passing a slice of meat to his niece.

"Thank you, Uncle Robert," Mary Elizabeth replied.

"I'm surprised the truant officials haven't been looking for your children. It is November, after all."

"John Bryce and Mary Elizabeth were in an exclusive private school in Edinburgh. Besides, they've not missed too much. They came up with their father on your wedding day."

"You're absolutely right. Still, you don't want them falling behind in their studies with a school close by."

"I'm not sure I want them going to a village one. What sort of children attend?"

"You're being a snob, Margaret. There is nothing wrong with the Kendonald School. And, if you are so concerned then take your children back to Edinburgh." The words spilled out before Robert had a chance to take them back.

"Finish your meals quickly, children. We're catching the next train home. I'll not stay in this house and have my brother who is in love with a harlot who married him for his wealth insult me. Now she has it, she's run off."

Robert dropped into his chair. Things hadn't gone the way he hoped. He loved having his sister and her children at Weetshill. They were company for Jenny. Since Sarah's disappearance, having them there had been a Godsend for him and his stepdaughter.

"Sorry to intrude, sir, but Doctor Burnett is here," the butler announced.

"Thank you, Archibald. Show him into the library and I'll be with him in a moment."

"Aye, sir."

"I am so sorry, dearest Margaret. I didn't mean that. Of course I want you and the children to stay here. And you are right Jenny needs to be in school, too. Why don't we go and speak with the schoolmaster tomorrow?" he stood. "If you'll excuse me, I must go to Doctor Burnett."

Robert left the dining room, wondering about sending Jenny to school. With her stuttering problem and her seizures, wouldn't it be better to hire a governess? Get someone to come to Weetshill for her, and the other children? Once he ensured Jenny was fine, he would discuss the matter with Margaret.

"Ah, Doctor Burnett, so kind of you to come so quickly," Robert greeted entering the library.

"Miss Jenny isn't well?"

"She had a seizure. I want to ensure there are no lasting effects from it."

"Very well. Shall we go see her?" the doctor responded.

Robert led the way to Jenny's room. His mind jumped from one thought to another. Governess. Sarah. Jenny. Village school, Jenny, experience at the stone circle which took him to a different time. "Here we are, Doctor," he stated and knocked on the door before opening it.

Jenny sat on the dressing table stool and Janet stood behind her brushing the little girl's hair. "I'll leave you now, sir. Wee Jenny is ready for bed," the young maid stated before she scurried past the men into the corridor.

"Thank you, Janet," Robert called after her.

"Well there, lassie, let's have a look at you," Doctor Burnett comforted. "Robert here was worried about you."

"F-father?" she asked.

"It's all right, Jenny. I'll be right here," Robert answered sitting in the rocking chair near the window. The furnishings in this room were much like in Sarah's. The only difference was the huge dollhouse and all the accoutrements that went with it. The thought of his missing bride made him wistful and he sighed.

Jenny scrambled off the stool and bounded over to the doctor. "S-see, J-jenny f-fine."

Doctor Burnett took his stethoscope out of his bag and handed it to Jenny. "Can you look after it while I get a few more things?"

She nodded and immediately put it around her neck and placed the horn on her chest. "J-jenny n-not h-hear anything."

"That's because, these have to be in your ears," the doctor replied and put the ear pieces where they needed to be. "Now can you hear?"

Jenny listened then smiled. A moment later, she had the horn pressed against the physician's chest.

"Who is the doctor and who is the patient here," he chuckled.

Even Robert laughed.

After looking in Jenny's eyes and mouth, the physician took her pulse and felt the glands in her neck. He wrestled his stethoscope back and pronounced the little girl to be in fine fettle.

"It's such a relief." Robert stood and made his way to the physician and his patient.

While the doctor gathered his equipment and returned it to his bag, Robert helped Jenny into bed. "I told you I wanted you to have an early night after today," he reiterated.

Once he had her tucked in and kissed goodnight, Robert escorted Doctor Burnett downstairs. "Thank you so much for coming. I was worried about Jenny, especially after she had another seizure. I've never seen one this bad before."

"She's a fine wee lassie. I don't think you have much to worry about, although when your wife was here, she was in better health. What on earth has happened, Robert?"

"It was rather sudden. She had to return home on urgent family business," Robert lied. He couldn't tell the man Sarah had returned to the future, even if that's what happened.

"Aye, well I must be going," Doctor Burnett stated and reached out to shake Robert's hand.

"Could I bother you for a moment longer? Please?"

"Archibald told me you had sat down to your meal. I must let you get back to it."

"No, this is important." Robert opened the library door and ushered the doctor in. "Dram?" he asked walking to the table where the family kept the decanter and glasses.

"Aye, thank you. That would be sublime."

Robert poured two glasses and walked to the sofa. "Sit," he beckoned with a nod of his head.

Doctor Burnett sat in the armchair and placed his bag on the floor beside him.

Once his guest settled in his seat, Robert handed the man his drink and sat at the end of the sofa. "Earlier, Margaret and I discussed enrolling the children in the village school in Kendonald."

"You mean they're not attending school?"

"No. And before you scold me for it, I know they should be. Margaret's children, John Bryce and Mary Elizabeth, attended school in Edinburgh. They have only been away from their studies for a few days. Jenny, well, she's never been. Other than Sarah working with her, we'd never discussed sending her."

"And you want my opinion," Doctor Burnett replied.

"Please." Robert shifted closer to the edge of the sofa.

"Well, Jenny should be with other children."

"She gets it here with her cousins," Robert stated.

"Aye, but it isn't quite the same. But, children can be quite cruel. I would expect Jenny would endure a lot of taunting because of her seizures and stuttering."

"I couldn't stand for that. I wouldn't stand for that," Robert yelled unable to bear the thought of Jenny being tormented.

"I know. I'm speculating out loud. You did ask for my opinion."

"If I don't enroll Jenny in the village school, what are my options?"

"Well, you could always hire a governess. Jenny would get her education. Better still she wouldn't be the subject of the village children's cruelty."

"Thank you, Doctor, thank you," Robert said and shook the physician's hand. "I had pondered the idea of a governess, not just for Jenny but for my niece and nephew, too. But how do I find one?"

"That's a matter best discussed with your sister. She might know of someone in Edinburgh. Children go off to boarding school leaving governesses to find alternate positions."

"I will. Would you like to stay and dine with us? There is plenty of food."

"No, I'll pass on your kind invitation. I'll leave you now so you can get back to your meal," Doctor Burnett replied placing his glass on the coffee table. He picked up his bag and walked to the library door. "I hope my visit has put your mind at rest."

"It has, Doctor. It has." Robert followed his guest to the front door and bid him farewell before rejoining the others in the dining room to continue his meal.

"Mrs. MacEwen ...," Margaret began.

"I've solved our problems. We'll hire a governess," Robert interrupted. "One who can teach your children and Jenny. Doctor Burnett thought it wouldn't be right for the wee lassie to attend the village school. The children might taunt her about her conditions."

"That's all well and good. I was trying to tell you Mrs. MacEwen took your plate back to the kitchen so cook could put it in the warming oven."

"Thank you."

"I *do* like the idea of a governess," Margaret replied, dabbing her napkin at the corners of her mouth.

"The thought had crossed my mind. It wasn't until I spoke with Doctor Burnett I decided that was our best course of action. He also suggested you might know of someone in Edinburgh interested in such a position."

"I'll write George this evening and ask him to put a notice up in the shop. I'm sure there are some suitable young women who would be happy of the employment."

"Preferably one with experience who will soon be finding herself out of work."

"Yes, Robert, that goes without saying."

John Bryce and Mary Elizabeth looked at their uncle, then their mother, and each other. "But what if we don't want a governess," the boy blurted out.

"The matter isn't open for discussion. You and your sister need an education. It will be to keep you up-to-date with your studies. You'll be going off to higher education soon," Margaret stated. "Now if you children are finished, you can be excused."

Amid much grumbling, the siblings left the room.

"Aye, I thought I heard voices. I'll bring your plate back right away." Mrs. MacEwen disappeared behind the closed door. She returned a few moments later carrying Robert's plate in two heavy tea towels. "It be very hot, sir, so be careful," she advised sitting it on the table in front of him.

"Thank you, Mrs. MacEwen. That will be all." Robert dismissed the housekeeper leaving him and Margaret alone.

"Robert, I'm sorry, I didn't mean those terrible things I said about Sarah earlier. They came out in anger and frustration."

"I know you didn't. I accept your apology."

"Is wee Jenny all right?" Margaret asked. "Seeing her in that way was terribly frightening. You know it didn't happen so often when Sarah was here."

"I know. I don't need reminding," Robert snapped. He popped a piece of meat into his mouth, chewed and swallowed. "I'm sorry. I shouldn't have reacted that way."

"I shouldn't have mentioned it. I do hope Sarah returns soon, for Jenny's sake as much as anyone else's. I'll leave you to finish your meal in peace and I'll go pen the letter to George."

Margaret sat down behind the desk and gathered her writing accoutrements. When the butler entered, she was staring at the library's fireplace.

"Are you warm enough, Mrs. Esslemont?" Archibald asked.

"I was about to stoke up the fire some more when you came in."

"Allow me," he replied picking up two logs and placing them on the grate. Afterwards, he took the poker and stirred the coals and soon the fire crackled to life. "Is there anything else, ma'am?"

"That's all for now, Archibald, but I will have a letter for the morning post."

"Aye, put it in the bag by the front door and it will go," he replied, leaving the room and closing the door behind him.

1st November, 1886

My dearest George,

The children and I miss you so much. I hope you soon sell the shop so you can return to Weetshill and be with us.

Robert and I need your help with a matter concerning the children, ours and Jenny. My brother doesn't feel the village school is appropriate for the wee lassie. Our children need to continue their education as well. To that end, I need you to seek out and employ a suitable governess.

When you finalize the arrangements, please let me know. Robert and I will arrange to meet her at the Weetshill railway station.

Your loving wife,

Margaret

After addressing the envelope and inserting the letter, Margaret pondered what Robert said. What if there was something to those mystic lines, or ley lines, or whatever kind of lines they were? She knew as children, he had seen things at the stone circle she never did. Was the stone circle part of a window through time no one understood or knew was there? Or did Robert and Sarah know of it and that's how they were able to cross into each other's lives? She didn't understand it and all this thinking about time and place hurt her head. Margaret sealed the envelope and walked to the door.

Distracted by a flash of light outside the window, Margaret stopped. She peered through the glass that had begun to frost up around the edges. It was too late for thunderstorms. Was it the headlamp of a carriage coming up the lane? The only illumination outside was the stars. At random intervals huge moving clouds extinguished them. A storm was brewing. One that would bring snow and sleet meaning another day or more of the children cooped up indoors. It wasn't so bad if they stayed up in her late brother's room. Instead, they ran screeching through the house, up and down the stairs, too.

4

Sarah woke to a darkened room. It took her a few minutes to get her bearings. She soon realized she was in her hospital bed like they had told her and not back at Weetshill mansion.

Disappointed she began to cry. She loved Robert with all her heart and her time in the past seemed too real to be a dream. Fumbling in the dark, she found the cord for the call button and pushed it.

A few moments later, a nurse appeared in the doorway. "I heard you had come out of your coma when I came on duty," she chatted. "What can I get you, Sarah? I'm Jill, by the way."

"Water."

The nurse poured a bit into the Styrofoam cup and like David had done earlier, helped Sarah so she could take a sip.

"My throat is so sore and my mouth is always dry," Sarah spluttered as she spoke and tried to drink at the same time.

Placing the cup on the table, the caregiver raised the head of Sarah's bed, and plumped the pillows. "Anything else before I leave you?" she asked.

"My hair is a complete disaster. Is there any chance of getting it washed?"

"Sure. It's too late tonight but I'll leave word at the desk and whoever is on duty tomorrow can do it for you. How's that?"

"Brilliant. Thank you."

After she left, Sarah stared off into the corner where she had seen the air shimmer and Robert and Jenny appear.

The street lights cast an eerie, orange glow through the fog and around the edges of the drawn window shade. A tear slid down Sarah's cheek and she swiped it away with the back of her hand.

Robert tossed and turned unable to sleep. He didn't feel right about sleeping in their marital bed alone. The sheets and pillow smelled of the toilet water Sarah used. The scent magnified his hurt and loneliness. After what seemed like an eternity, he gave in and

28

returned to his old room. Padding down the corridor in his nightshirt and bare feet, he met Dougal, the valet. "Would you see the fire is lit in my bed chamber and put the warmer under the blankets, please?"

"Aye, sir. But can I ask why when you's got a fine room down yonder," he pointed and continued, "that's got a fire lit and a warm bed?"

"It doesn't seem right sleeping there without Sarah. When she returns, we will sleep there as man and wife again. Until such time comes, I can't bear to sleep in that bed alone."

The valet nodded and opened the door to the requested room.

Rather than follow Dougal, Robert walked to the room Sarah used before their marriage. It was dark and cold, not even a hint of fire in the grate. He lit one of the paraffin lamps and carried it to the dressing table. Sitting on the stool, he stared at his dim reflection in the mirror. Looking down he saw the amber encrusted trinket box. Wasn't that where Sarah suggested he look for her engagement and wedding rings? He slid the precious item across the table towards him and lifted the lid. After removing brooches, combs, and still more adornments, he reached the bottom. It was empty. About to replace the contents, he saw something in the shadows and stopped. Hidden by the trinket box's earlier position lay the missing jewelry. Maybe Sarah thought she put them inside?

Clutching them in his fist, he returned to his bedroom and shivered. Even though Dougal had lit the fire, it remained cool and damp. Maybe he should go back to their shared room. At least it was warm – or should be.

The valet appeared a few moments later with the bed warmer and slipped it under the top covers. "Shan't be long, sir, and your bed wi' be warm. I hopes you get a good night's rest."

"Thank you, Dougal," Robert replied climbing in and pulling up the covers. Sinking down into the pillows and the soft, feather mattress, he felt somewhat at ease. He prayed the change in room would allow him to get a decent night's sleep.

After the door closed behind the valet, Robert opened the drawer in his bedside table. He found a small, navy blue, velvet drawstring bag and dropped Sarah's rings inside. He put it back then turned the lamp down on his bedside table and rolled over facing the now roaring fire in the grate. He watched the flames flicker and dance over the logs and thought of Sarah. He lost her once when they took her off to the asylum and the pain during her absence was unbearable. This time was worse though, because he had seen her.

Spoken to her. Touched her. But she never returned to Weetshill with him. Was she trapped in wherever that place was he saw her? How could he get her back to Weetshill? There had to be a way. In the morning, he would go to the stone circle. Maybe the answer lay there at the ancient site.

5

A student nurse appeared by Sarah's bed. She carried two buckets and a plastic, kidney bean shaped pan. A towel tucked under her arm and a bottle of shampoo in one of her tunic pockets. "You wanted a shampoo?"

"Please."

"My name is Ailsa, what's yours?" she asked smiling.

"I'm Sarah."

At the sink in the room, the young girl filled one of the buckets. "If I've made this too hot for you, you let me know."

"I will."

The young girl lowered the head of the bed until it was flat and the height dropped to its lowest position. Ailsa moved the side rail and helped Sarah shift positions so her head hung over the edge. Plastic scraped on tile. "Just getting the bucket in position," the girl explained as she continued her preparations.

She poured the first pan of water on Sarah starting at her forehead and letting it soak her entire scalp.

"Too hot?"

"No, it feels wonderful," Sarah replied.

When Ailsa squeezed the shampoo bottle, it burped. "Shoot! Got a favorite shampoo and conditioner?"

"Yes."

"Next time you have visitors, ask them to bring it in to you. Same with any other personal things you might want. Your pillow, duvet, stuffed animal, makeup, anything that will make you feel better."

"Thanks I will."

Sarah relaxed as Ailsa massaged the shampoo into her scalp; the girl's touch gentle. All too soon, the young nurse rinsed her hair, but even having the water poured over her head felt wonderful. Hearing it drip into the bucket sounded like the burn down the road from the farm babbling over the rocks. Once Ailsa squeezed the excess water out, she wound the towel like a turban around Sarah's head.

A couple of button pushes returned the bed to its earlier position.

"I'll take this stuff away and be back to brush your hair for you."

"But, I don't have a brush."

"No worries," Ailsa replied and disappeared out the door.

Sarah leaned back against her pillow. Having clean hair felt amazing. The student nurse's suggestion of having personal effects brought to the hospital got her thinking. She would definitely ask her mother to bring some things to her. She had to decide what was most important – what she couldn't live without.

The student nurse returned removing a plastic hairbrush from the clamshell packaging.

"I can't take it. I can't pay you. I've got no money."

"I got it at Boots on clearance. It's not a big deal," Ailsa replied un-wrapping the towel.

"If you're sure. I can have my mum give you some money next time she's in. And if you're not here, she can leave it with me."

Not answering, Ailsa went to work on Sarah's hair. It didn't hurt until she reached the back of her head. The memories of Mrs. MacEwen looking after her the first night at Weetshill flooded back.

Scorching tears ran down Sarah's cheeks. She was so happy with Robert and everyone else at the mansion in the past. What cruel twist of fate landed her here in ICU at Aberdeen Royal Infirmary?

Robert's reflection in the mirror over his washstand wasn't a pretty sight. Dark circles and bags under his eyes indicated his sleep was fitful at best, if he even slept at all.

"Mornin', sir," Dougal announced knocking and entering. "Can I get you anything?" The valet carried Robert's suit over his arm. He laid it on the bed before getting fresh clothes out of the wardrobe, then picked it back up and started to leave.

"Dougal, will you see that my overcoat, hat and gloves are waiting by the front door for when I finish breakfast?"

"Aye, sir."

The door clicked shut leaving Robert alone again. "Sarah please come back to us," he begged aloud.

Moving in slow motion, he shaved and dressed, unmotivated without Sarah in his life. He tried to put on a brave front for Jenny but was it enough? The wee lassie missed Sarah and try as he might, he couldn't take his wife's place. Before leaving his bedroom, Robert walked to the window. He drank in the surrounding vista starting with the forest on the hill. Trees providing firewood for the mansion. Off to the right a part of the barn stood partly obscured by the woodland. To the left were the hills where they hunted grouse every year but this. Compounding his melancholy, were thoughts of his grandfather's death.

Unable to put it off any longer, Robert snatched the velvet bag out of his bedside table. He tucked it into his inside breast pocket then made his way to the breakfast room. When he pushed open the door, Margaret was already at the table. "Good morning," he lied trying to sound cheery.

"And to you, Robert. My, you look a fright this morning. I hope Jenny doesn't see you looking like that. You'll scare the life out of her," she greeted then walked to her brother and hugged him. "I know what you're going through. I miss George, too."

"It's hardly the same, now is it?"

"No, I suppose not but ..."

"I wish I knew the answers," Robert mumbled. He served his breakfast from the selections on the sideboard. "Have the children eaten yet?"

"Yes, and they're off playing upstairs."

"Good. After breakfast, I'm going over to the stone circle at Gleanstane." He carried his meal to the table.

"Is that a good idea?"

"I don't know. I know I can't sit here and do nothing. I'm hoping by going there I'll see Sarah, wherever or whenever she is, and be able to bring her back with me."

Margaret approached his chair, her skirts rustling, leaned over and hugged him. "Please don't be disappointed when it doesn't work."

"How do you know it won't?" he demanded. "I'm going there now. I'll not stay here another minute."

"Please wait, Robert. I didn't mean it that way," she begged.

"Thank you, Archibald," Robert praised while the butler helped him into his overcoat. "I'm not sure how long I'll be but anything requiring my attendance can wait until I return."

"Aye, sir. Your hat and gloves, sir," he replied handing the remaining items to his employer.

Robert slipped his hands into his gloves and took his bowler from the butler who opened the front door for him.

Placing his hat on his head, he sauntered up the laneway. He knew in his heart what he hoped to discover at the stone circle was pure fantasy. Still, if there were any chance of finding a way to bring

Sarah back, it was worth it. Although it was cold, there was no snow yet, at least none that stayed. Still, the wind was bitter and made worse when it came up in gusts at the stone circle on the hill.

He sat on the fallen boulder where he'd seen Sarah so many times when she was a little girl. He wondered how that was possible. His love for her started back then. His heart ached now with sadness, knowing the possibility he would never see her again. Never be able to hold her in his arms and tell her how much he loved her.

An ingenious idea flashed in Robert's mind. Once he returned to Weetshill, he would write to Professor Ross. Ask his opinion. No. He would invite him to spend some time at Weetshill. They could discuss Robert's conundrum away from the University and the scoffing people there. It hadn't brought Sarah back to him but Robert felt a huge weight lifting from his shoulders. He couldn't imagine the scholar turning his invitation down. He recalled how well Sarah and Ian Ross had got on that night during the hunting party's stay at the mansion. Without a doubt, the man would be able to offer an opinion if not help.

Robert leapt to his feet. He trotted over the hill to the narrow road winding past the Kendonald Free Church and manse. He continued at that pace until he reached the laneway to Weetshill mansion.

The butler opened the front door for his employer. "You look half frozen, sir," he uttered.

A gust of wind brought a few dried autumn leaves into the mansion along with Robert. "But my heart is warm, Archibald. My heart is warm. That's what matters at the end of the day isn't it?" A wave of horror enveloped him. He realized he'd spoken in the same repetitive manner Horatio Christie used. Shaking his head and scolding himself, he removed his hat and gloves and placed them on the bench.

"Get you into the library and in front of the fire, sir," the butler clucked helping Robert out of his overcoat.

Inside the library, Robert stood in front of the huge fireplace. He rubbed his hands together to warm them, surprised even though he had worn gloves, they were this cold. Until his fingers thawed, he would never be able to hold a pen, let alone write a letter.

Bit by bit, the chill left Robert's body. He looked at the decanter of whisky then at the mantle clock. It wasn't yet midday. He knew he shouldn't be taking a drink this early. But, it did have great warming and restorative properties he reasoned. After a short debate with his conscience, he summoned the butler, asked for tea and made his way to the desk.

Pen nib prepared, Robert opened the inkwell. He took a sheet of paper out of the center top drawer of the desk and placed it on the blotter. He needed to phrase this letter with the utmost caution.

2nd November, 1886

Mr. Ian Ross
Professor of Archaeology
University of Aberdeen

My dear Mr. Ross,

I recall when you and the rest of the hunting party visited Weetshill in August, you discussed mystical lines and sacred places with ~~Miss Shand~~ my wife. It was a subject you both held a keen interest in.

I would very much like to continue that conversation. If you could bring any documents related to the subject with you, I would be most pleased.

Should you be able to join us, I would expect your arrival to Weetshill Railway Station, 6th November. You will of course, be welcome to spend the night as my guest.

Sincerely yours,

Robert A. Robertson
Laird, Weetshill

Satisfied with his letter, Robert readied it for the post. He started across the room to put it in the bag in the great hall. The door pulled open easier than he expected. He jumped back, startled seeing his sister in front of him.

"You look much better than you did earlier. The fresh air did you the world," Margaret stated. She brushed past him to the chair and her mending basket.

"Aye, very much. I've written to Professor Ross and invited him to visit at week's end."

"Oh?" She found it difficult to understand why her brother invited a guest while he grieved for Sarah. And if what Robert had told her about Sarah was true, how did he propose to explain it to people? In her mind, keeping people's visits short was the prudent thing to do.

Margaret stood and followed him into the great hall. "Do you think having overnight guests is a good idea with you in the state you're in?"

"I think it is just the thing to do," Robert replied. "Now if you'll excuse me, I'm going to read the paper." He sidestepped her and entered the library.

Following close behind, Margaret found him with his face buried in *The Aberdeen's Journal.*

Resigned to his decision, she sat down and picked up one of John Bryce's socks he poked the toe through. Sighing, she threaded her darning needle and began the task. Her son was so much harder on his clothes than his sister. Margaret hoped it was due to his age and the fact he was a boy. Distracted by her thoughts, she pricked her thumb with the sharp needle. The first drop of blood appeared and she put her injured digit in her mouth and sucked on it.

"Mama, tomorrow is my birthday," Mary Elizabeth announced bursting into the room. "Have you bought me a gift yet? Will I get it at breakfast time like I did in Edinburgh?"

Margaret's face fell. With everything that had happened, her daughter's upcoming birthday hadn't crossed her mind. This was a first. She had never forgotten either of her children's birthdays before. "Drat," she declared.

"You forgot me, mama?" the little girl asked.

"No, I stuck myself with this needle. That's all. Off you go and play now. We might do things a little different now we're here. After all, it *is* your Uncle's home."

"Please Uncle Robert, can I get my birthday present at breakfast time?"

He put his newspaper down and pulled his niece onto his lap. "Well," he drawled, "When it comes right down to it, it will be up to your mother. Now do as she said and off you go."

Mary Elizabeth skipped out of the library. She slammed the door behind her, rattling the windowpanes.

"Thank you. Didn't you see me gesturing at you?"

"Yes," he quipped. "You forgot her birthday didn't you?"

Margaret hung her head, too ashamed to admit she had done such a thing.

"You did," Robert chuckled. "Oh my, this *is* hilarious."

"It is not," she countered and slammed her mending back into the basket before standing up and pacing. "What am I going to do?"

"I don't know. But you'll think of something."

Margaret whipped around and squealed because Robert stood right in front of her.

"Take Mary Elizabeth to Duninsch tomorrow. Let her choose her birthday gift. I'll see Callum is ready to take you both after breakfast tomorrow."

"What a splendid idea," Margaret exclaimed. Her mood changed. "When John Bryce and Jenny discover I'm taking Mary Elizabeth on an outing, they will be jealous."

"You let me worry about them. You and your daughter go out and have a lovely day – just the two of you."

"Thank you." Margaret rested her hands on Robert's shoulders and kissed his cheek.

The next morning brought a new rotation of nurses. The one assigned to Sarah's care was all business and didn't take time to talk with her. Checked her vitals, wrote the numbers in her chart and nothing else. She even wore her ID badge flipped backwards so Sarah couldn't see her name.

Soon the smell of breakfast trays filled the air. A cooked breakfast was something Sarah craved. All she received was a bottle of *Ensure*. The nurse opened the container and stuck a straw in it. She pulled the tray table across Sarah's bed, placed the bottle on it for her and left.

Sarah struggled to get into a position so she could pick up the nutritional shake and take a sip. Strawberry – her least favorite flavor. When she reached to put it back on the table, a movement by the door surprised her. "Wh-what are you doing here?" she seethed.

"Please Sarah. I need to talk to you. Your mother told me you were awake now so we came to see you."

"We? What's this we?"

"Blair is here, too."

"I have nothing to say to either one of you. You're a pair of traitors. Y-you used to be my best friend, Niamh. How could you steal my boyfriend the first time I turned my back?"

"It wasn't like that, Sarah. Please, you must believe me. It just kind of happened."

"And where is Blair? I thought you said he was here, too."

Niamh turned around. "He was right with me. Blair, sweetie, where are you?" she called.

He stepped through the doorway.

"I hate the pair of you. I don't ever want to see either of you again," Sarah screeched. She wanted to hurt them the way they had hurt her. "Get out," she yelled picking up the container. With what strength she could muster, Sarah tossed it, hitting Niamh. The contents spilled out all over her white top, staining it pink.

"You cow," Niamh cried and turned to rush out of the room. In the doorway, she ran into a man wearing the hospital regulation uniform and a stethoscope draped around his neck.

"I heard the noise all the way down the corridor. How did you get in here? It's only family allowed at this point. Besides visiting hours haven't even started yet. You've disturbed my patient. It's time you were leaving." David extended his arm behind Niamh and turned her towards the door and followed her and Blair out of the room.

A short time later, he returned. "They're away. I saw them get on the lift. They won't be bothering you anytime soon. Are you all right?"

By now, Sarah sobbed out of control. David walked to her bed and put one arm around her shoulders. She grabbed the front of his tunic in both hands and buried her face in his chest. With his free arm, he rubbed her back.

Little by little, her blubbering stopped. Still, her body convulsed as she struggled to regain her composure.

"Care to tell me what that was all about?" David asked.

Sarah shook her head.

"Sometimes it helps to talk about it," he replied.

"I never want to see them again," she wailed. "They betrayed me. He – Blair – was my boyfriend. I was so sure he'd been acting weird because he was going to ask me to marry him. We'd been together for ages. It seemed the next logical step for us. Th-then, I caught him snogging Niamh's face off."

"I'll let them know at the desk, if either one of them show up here again, they're not allowed to see you. I'll leave word at the main entrance, too. With the number of people coming and going down there, they could slip past security. And I promise you, if I see either one of them again, unless they're a patient, I will show them the door."

Sarah pulled back and looked up into David's hazel eyes. Except for the color, they were reminiscent of Robert's golden brown ones. Still, they had that same genuine caring look in them. "Thank you," she whispered.

David extracted himself from Sarah's grip. He reached to the foot of her bed for her chart and scanned the notes from the night nurse's checks on her. He took her vitals again but everything was out of whack from the earlier upset, so he didn't record them.

"I'll be back later to see how you're doing. Fingers crossed, by then you won't be so upset."

"When am I going to get out of bed?"

"Can't say. It's for Doctor Compton to decide."

Sarah sank back into her pillows, dejected by his comment. By the sounds of things, she would be bedridden for quite some time.

David stopped by the door and turned to her. "Think maybe you've got a smile in there for me?"

She nodded, gave him half a smile and turned away. Right now she wasn't in the mood. Happiness was the furthest thing from her mind. The raw hurt that overcame her when she caught Blair and Niamh rushed back. Sarah broke down into gut-wrenching, tortured sobs again. David was kind and caring but he wasn't Robert and he was the man she needed and wanted.

6

David paused, leaned down then returned to Sarah's bed. He bent over and picked something up off the floor. "What the ...?"

"What?"

"It looks like it might have been food at one time. Looks fossilized now."

"Gross," she replied making a face.

Concerned over the petrified object on the floor, David wondered for how long? If it had been there any length of time, the cleaning staff wasn't doing a good job. As it was, the NHS had come under fire more than once in recent years for the lack of cleanliness in their hospitals. Aberdeen Royal Infirmary had an outbreak of MRSA and a winter vomiting bug.

"Feeling any better now?" he asked. Despite the cleaning job bothering him, Sarah's reaction to his comment warmed his heart. Maybe she had turned the corner on the road to recovery.

"N-not really," Sarah managed through her ragged breaths.

When the lunch trolley arrived, Sarah's meal included yet another bottle of *Ensure*. This time she also got a small container of vanilla yogurt. At least they didn't lumber her with strawberry again. This time it was chocolate but it didn't appeal to her any more than the morning's offering had.

About one-thirty, a man of East Indian extraction came in to her room. He had black hair, greying around the temples. Dressed in similar fashion to Doctor Compton the first time she met him. A few coarse black hairs poked out of the open neck of his pressed, long sleeved, cream colored shirt. Instead of dress trousers, this man wore a pair of tan chinos.

"Who are you?" Sarah asked.

"I am Mr. Youssef. I am the head of the trauma team that performed the surgery on your legs." He looked at her toes poking out from the bandages on her leg in the external traction device and squeezed them. Then he pulled the covers back and examined her other leg. "Very nice. Very, very nice. Healing well." The surgeon pulled a chair up and sat beside the bed. "Your legs were badly broken. We removed bone fragments, dirt and damaged soft tissue from the wounds. The impact fractured your fibulas, the small bones in your lower legs, in one place so we were able to set them. Your tibias, though, shattered. They bore the brunt of the collision. The breaks were in a good position. There were enough large fragments we were able to insert a long nail down through the center of the bone."

The surgeon's graphic description nauseated Sarah. She reached for her water glass and took a sip.

"Because of the damage to the soft tissue in your lower legs, I brought in the plastic surgery team. Miss McIntosh will be along to see you and explain."

"Will I be able to walk again?"

"Oh my, yes. You'll have to undergo physiotherapy for some time, but yes, you will walk again."

"What about travel? With this metal in my legs I'll never be able to go anyplace where I have to pass through a metal detector."

"Not to worry, my child. Before you go through the detector, explain you've had major orthopedic surgery. Show them your scars, although we trust they will be well healed by the time you're ready to travel. We'll also ensure you have an official card or letter to carry with you."

Sarah breathed a sigh of relief. Confining her travels to mainland Britain wasn't something she looked forward to.

"I'll say my goodbyes now and get a physio schedule set up. When it is time, one of the nurses will come for you."

Alone in her room again, Sarah's mind raced. An accident explained why her one leg was in that cage thing. But why couldn't she remember it? Had she blocked it from her mind?

Before she had a chance to dwell on her predicament any further, her mother and sister arrived.

"How are you feeling today," Mrs. Shand asked. She strode to the bed and plumped Sarah's pillows.

Rachel stood near the window, looking disinterested in being there. She pulled her mobile out and started jabbing at the screen.

"You know you're not supposed to have that on in here," Mrs. Shand scolded.

Sarah remembered her phone. She hadn't lost it after all. Robert brought it to her. He mentioned Jenny found it along the tree line.

"Mum," she began. "Can you bring me the charger for my iPhone?"

"Why do you need it if you've lost your phone?"

"I have it now but it needs charging."

"But it wasn't with the things they gave me when you were first brought in."

Sarah knew where it came from but she couldn't tell her mother. "Maybe they found it afterwards," she offered. "It's in my bedside table. You can check."

Mrs. Shand opened the drawer and there was the missing device.

"And my makeup, too, please?"

"What do you need that stuff for in here?" her mother asked.

Tugging at the sheets, Sarah spoke. "The student nurse who washed my hair suggested I have some of my things from home. Can you bring my pillow, shampoo and conditioner and makeup."

"We can bring those things in for you the next time we come," Mrs. Shand said.

"And besides, if I don't look like a bag of dirt, I won't feel quite so much like one."

"You don't look like a bag of dirt. Who on earth told you that?"

"No one."

"Do I have to stay here, Mum?" Rachel interrupted. "Jacquie wants to meet me at the Bon Accord Centre. I told her I got my hair done and she wants to see it."

"It's a long way from here. How will you get there?"

"Duh … bus?"

"Enough cheek, young lady. I suppose you might as well go. I'll pick you up there at half five."

"That's not much time. Can't you pick me up at the train in Duninsch later tonight? I'll catch the six-twenty," she confirmed, looking at her phone. "If it's on time, I'll get in to Duninsch about five to seven."

"Oh all right, go. You won't give me a minute's peace until you do."

"Bye, Mum. Thanks." Rachel gave her mother a hug. "Bye, Sarah," she muttered and bounded out the door.

"It's a wonder your sister has any hair left. The number of times she's colored it, straightened it, and who knows what else," Mrs. Shand mused.

Sarah nodded. Her sister changed her appearance almost weekly it seemed. "She didn't stay long. Couldn't get out of here fast enough," she quipped.

"She's not one for hospitals, is our Rachel."

"But she was here. She was here when I came to."

"I almost had to tie her to the chair. Your father sends his love."

"That's nice. When's he coming to see me?"

"I doubt it will be before the weekend. You know he's busy with getting the farm ready for winter. Have you had your CT scan yet?"

"No, but Mr. Youssef was in to see me. He says my legs are coming along well. Said the plastic surgeon would pop in, too."

A tear dripped down Mrs. Shand's cheek and she turned her back to Sarah. "How nice."

Sarah knew her mother was crying but didn't say anything. She supposed if it were the other way around, she would be, too.

"Niamh and Blair showed up here this morning. He stayed in the doorway and let her do all the talking."

"How did they get in? It's supposed to be family. I don't want you getting upset."

"It's okay, Mum. I doubt they'll be back any time soon. I chucked my *Ensure* from breakfast all over Niamh. David, the student doctor, escorted them out. He's left word at the desk on this floor and with security at the main entrance to not let them in."

"David does seem like a nice young man," Mrs. Shand replied.

"Yeah, and you thought Blair was in the beginning, too, and he turned out to be a proper loser."

They chatted, not about anything in particular, longer. Each time Sarah made a move to shift to a more comfortable position her mother sprang to her bedside to help. Not able to wait any longer, she brought the subject up again. "Mum, I know you saw Robert, Jenny and me. You can deny it all you want but when I first mentioned it to you, you got all defensive. I need to know was I wearing a ruby and diamond ring and a plain gold band?"

"I-I, oh look at the time. I have to be going. Get home and get supper on for your father." Mrs. Shand leaned down, kissed Sarah's forehead and fled from the room.

Since her sister's accident, life at Gordonsfield was no longer the same. Rachel heard her parents fight often and over the least little things. Her mother spent most of her time at the hospital. When Rachel wasn't getting dragged along, too, it was up to her to make supper and wash the dishes afterwards. The cooking and washing up weren't a big deal to her. It was the tension in the house that bothered her most. When she was home, she walked on eggshells for fear of causing her father or mother to fly into a rage. The only time she could be herself was at school or her part-time job at the small department store in Huntly. Sure, she loved Sarah but she resented the situation she'd put the family in. Rachel looked forward to the period of normalcy she would have when she met up with her friend.

Inside the bus shelter, she pulled her fleece-lined beanie from her coat pocket. She jammed it on her head wanting to surprise Jacquie when they met inside the mall entrance on Schoolhill.

The bus arrived and the driver opened the door. Rachel boarded and dropped her fare through the slot. She found a seat and settled in for the twenty-minute ride to the Bon Accord Centre.

Gunmetal grey clouds filled the sky and a steady drizzle fell. The somber scene outside echoed through the silence. The only sound was the audible shwoop, shwoop of the wipers gliding over the windscreen. On a sunny day, the granite buildings sparkled but on days like this, they loomed dark and menacing. The streetlights reflected in luminous pools on the wet tarmac. Since the time change, it got dark much earlier and with the inclement weather, earlier still.

At least there weren't a lot of passengers getting on or off so the ride to Union Street didn't take long. It wouldn't have mattered which bus Rachel took to get to the mall, she would have had to walk the last bit. The one she took happened to be the first one to arrive at the stop outside the hospital.

Rather than cut through the St. Nicholas kirkyard, she stayed on the streets. That place was creepy at the best of times and after dark even worse. The only lights were on the church near the back, closer to Schoolhill than Union Street.

Commuters walking towards the railway station impeded her progress. If she soon didn't get to the mall, there wouldn't be any sense in going. It closed at six and she would have to catch the train to Duninsch.

Exhausted when she arrived at the entrance, Rachel wanted to find a bench and catch her breath. Jacquie rushed outside to meet her. "Let me see," she babbled.

"Let's go inside where the light is better," Rachel suggested. Wrapping her arm through her friend's, they walked inside.

Once in the mall, Rachel pulled her hat off and shook her head before combing her hair with her fingers.

"Ooh, I love it," Jacquie squealed and reached out to touch Rachel's newest look. Cut in a bob with jagged layers at the back, the base color was black, almost a blue-black it was so dark. Throughout, bright neon pink and orange foils completed the appearance. "It's so soft. I thought it would be coarse and dry."

"The stylist put oil in it. And salons always have the best products."

"So how much did it cost?"

"For the cut, color, foils, shampoo, conditioner and oil treatment, almost two hundred pounds."

"And you'll change it again when your roots start to show."

Rachel grinned, knowing full well her friend was right.

"I think your hair has a chemical dependency," Jacquie joked. "I bet you don't even know what your natural color is anymore."

"Brown. But not a nice, rich brown like Sarah's. Mine's plain, flat and mousy."

"It's a good thing you've got a job so you can support your habit. Maybe you need an intervention?"

Rachel wanted to tell her friend to do one, but kept a civil tongue and smiled instead.

"Shall we shop?"

"Was there any doubt?"

The girls linked arms and wandered through the mall window shopping along the way. They entered a few stores and tried some things on.

Rachel struggled into a pair of skinny jeans. Bending over to put her other leg in, she lost her balance. Hopping on one foot trying to regain it, she stumbled backwards into the door which hadn't latched. The next thing she knew, she was on her back, half-dressed on the floor in the main part of the shop.

Jacquie collapsed in a pile of giggles onto one of the nearby chairs. She was of no use to anyone.

Looking around to make sure no one else saw her incident, Rachel got on her hands and knees. With her cheeks burning with embarrassment, she scrabbled back into the cramped dressing room.

Changed back into her own clothes, she and Jacquie, still laughing, left the store. Rachel deposited the source of her humiliation on the counter before the clerk had a chance to speak.

Outside the shop, Jacquie looked at her friend. "That was priceless," she howled.

The heat returned to Rachel's cheeks. "I'm glad you find it so funny," she spat trying to remain angry but found it impossible. Before long she, too, dissolved into fits of laughter.

The girls wandered through the mall until Rachel spotted the time on one of the overhead clocks. "Oh shoot, I've got to go or I'll miss my train. Told mum I'd be on the six-twenty and I still have to buy my ticket."

"I'll walk you to the station," Jacquie offered.

"No, you're all right." Rachel hugged her friend then dashed to the exit.

Like it or not, she would have to cut through the St. Nicholas kirkyard. It was the fastest route to the station. The headstones cast eerie shadows in the low light. Rachel began to run and didn't stop until she reached the ticket window. "Duninsch, one way," she panted, her chest heaving.

Dropping into one of the few empty seats in the carriage, Rachel pulled out her phone. Six-fifteen. She had made it with five minutes to spare.

7

Moira Shand closed the back door, leaned against it and sighed. When Sarah was unconscious, the trips to the hospital had been tiring enough. Now that she was awake, they were more so, if that was possible.

"You're home," Jimmy observed stepping out of his office.

She was so tired she couldn't even come up with a comeback for his statement. After all, she was standing in the back hall about six feet away from him. Of course, she was home. Her eyes filled with burning tears.

Seconds later, Jimmy was at her side. "You look shattered, love," he whispered, pulling her to him and wrapping his arms around her.

Moira leaned against him and held him close. His kiss on the top of her head was soft. On the verge of breaking down, she sighed a ragged breath.

Jimmy disengaged himself from her grip and walked her to the family dining room. "You sit here on the sofa," he ordered and handed her the remote for the TV. "Put your feet up and rest. I'll fix you something to eat and a cup of tea."

"Thank you." She slipped her coat and shoes off, pulled the throw off the back of the couch and covered up with it.

"Where's Rachel? She not come home with you?" Jimmy asked, poking his head out of the galley kitchen.

"No. She met Jacquie at the Bon Accord Centre and is taking the train home. Someone will have to pick her up at the Duninsch railway station for seven o'clock."

"Cheese and tomato sandwich okay?" he called out over the clatter of dishes and cutlery.

Moira heard him but didn't have the energy to reply. She snuggled under the blanket and thought about her family, starting with her husband. Jimmy was a good man, despite being quick tempered. She'd never seen him angry enough he would actually hit someone. He was bluster. When he found out about Blair dumping Sarah, had he got his hands on the lad, she wasn't so sure. Sarah took after her father when it came to being quick-tempered. But once she started dating Blair, she had calmed down a great deal. Rachel was the exact opposite of her older sister. She didn't let anything bother her. Still she could be a bit of a handful by times. Moira put it down to her youngest daughter's age. She was pushing the limits to see how far she could go. Back to Jimmy, if a boy ever hurt either of his girls, woe betide the lad who did it. Blair should consider himself lucky she prevented her husband from going after him.

Murphy meowed and jumped up onto her. He stomped on her in circles until he found a comfortable position then lay down. But he was far from still. He kneaded his front paws over and over in her chest. In the end, Moira had to push him off.

"Your sandwich and tea are ready, love," Jimmy declared. "I put them on the table for you."

"Mmm," she groaned and threw the blanket off.

He helped her off the couch and over to the table. "Here you go, love. I've got some paperwork to catch up on so I'll let you eat in peace."

"Don't go, Jimmy. Please, I need to talk to you."

He pulled his chair out, sat down and held her hand. "What's wrong?"

"It's Sarah."

"What about Sarah? She's not taken a turn, has she?"

"No." Moira rested her forehead on the fingertips of her other hand. "It's this business about her having been back in the past."

"Didn't you say the doctor said it could be her subconscious processing her injuries?"

"Something like that. But she's so adamant. She's determined she traveled back in time. She says we saw her, her husband and the wee girl they adopted. Jimmy, I think she needs professional help."

"You mean a shrink?" he yelled, jumping up from the table. "No girl of mine is going to see one of those head doctors."

"We can help her get through her physical injuries but not her mind. She needs more than we can give her."

"I told you no shrinks," Jimmy bellowed. He turned and stormed out of the room, slamming the door behind him.

Moira sat in stunned silence. Her appetite had vanished. She picked up the plate with her sandwich on it and took it out to the kitchen. She was about to toss it in the bin but thought better of it and put it in a re-sealable plastic bag and placed it in the fridge. Someone would eat it tomorrow.

She turned the lights out and the TV off. A beam of light shone from under the office door. Closing the family dining room door behind her, Moira walked to the stairs. She paused for a moment at the foot, debated about going in and trying to talk sense into her husband. In the end, she decided to leave it for another time. She was too shattered tonight to take on that battle. "I'm going to bed. Don't forget to pick Rachel up at the railway station," she called.

Jimmy pushed his chair away from the desk and leaned back. He still fumed over his conversation with Moira about Sarah getting professional help.

He likened himself to a cartoon character with steam coming out his ears. The top blowing off his head and more vapor with springs and other parts escaping from there.

Lacing his fingers behind his head, he stared at the ceiling and sighed. He shouldn't have taken his frustration over Sarah and her situation out on his wife. Still, he couldn't bring himself to consent to his eldest daughter seeing a head doctor.

The screen on his computer went black. Jimmy grabbed the edge of the desk and pulled himself forward. He wiggled the mouse on its mat and the screen returned to life. He brought up a search engine but once it loaded, he didn't know what to type into it. Brain injury, dream interpretation, serious injuries?

Instead, he typed in Weetshill mansion and got more information than he thought possible. Deciding which result to read proved difficult. He finally picked one on the history of the house.

Engrossed in reading it, when the phone rang, he jumped. He fumbled on the desk for the cordless handset which had become buried under a stack of papers. Pushing the talk button, he answered, "Gordonsfield Farm."

"Are you or mum coming to get me at the railway station?" Rachel demanded.

Mr. Shand looked at the clock on the lower right of the computer screen. It was almost seven-thirty and his daughter's train was due in half an hour ago. "I'll be right there. Sorry, I was on the computer and lost track of time."

"Fine, but so you know, it's freezing out here."

"On my way." He pushed the end button, dropped the phone and scooped up his keys. Inside the back door, he shrugged into a coat and slipped on a pair of Wellington boots.

Rachel walked to the carpark to wait for her father. The stand of trees lining the side across from the platform did nothing to block the wind. It whistled between them and the station building.

Since calling home for someone to come pick her up, the wind had blown a fog in from the North Sea. That made the night even more cold and damp than it had been in Aberdeen.

Returning to the platform she huddled next to the building under the light. Its orange glow looked eerie and ghost-like in the mist. Rachel checked her phone for the time. She figured it would take her father about fifteen minutes to get from home to the railway station.

She checked her phone again to see how much time had elapsed. About twenty minutes later, headlights appeared at the entrance of the carpark. Thinking it was her ride, Rachel started towards them. The vehicle came closer then turned around and left.

When her father finally arrived, he drove to the station building before stopping.

"Took you long enough," she sniped, climbing into the car. "It's freezing out there."

"In case you hadn't noticed, missie, it's foggy as all get out and you can't see past the bonnet of the car."

Once Rachel fastened her seatbelt, Mr. Shand drove off. She watched the glow from the street lights disappear in the passenger side wing mirror.

While fiddling with the car radio to find a station with music she liked, something moved in front of the car. Rachel screamed. Mr. Shand jammed on the brakes, bringing the car to a screeching halt.

"Dammit, Rachel, what were you thinking?" he bellowed.

"Didn't you see it? A flash of something light in front of the car. Like maybe a deer or something ran across the road."

"I think you're spending too much time at the hospital with your sister. You're imagining things just like her."

Rachel flounced back in her seat and folded her arms against her chest. Despite her father not believing her, she had seen something and didn't want him to hit it.

When they arrived home, she bolted from the car, ran upstairs, and slammed her bedroom door.

8

The next morning, Jimmy Shand climbed into the cab of his John Deere tractor. He reached for the key he'd left in the ignition but before touching it, he stopped. Leaning back in the seat, he sighed and thought of Sarah. Overjoyed she was out of the coma, he worried over how her injuries affected her.

From the time he and Moira brought Sarah home from the hospital as an infant, she had a distinct personality. It developed along with her as she grew up. Headstrong, independent and stubborn. Not long after she started dating Blair her personality made a one hundred and eighty degree turn.

Moira thought the lad was good for Sarah. He'd calmed her down. She was no longer quick-tempered. Jimmy noticed before Sarah's accident, she had become subservient and followed Blair's every lead.

He scrubbed his hands down his face then started the engine. Preparations for winter were behind and he would have to put in even longer days than usual to get back on track.

Driving into the field, he picked up one of the round bales of hay with the forks on the front of the tractor. He drove up the hill to the field where the stone circle stood. He dropped the bundle onto the ground and scrambled out.

A strong gust of bitter wind almost knocked him off his feet and he stumbled into the tractor. Jimmy tramped around the vehicle where he sheltered from the wind. He fumbled in his coveralls for his pocket knife. He sliced through the plastic and pulled it away from the hay.

By now his nosey beasts, which is how he referred to his cattle, had surrounded him. He pushed his way through the herd to get to their trough to ensure it hadn't frozen over during the night.

Between the large metal tub and his current location he could see the upright stones. Striding to the fallen boulder, he brushed the light skiff of snow off its surface then sat down.

Mr. Shand thought of the number of results in his internet search of Weetshill. Maybe Sarah had done the same and that's why she was so obsessed with the place. He had looked at one. Maybe the others had more information about the families who lived there over the years. He only knew what he'd heard about the place and now what he'd skimmed over the previous night.

He had too much work ahead of him to hang about dawdling. Standing, he brushed the seat of his coveralls off, climbed back in to his tractor and fired the engine.

Once everyone had their breakfasts, Margaret looked straight at John Bryce. "I'm taking your sister shopping in Duninsch today for her birthday. I want you to behave yourself for your Uncle Robert and be nice to Jenny."

"Aw, why does Mary Elizabeth get to go alone with you and not me, too?"

"I said I was taking her shopping for her birthday."

"Will you take me on my birthday?"

"I think that's something best left to your father or your Uncle Robert."

"Wh-what about J-Jenny?" the little girl asked.

"I'm quite certain Sarah will be back in time to take you and if not, then I would love to."

"Mama, can we go to Aberdeen instead? I've never heard of Duninsch before so it can't be very big. At least I've heard of Aberdeen. It would be more like Edinburgh … please."

"Very well, then." Margaret couldn't refuse her daughter's request since she'd forgotten the child's birthday. "We'll make a day of it. Shopping, lunch, more shopping then back home, here."

"Yes, please, mama."

When Archibald entered the room, he announced, "Callum is waiting wi' the carriage ma'am."

"Thank you," Robert commented. "Would you let him know there's been a change of plan? He'll be taking Margaret and Mary Elizabeth to Weetshill railway station rather than Duninsch. He's to pick them up there … at what time, Margaret?"

"He can come with me when I purchase our tickets. I'll advise him then."

"Very well, ma'am. I shall tell him," the butler replied retreating from the room.

"Finish your breakfast now, Mary Elizabeth," Margaret stated.

She picked up her napkin and patted her lips clean.

Within the half hour, Mary Elizabeth and her mother boarded the carriage. Robert, John Bryce and Jenny stood outside the front door and waved them off.

The young girl waved from the window. This was her first proper outing with just she and her mother. On previous trips, either her brother was with them or it was the entire family.

At the station, Mary Elizabeth waited in anticipation of her day out. She hopped from one foot to the other like she needed the bathroom. Her mother paid their fare and instructed the coachman of their return time.

When Margaret placed the ticket in her hand, she gasped with delight. She never got to hold her own ticket before. On previous train trips, either her mother or father had always held them.

"Don't lose it now, Mary Elizabeth. You need to give it to the conductor on the train."

"I know, mama. I'm not a baby anymore." Disappointed her mother still thought of her as a child, she sighed. After all, today was her ninth birthday. She was almost grown up.

The train pulled in to the platform in a cloud of coal smoke and steam. Mary Elizabeth curled her nose at the smell. She'd heard adults say what the smell was but she couldn't think of it. All she could liken it to was rotten eggs.

She clambered onto the train and followed her mother to their seats. Within minutes, the train lurched into motion. Their adventure in Aberdeen was about to begin.

The hillfort on the top of Dunnideer disappeared, obstructed from view by the mountain. Bennachie grew larger until it, too, was no longer visible. Cows and sheep grazed in the fields along the railway. Soon the rural setting gave way to the granite buildings of Aberdeen.

Mary Elizabeth inched forward on her seat until she perched on the very edge. She craned her neck to see everything. When she came with her father and brother for Uncle Robert's wedding, it was nighttime. She'd missed most of it because she'd fallen asleep.

Soon the train came to a stop in the joint station. Margaret took her hand and they walked one in front of the other down the narrow aisle and out the carriage door.

Margaret led her daughter to Union Street. The sky had clouded over and threatened rain. She didn't want them to get caught in a sudden downpour.

She stopped in front of Milne, Lowe & Co., one of the shops she had frequented shopping for Sarah's wedding. Back then, the store had some darling little girls' dresses and a large assortment of hair ribbons. She hoped they still did and her daughter would agree.

The train had been late arriving at Weetshill station. To accomplish everything as planned, they wouldn't have time to linger.

Mary Elizabeth dashed through the shop's door to the display of dresses. When Margaret approached, her daughter emerged from the array of clothing. She held up a brown, velvet dress with ivory colored lace trim around the neck and sleeves. The high waist was also adorned the same. "It's bee-eautiful," she exclaimed. "Can I have this one?"

"Don't you want something brighter? This emerald green one is quite lovely. So is the royal blue." The rich color reminded Margaret of the portrait of her grandparents hanging at Weetshill.

"But I like this one."

Margaret spoke with the young female clerk. She led them to a small room where the little girl could try the garment on.

The dress fit Mary Elizabeth better than a custom-made one from a dressmaker's. They also purchased ivory velvet hair ribbons, and pairs of ivory and brown stockings.

"Thank you, mama," the little girl gushed. "This is the bestest birthday ever."

Margaret hugged her and kissed her cheek. Robert's suggestion of a day out for them was a great success so far. This would be the way they would celebrate Mary Elizabeth's birthday from now on.

Laden with the bundles from Milne, Lowe & Co., the two returned to Union Street. It was busier now than when they entered the shop. The clock on the Tolbooth chimed one o'clock. Bumped and jostled, Margaret kept a firm grip on her daughter with one hand and their packages with the other.

After a stop for a bowl of stew and bread, and a pot of tea, Margaret took Mary Elizabeth to Jackson's on Upperkirkgate for a new pair of shoes. "You can't have a new dress and not get shoes, too."

"Thank you, mama."

"You're a big girl now, so big girl shoes are in order."

Mary Elizabeth clapped her hands in response.

It took some time to decide but the mutual choice was a brown leather pair with hook and eye closures.

"Fine day, ladies?" Callum asked taking the packages from Margaret and escorting them to the waiting carriage.

"Yes, thank you," Margaret replied.

Mary Elizabeth had run ahead and waited for them to catch up. "Hurry up mama. I want to show Jenny and John Bryce my birthday presents."

Margaret shook her head and chuckled but picked up her pace the remainder of the distance. "Thank you for making yourself available to us today, Callum. We had a most enjoyable time."

"You's welcome, Mrs. Esslemont. I's just doin' me job."

The mother and daughter settled themselves in the carriage. Callum closed the door and climbed into the driver's seat. A flick of the reins and they were on their way back to Weetshill mansion.

First thing in the morning, Sarah woke to her bed moving. "What's going on?"

"Taking you down for your CT scan."

"Now?"

The porter, wearing a green polo shirt and navy trousers, didn't answer. When they arrived outside the CT suite, he spoke to someone there and left Sarah, bed and all, in the corridor.

Unconscious at the time of the first scan, she didn't know what to expect. By the time a technician came for her, she'd become nervous. He moved Sarah off her bed and onto the stretcher-like part of the scanner and strapped her head in place.

"The scan doesn't take too long. We'll get a few pictures and you'll be on your way back to your room."

"Okay," Sarah answered, afraid of the unknown. She wished she had the time to contact her mum and have her at her side. After it was over, she admonished herself for being a wimp.

Sarah sank into a deep depression. Unable to come to terms with her situation, she worried everyone.

Doctor Compton stopped in on his rounds. He checked her chart. "We're all concerned about your state of mind – your poor mother in particular. I'm going to set up a psych consult for you."

"I don't need to see a shrink," Sarah cried. "I want to be back at Weetshill with Robert and Jenny where I belong."

"That's it. You don't belong at Weetshill, my dear child."

"I'm *not* a child and I *do* belong at Weetshill," she shrieked.

"Get some rest. You need to keep your strength up. You'll be starting physiotherapy soon." He patted her hand and left.

Sarah seethed. She didn't like the way everyone patronized her. Doctors, nurses, they were all the same. Well, except maybe David. He didn't treat her like she was a child with a vivid imagination.

"What do you want?" Sarah snapped at the woman who stood in the doorway.

"I'm Miss McIntosh. Mr. Youssef has been to see you, I trust?"

"Yes."

"He told you I would be along, too?"

Sarah nodded.

"May I?" The surgeon put her hand on the back of the chair.

"Suit yourself."

Miss McIntosh sat down, crossed her legs and adjusted her skirt. "We had to remove a considerable amount of damaged tissue from around the main impact site in your legs. Due to the severity of your injuries, we couldn't suture the wound closed." The plastic surgeon explained the procedure to Sarah. "Here, let me show you."

Sarah tried to sit up but couldn't.

The surgeon raised the head of the bed and pulled the blanket down. She folded Sarah's nightgown back and inspected her legs. "We took the skin grafts from your thighs." She outlined each area with her index finger. "You'll be able to see it better once you're more mobile."

With a gentle movement, Miss McIntosh removed the bandages from her patient's leg. She inspected the surgical site on Sarah's shin then lifted the bandages near the pins in Sarah's other leg, too. "Everything is healing wonderfully. You're a very lucky girl."

"I don't feel so lucky."

"You will have scarring but it will fade in time. I must go now but I will be back again."

Soon after the plastic surgeon left her room, Rachel arrived. "Sarah, read this," she blurted rushing to the bed. "I came across this article in *The Press and Journal*. I *had* to bring it to you."

"Where's Mum?"

"At home with Gran. Dad will be here tonight."

"How did you get into Aberdeen?"

"The Leslies from down by Grannie and Grandpa Shand's were coming in and stopped to see if we wanted a lift. The charger for your iPhone, shampoo, conditioner, and your makeup are in this bag.

Mum is going to bring your pillow and duvet when she comes."

"You can put my stuff in the drawer for now," Sarah replied pointing to the bedside table where her mobile lay.

"Don't you want to see the article?"

"Duh, yeah."

Hands shaking, Rachel handed her the newspaper. "Right there, Sarah." She pointed to the headline.

When she saw the photograph of Weetshill in its ruined state, Sarah's eyes filled with tears. The text in the body of the article was impossible to read at that moment. She looked away and focused on the far wall then returned her attention to the paper.

TRAGEDY STRIKES AT WEETSHILL YET AGAIN

One child died and another suffered serious injuries yesterday at the derelict Weetshill mansion. A cornice block tumbled to the ground striking the youngsters.

The children were on holiday from Canada and staying at nearby Mains of Weetshill at the time of the tragedy. The grieving parents remain at Royal Aberdeen Children's Hospital with their injured child.

On 30th October, 1887, a fire tore through one wing of the mansion. It resulted in the death of the young laird, Robert Robertson. Other members of the household staff were also injured. The fire was especially tragic as it happened on the laird's first wedding anniversary. No trace of his bride was ever found, leaving people to suspect the fire may have been set intentionally.

Newspaper staff could not reach the owners of the B-listed mansion for comment. Since the 1950s, when the roof was removed, a high fence has surrounded it. Tales abound of the handsome young laird haunting Weetshill. These stories continue to bring people out to see if they can see his ghost.

"I have to get back there and stop the fire from happening," Sarah proclaimed. "There was no mention of a wee girl? Our Jenny?" What happened? How did the fire start? She needed to find out. "Rachel, I need you to do me a huge favor."

"Great. What is it?" she moaned.

"I need you to find out everything you can about the Laird's wedding. I need to know the full name of his bride and the circumstances of the fire. Anything else you can find out from the marriage date on 30th October, 1886 through to after the fire."

"Sarah, I don't know why this is so important to you. I think you're off your trolley."

Convincing her family she had spent time in the past was next to impossible but Sarah knew it was real. She had to find a way to prove it beyond doubt. "Please tell me you'll do it."

"But I don't even know where to start? How am I going to find anything for you?"

"Newspapers get microfilmed. I don't know. Maybe *The Press and Journal's* head office? Library? I'm not sure either. I know I can't do it stuck in here."

"All right, I'll do it. Yeesh. You're like a dog with a bone when it comes to Weetshill."

Sarah related her incredible story to her sister in great detail. It was the only way she thought she could get Rachel to believe her. "I'll bet you find the bride's full name was Anna Sarah Shand and she was from Musselburgh. You saw us – Robert, Jenny and me. It was Halloween. You made a smart comment about our clothing.

9

David entered the room and Sarah stopped mid-word. "Go on with what you were telling your sister. From what I heard, it all sounds fascinating."

"Oh, all right. But you have to promise you won't think I'm crazy."

"It's a deal."

Sarah started over. Names, dates, places; the minutest details of the past. Details only someone who had been there would know. While she talked, David spotted the open newspaper on the bedside table. He picked it up and looked at it.

Weetshill mansion. When they first met, Sarah had talked about it. It sounded familiar then and seeing the article in print, made it seem more so. Even the photograph of the derelict building looked familiar to him. Still, he couldn't place where he had seen it before. "I'm off home to my mum's, at Williamsmuir, after my shift tonight. She's been doing some genealogical research. I want to tell her what you've told me. She might be able to make sense of it all. Do you mind if I take this newspaper with me?"

"Yes, I do."

"No worries, I'll pick up a copy at the newsagent's. I best be off. Get back on duty before I'm reprimanded for spending too much time with you."

"Will you stop and see me later?"

"Yes, I'm working this unit tonight but I doubt you'll see me. You'll be asleep by that time."

Sarah watched David leave her room.

"He's cute, Sarah," Rachel giggled once he was out of earshot.

"I know. He looks and sounds so much like my Robert, it's scary."

"Think his mum will have any clues for you?"

"I doubt it. I think he was being nice."

Sarah visited with her sister until she dozed off. She woke to a kiss on her forehead. "Dad."

"Your mum is very relieved you're awake. It's been a fraught time for her."

"And you?"

"I've been worried, too, you daft thing."

"I suppose she told you I'm crazy."

"No, she didn't. She did tell me some about your dream, though."

"It wasn't a dream. It was real. I don't know how but it was," Sarah insisted, punching the mattress on either side of her.

"I'm sure you believe that."

"I do, Dad. It *was* real. I know you don't believe me. Our house wasn't built yet. The barn was different. The only house on our property is the ruin in the field behind ours. The stone circle looked the same but the fields around it were different."

"Dammit, Sarah. You're not making any sense."

"I have to say it now while it's fresh in my mind. I'm afraid if I don't, I'll forget it. I don't want to – not even a moment of it."

"Go on then."

"I remember the Kendonald Free Church and manse, but they don't exist. Or did they?"

"They did and still do. The church is the workshop and the old manse is the farmhouse up over the road at Wardlair."

"They're real? So it's not a dream," Sarah pondered. She paused for a moment before asking, "What about Gleanstane, Dad? Whatever became of the big house over the hill from the stone circle?"

Mr. Shand ran his hand through his thinning hair. "I don't know that much about it," he sighed. "Why do you need to know all this anyway?" he groaned. "It was a dream you had while you were in the coma. Probably all those drugs they kept you pumped full of caused them."

"I know you don't believe me, Dad, but I *really* was at Weetshill in 1886. I can't explain how but I know I was. Please, tell me about Gleanstane."

"There was some sort of scandal and the big house burned down sometime in the late 1880s."

"I know what the scandal was. Horatio Christie fathered a child with his daughter. Their dirty little secret came out before Robert and I got married and the two of them disappeared."

"I don't want to hear another word of this," Mr. Shand hollered. "You *had* a dream. You did *not* go back into the past."

Sarah's bottom lip quivered. She was about to burst into tears but didn't want to break down in front of her father. She did go back into the past. She knew it wasn't a dream. She took a deep breath, "You need to read the piece in *The Press and Journal* that Rachel brought in. I was there, Dad, at Weetshill. I'm the young bride they think may have started the fire." Sarah thrust the newspaper, still opened to the page, into her father's hands.

"It's your imagination, sweetie. There's no way that could have happened," he replied, his voice much softer now.

"But it did," she insisted.

"If you say so."

"Daddy, I need a hug." Sarah reached up and put her arms around her father's neck.

Mr. Shand leaned closer and put his arms around her in a gentle hug. "Better?"

"Yes."

"Well there, missie, we best be making tracks for Kendonald and let your sister rest." He looked at Rachel, who had remained quiet the entire time her father had been there.

"Bye, Dad. Come back again soon, okay?"

"Try and keep me away," he replied and leaned down and kissed the top of Sarah's head.

"You'll do me that favor, Rachel, please?"

"If it's so important to you, then yes."

10

Margaret burst into the library, a letter clutched in one hand and its envelope in the other. "This is wonderful news, Robert. We'll have a governess in two weeks' time."

"Imagine. That's much faster than I expected." He placed his newspaper on the coffee table.

"George knows this lady. At the present, she's working for one of the merchant's near the shop. He says here in his letter the gentleman's employing a tutor for his son to prepare him for boarding school. The current governess will be seeking work. He goes on to say this couldn't have happened at a better time."

"Shouldn't we meet with the woman first? Discuss the requirements of the position rather than take her on sight unseen?"

"George wouldn't send us someone who wasn't worthy."

"I know, Margaret, but we want someone who is going to fit into our routine and who the children like. Write back to George and tell him we want to meet with this woman before taking her on. I'll pay her return train fare from Edinburgh to Duninsch if we decide she's not suitable. Still, she should bring her belongings. Did George mention her name?"

Margaret scanned the letter again. "Yes, here it is. She's a Miss Constance Balfour."

"Hmm," Robert muttered, "Oh and include she is to bring references so we might check them."

"I'll do it right now. Should I send it by special messenger so it arrives sooner?" Margaret asked walking to the desk.

A few moments later, she finished writing the letter. She read it aloud for Robert's approval and once he gave her the nod, she prepared it for sending.

When she returned a few moments later, Margaret said the butler ensured it left straight away.

Robert nodded and went back to his newspaper.

"Can we go out and play in the snow?" John Bryce asked.

"What snow?" his mother asked.

"Look outside, mother. Haven't you seen it?"

Margaret walked to the window and pulled the curtain aside. There had to be six inches on the ground.

Robert joined her. "Aye, remember those days when we frolicked in the snow?"

"Make sure you bundle up and have a hat, muffler and mittens."

"Thank you so much, mother," he hooted, hugging his mother and bursting out into the great hall. "She said we can, Mary Elizabeth," he hollered.

"Jenny, too?"

"I didn't ask that."

"Yes, Jenny, too," Robert called out from the library.

Soon the three children romped in the snow. Robert and Margaret watched from the window. "They'll catch their deaths out there," she whispered rubbing her hands on her arms.

"Don't be such a fuss budget. They'll be fine. Morag will fix them up with a hot drink when they come in and their wet clothes will dry. Besides, look at how much fun they're having."

Shrieks and laughter from outside permeated the walls of Weetshill mansion.

11

Rachel hopped from one foot to the other to keep warm on the pavement on Rosemount Viaduct opposite the Central Library. Despite the bright sunshine, the temperature was much colder than it had been. An east wind blew in off the North Sea.

It would be so easy to lie to Sarah and say she couldn't find any information. At the same time, her sister entrusting her with this task had piqued even her own curiosity. The whole thing sounded like something out of an episode of *Doctor Who*.

When the light changed and the walk signal switched on, she scampered across the street and up the steps. Rachel pulled the heavy door open and stepped inside. The building was enormous. Would she ever find the needle in a haystack Sarah had sent her to find in a place this huge?

Feeling lost and overwhelmed, Rachel spotted a nearby information desk and walked over. "I need to look up some information from back in the 1880s."

"What type of information?" the clerk, with jet black hair, heavy black eyeliner and lashes asked.

"Newspapers and some family history."

The girl came around the reception desk. She wore a pleated, grey skirt, white over-the-knee socks, and a pair Doc Marten boots. If not for the bit of color, Rachel could swear the girl was a Goth. Black nail varnish covered her short fingernails.

"I'll show you where to go. Follow me."

She escorted Rachel back into the foyer and pointed to the stairs. "Local Studies are up there. Someone there will be able to help you."

Pulling the wooden door open with trepidation, Rachel stepped through. To her left was another information desk. A grey-haired woman typing something into the computer looked up.

"Can I help you?"

Rachel repeated her request. She looked around the room trying to see everything all at once.

"This way," the woman indicated standing. She led Rachel to the row of microfilm readers on the far side of the room. "We've digitized some of our collection but you're most apt to find what you're looking for on these. The reels are in the cabinets here. All but one of these machines prints and copies are twenty-five pence each. Do you know how to load the reels on?"

Rachel shook her head.

"I'll show you. What month and year do you want to start with?"

"October/November 1887."

The librarian found the reel holding those two months and loaded it onto the reader for Rachel. "This button turns it on. This is forward and back. Depending on how far you turn it in either direction is how fast it goes. And this one is print," she instructed before leaving.

On her own, Rachel turned the knob and the newspaper images flew past on the screen in a blur. She slowed the machine down a few times, checking for a date to see how close she was to where she needed to be.

She worked her way through the reel of microfilm to 30 October 1887. While she did, Rachel drummed her fingers on the film reader's table. She hoped she would find something soon because this was boring. It took some time to reach the date she was looking for. When she found it, she focused her attention on the image on the screen in front of her. Scanning the entire front page of the 30th October edition, Rachel saw nothing. She went through the rest of that date with the same result.

When she was about to give up, something on page four of the 3rd November newspaper caught her eye. It jumped off the microfilmed page like a flashing neon sign.

WEETSHILL MANSION PARTLY DESTROYED – LAIRD PERISHES IN BLAZE

With the utmost sadness, we report the death of one of Aberdeenshire's most revered men. Robert Andrew Robertson perished on Sunday last, 30 October, when fire consumed part of his stately home.

Weetshill is a large holding between Duninsch and Kendonald. It has been in the Robertson family for seven generations.

At the time of its discovery, the fire was too far advanced to quell the conflagration. The valiant efforts of the Laird's servants and tenants were for naught. Flames were visible for miles and the ominous red-orange glow even further.

Mr. Robertson's valet discovered the body of the Laird in his bed where he succumbed to the smoke. His was the only room in the mansion burned in this terrible fire.

Besides the Laird's servants, his sister and her family were also staying at Weetshill. They all escaped with their lives, even the Laird's adopted daughter, Jenny.

An air of mystery lingers. The Laird's wife of one year has vanished. The couple celebrated their anniversary on the day of the tragedy. It is unknown if she had anything to do with the fire. Kendonald's Police Constable Skinner is leading the investigation. He expects to enlist the aid of other members of the Aberdeenshire Constabulary.

Rachel read and re-read the article before printing it. Had Sarah read something about Weetshill before her accident? How else could she know the names? Or had her sister somehow travelled back in time? She scanned the remaining images on the reel. She saw no further information on the fire. Nothing about the Laird's funeral, or anything else to do with Weetshill mansion.

Pulling the printout from the machine, Rachel made sure it was legible then folded it up and tucked it in her bag. She knew the price for copies and a sign by the machines indicated it. There was no place near the microfilm machines to pay and she didn't have to insert coins to print.

She found her way to the shelves and scanned the books for anything about the mansion and the Robertsons. They had a publication on Weetshill but it was before 1886. It pertained to the history of the house rather than the occupants.

"Is there something I can help you find?" a disembodied, male voice asked.

Rachel turned around. There was no one there. Through a gap over top of the books, a grey-haired man bent over one of the display cases where the sound seemed to originate from. Had he been the person who had spoken to her?

"Do you work here?"

"Not work but I volunteer," the phantom voice replied.

Walking by the cabinet, Rachel found it odd he held his glasses in one hand, yet used a magnifying glass. Still his nose almost touched the map he was so engrossed in. When she reached the end, she perused the titles on the shelves behind him. With the Robertsons being a prominent family, there had to be something on them in the library. "You don't happen to know if there's a book here on the Robertsons who own Weetshill, do you."

He straightened up, stretched and disappeared. A few moments later, he returned holding the same book Rachel had looked through.

"Thanks but I've already seen that one. Is there something written about the family?"

"There used to be. I've not seen it in a long time. Before you leave, ask at the desk."

"Did you find everything you were looking for?" the librarian asked looking up from her computer.

"Just the one newspaper article. Do you have anything on the Robertsons of Weetshill? I didn't see anything on the shelves. The man back there said to ask you. He seems to think there was at one time."

"Oh, that would be Art. He would know. I swear he knows every publication here in Local Studies," the woman replied. "I can help you look for it if you'd like."

Consulting her watch, Rachel couldn't believe the time. She had spent the better part of three hours there. "I-I don't have time today," she stammered. "Maybe another time, I'll take this for now." She paid for the photocopy hoping it would appease Sarah. At least make her forget about continuing the search into the past.

"I'll get Art to give me a hand. We'll have a look about and see if we can find anything on the family and leave it here at the desk. The next time you're in, you can ask whoever is on duty for it."

"Thanks. That's brilliant."

When Rachel stepped out of the library, Niamh and Blair walked past. They stopped at the Union Terrace crossing. She hoped they didn't see her. They were the last two people she wanted to see. Niamh draped herself over Blair and held her left hand out with her fingers spread. As she waggled them, Rachel saw a diamond ring and a sizeable one, too. She had to get to the hospital and tell Sarah. But could she do that to her? Waltz into the hospital room and tell her Blair had asked Niamh to marry him? And given her a diamond ring? No. She would have to tell Sarah some time but not today and not that way.

12

The next day one of the nurses removed Sarah's IV and catheter. It was the first step towards feeling human again. After washing, she applied her makeup. At least now when she looked at her reflection in the mirror, she didn't look quite so corpse-like. She had some color, albeit false.

Another nurse helped her out of bed and into a wheelchair. She adjusted the footrests elevating Sarah's legs so the cage on her one leg didn't bind anywhere. When she left, Sarah lifted the top edge of the bandage. Glimpsing the metal piercing her skin she was almost sick. She leaned forward and inspected her other leg, too. Now without the bandages, she thought it looked disgusting. The impact site appeared caved in. Spider webs of red scars fanned out from it. She'd never be able to wear shorts or dresses again. Not with a leg looking like that. She began to cry.

Mr. Youssef walked past her door but backed up and stuck his head around the frame. "Are you all right, Miss Shand?"

She shook her head in response.

He pulled over a plastic chair and sat backwards on it with his arms folded on its back. "Tell me, my dear, whatever is it?"

"My legs, they're awful looking."

The surgeon looked at her un-bandaged leg. "It looks fine to me. Give yourself time to heal. It will be good as new in time."

"Look," Sarah stabbed her finger at the spot on her shin upsetting her so much. "That. You call that fine?"

"The bone hasn't completely joined together yet. It all takes time. Be patient, my dear."

Patience wasn't one of Sarah's strong suits. It never had been and now that she was in hospital, at the mercy of the doctors and nurses, it wore thinner each day. There was nothing to do but stare at the walls or the ceiling. The design in the tiles swirled and made her dizzy if she looked at them for too long.

Mr. Youssef removed a tissue from the box and handed it to her. "Take this."

Sarah wiped her eyes and blew her nose.

"I'm going to order some x-rays. We'll see how well your legs are coming along. Maybe within a day or two, we'll be able to take you back to theatre and remove your external fixator. Cheer up, dear girl. Things could be far worse."

After he left, Sarah punched the arms of her chair over and over. Her frustration over not being able to do things for herself had hit the breaking point. A voice whispered to her, "Stop. Don't do that to yourself, Sarah."

She jerked her head up and looked around the room. No one was there other than her. Who had spoken? A strange sound buzzed in her ears and she clapped her hands over them to block it but the volume increased. The now familiar shimmering appeared in the corner and Robert appeared. When he reached her side, he kissed the top of her head then took her hand in his, lacing his fingers through hers. "Your face is a mess. What are you doing wearing that paint? You know I don't approve. It makes you look like a cheap trollop."

Sarah wiped her face trying to remove her makeup. Without a mirror to hand, she had no idea if her attempt was successful. She figured she had dark circles under her eyes running down her cheeks from her eyeliner and mascara. Waterproof, maybe. Tear-proof, not so much.

"That's better. You can clean yourself up later."

Robert's terseness wasn't typical. Something more than her wearing makeup bothered him.

"Jenny misses you so much, Sarah," he whispered, kneeling beside her. He cupped his hand around her cheek and stroked her face with his thumb.

"And I miss her, too."

His hand was warm and Sarah nuzzled into it craving his touch. "Why didn't she come with you?"

"This place frightens her. She had a seizure after she last saw you. She needs you, Sarah. I need you. You must get well and come back to us."

"I want to. But I don't know how." Sobs escaped from Sarah's lips. Her body convulsed with her cries.

"Maybe this will help," Robert soothed. He reached into the inside, breast pocket of his suit jacket and pulled out the velvet pouch. He handed it to Sarah. "Open it," he urged.

Hands shaking, Sarah poked her finger into the top of the bag and pulled it open. She turned it upside down and her missing jewelry fell into her lap. "My rings," she gasped. "I hope you didn't go out and replace them."

"No. I found them in your old room. Not in the trinket box but on the dressing table behind it." Robert tried to put the objects on Sarah but he couldn't get them past the second joint of her finger. "Your hands; they're so swollen."

Sarah began to cry. "Please hold me," she begged.

Robert shifted his position and wrapped his arms around her, drawing her as close to him as possible. With one hand, he stroked her long, brown hair.

His touch soothed her but at the same time frightened her. What if she could never get back to them? What if something happened to Jenny? She had already changed history by going back to the past once, hadn't she? But what would another journey do? "Tell me what to do Robert. Tell me how to get back to you and Jenny."

"I wish I knew the answer. I can't explain how I find my way here to you, now, in my future."

"Take these with you." She removed the rings and choked back a sob before returning them to the velvet bag.

"They're staying here with you where they belong." He lifted her hand and kissed it. "Keep them here. Maybe they're the key."

His touch became lighter until she could no longer feel him near her. Hoping he was still in the room, she whispered, "I love you. And tell Jenny I love her very much, too."

Not receiving a reply, Sarah raised her head to look for him again but there was no trace. He had vanished.

Later in the day, an orderly came and took Sarah to the x-ray department. She didn't want to get her hopes up. The prospect of having whatever Mr. Youssef called it removed was too much to think of. But it would be a huge step to regaining her independence.

13

"Look at you," David exclaimed. "When I left to go to my mum's, you were still in bed."

"They got me up not long after you left. I can get out of bed with help. I hate not being able to do things for myself."

"You were seriously injured, don't forget. It will take time."

"Time, that's all I've got," Sarah snapped. "I do nothing but stare at four walls all day. I want to get out and do things. I'm bored out of my skull."

"What about reading? I can get the nurses to leave you some magazines or the tabloids even. Now those would give you a right laugh. You'd soon quit feeling sorry for yourself."

Other peoples' problems might take Sarah's mind off her predicament. "Thanks," she mumbled.

"What about physio? Have you started yet?"

"No. At least it would give me something to do." Sarah smiled.

"I'll look into it for you?" He paused. "You know, you're quite pretty when you smile."

Sarah felt her cheeks burning and knew she was blushing. "Please."

David pulled out his BlackBerry and typing with his thumbs, entered a reminder.

"What did your mum say?"

"Well when I got there, she had the paper open to the article. It was on the coffee table so she has an interest in the piece, too. She said she was too busy this weekend to go through her trunk full of notes and other documents."

"How long will it be before she does?"

"I can't say for sure. But she will do it." She's going to try to look through them in the next while and she'll ring me if she finds something. Oh, and before I forget, my mum would love to meet you. She found your take on what happened during those few months at Weetshill intriguing. I hope you don't mind that I told her."

"I don't. I hope she doesn't think I'm crazy."

"Nah."

Disappointed David hadn't brought any information back to her, Sarah sighed. Without it, she had no idea how she could get back to Robert and Jenny.

"You got music on your iPhone?" he asked.

"I used to, why?"

"If it's still there you could listen to it. Help pass the time."

"No headphones or earbuds."

"I'll get you some. Pretty sure I've got an extra pair going back at my flat still in the packaging," David rambled. He typed another reminder into his BlackBerry. "Sorry but with the crazy hours I work here and study, if I don't make notes, I'll never remember to do a thing."

Sarah smiled and laughed. "Oh wait," she babbled. "I've got something to show you. She took the velvet drawstring bag from her pocket and dumped the contents into her hand. "My rings. I told you about them."

David took them from her. The plain gold band, and a ruby surrounded by diamonds appeared to be over one hundred years old.

"They're mine. It's my engagement ring from Robert and my wedding band."

"If these belong to you then try them on. If they're yours, they'll fit."

Her hands remained swollen from the IV fluids pumped into her during her comatose state. Sarah struggled to put the rings on the third finger of her left hand but she could only get them half way up.

"I'll take them to the desk for safe-keeping. If someone is missing them, they can retrieve them there."

"Please, you can't," Sarah begged. "They really are mine. Look how swollen my hands are. It's no wonder I can't get them on."

David had to agree Sarah's hands were puffy from the fluids. He looked closer at her. Even around her bright, emerald green eyes, there was swelling. He wanted to believe her but how was it possible she married a Laird on 30th October when she was in hospital.

"You don't believe me, do you?" Sarah mumbled.

"I think you're confused," he answered. Against his better judgment, he tucked the two pieces into the pocket of his tunic. "I'll hold on to them for you. How's that?"

"You promise you won't turn them in at the desk or to the police?"

"Why would you worry about me turning them in to the police?"

David asked.

"I've not stolen them. They *really* are mine. You have to believe me."

"I have to go. There are other patients I need to check on."

Sarah nodded and watched him leave the room. He had every reason not to believe what she'd told him, but those rings were hers. She knew they were. Robert knelt beside her chair the night before. He brought them to her.

Mr. Youssef stopped in about twenty minutes after David left. "I have excellent news for you my dear. I put a rush on your x-rays and I'm happy to tell you the bone in your leg lines up the way it should be. We'll be able to remove the external fixator. I'll check the theatre schedule and get you in there as soon as there is an available slot."

"That's brilliant," Sarah exclaimed. She couldn't wait to get rid of the ugly thing.

"You'll require a leg brace for about six to eight weeks. But all things considered that's a very minor detail."

"Leg brace?"

"Yes, my dear. It will go from your ankle to past your knee. But don't worry; it's hinged so you'll be able to bend your leg. It's molded plastic which wraps partway around your leg. It fastens in place with Velcro straps," he replied scribbling a likeness of what he talked about.

14

Robert paced back and forth on the railway platform, waiting for the train on which his esteemed guest would arrive. He pulled out the letter and read it again for the umpteenth time. Afterwards, he returned it to the inside breast pocket of his overcoat. Glancing up at the clock, he pulled his silver pocket watch out and checked the time. Both were within seconds of each other.

Since the snow came, the temperatures had hovered below freezing. The icy conditions complicated travel. Even dressed in a wool overcoat, Robert found it cold. Now though, the air was damp meaning more snow was in the offing but the skies remained clear.

A shrill whistle pierced the otherwise quiet air. The belching black smoke from the locomotive smudged the bright, blue sky. Another blast of the shrieking sound and the train chugged to a halt in front of the station.

The professor stepped onto the platform. Robert strode towards him. "Good to see you again, Ian," he greeted, shaking the man's hand. "Come, Callum has the carriage waiting for us. Do you have any other baggage?"

"No only these," Ian replied lifting his arms revealing a carpet bag and briefcase.

"Mrs. MacEwen has promised that luncheon will be ready for us on our return." Robert guided his companion by the right elbow.

"Where is your lovely wife? I thought she would have accompanied you."

Robert ignored him, happy they had reached the end of the station. They stood at the area where the coaches and their drivers waited for passengers. It would become awkward soon enough. He wanted to put the unpleasantness off for the foreseeable future.

Callum took the man's bags and opened the carriage door. He stood aside allowing the professor to board. Once he had, he placed the luggage on the floor.

Robert sat opposite the professor. He felt the man's eyes probing his from under a pair of thick black eyebrows. He cast his eyes towards the floor.

"I'm so looking forward to seeing your wife again, Robert. She is such a delightful lassie and I have to say I'm most envious of you. Not too many gentlemen have done so well for themselves as you."

"I suppose," Robert mumbled.

"Whatever is wrong? You're in a terrible state of vexation." Ian replied and placed his hand on Robert's thigh. "Tell me."

"It's nothing. Sarah had to return home," Robert lied. "Family emergency she said. I miss her."

"My condolences, my dear fellow. I'm quite sure she's feeling the same way. What of the wee lassie? Jenny's her name? How is she, or did she accompany your wife?"

"Jenny is fine. She's missing Sarah, too. She's at Weetshill with my sister and her two children."

"I'm pleased you have people with you during these difficult times." Ian settled back into his seat.

The carriage crunched to a stop in front of Weetshill. Robert opened the door to exit and almost stepped on his butler.

Recovering from his initial shock, he cleared his throat. "Archibald, will you attend to Ian's bags. That will allow Callum to return to the stables and look after the horse and carriage."

"Aye, sir. If you and Mr. Ross retire to the library, I'll be there straight away to fetch you both a whisky."

"No need. You take Ian's bags up to the room Mrs. MacEwen prepared for him. I'll get us each a dram," Robert replied, brushing past his servant. Ian's questions had been far too probing on the carriage ride and he needed a drink to steady his nerves.

As Robert approached the house, the grandfather clock chimed one o'clock. Within seconds the mantle clock in the library echoed, becoming louder as he opened the door. He hoped beyond all hope Sarah would be in the chair by the window but it was empty like his heart. He perked up at the sound of swishing skirts but disappointment washed over him when he saw his sister.

"Where is Professor Ross?" Margaret asked.

Robert hastened past her to greet his guest. "Forgive my manners, Ian. Most rude of me but I've not been quite myself since Sarah left."

"Apology accepted, my friend."

Breathing a sigh of relief, Robert escorted his guest into the library. "You remember my sister, Margaret?"

"Aye." Ian took her hand, bowed and planted his loose, damp lips to the back of it.

Margaret pulled her hand out of his grasp.

"Robert told me on the carriage ride here his wife, oh I can't think of her name at the moment. Lovely lassie though," the professor faltered, his face turning bright red.

"Sarah," Margaret replied.

"Yes, Sarah," Ian blurted, taking the glass from his host. "She had to return home on rather short notice."

"Margaret?" Robert asked.

She took the glass from her brother sending him back to the table for his own beverage.

"When I was up for the hunt August last, Miss Sh ... I mean Mrs. Robertson and I had such a wonderful chat. I hoped to be able to continue where we left off."

Feeling his sister's eyes staring at him, Robert squirmed. "Unpreventable, Ian, but I would love to discuss those things and more with you after our luncheon."

Soon afterwards, the butler announced the midday meal and they made their way to the dining room. "No children?" Robert asked taking his place at the head of the table after seating Margaret.

"Nae, sir. We fed them afore you so you can talk wi' out 'em buttin' in." Mrs. MacEwen ladled soup from the tureen on the sideboard before handing the filled bowls off to the maid. "There be fresh bread, too, sir. Morag were slicin' it when I broughts the broth in."

Without the three children's laughter and bickering the dining room was too quiet. Robert wished they could have eaten with the adults. A maid brought in a plate of thick sliced bread and the earthenware bowl with butter. She placed both on the table then exited the room without a sound.

Once they finished the soup course, the housekeeper placed a leg of lamb at the far end of the table. Archibald carved and served. The maids brought bowls of potatoes and carrots in. Mrs. MacEwen saw to it everyone received a generous helping.

"I brought the material you requested, Robert. When and where would you like to discuss it?" Ian asked before taking a sip of the wine the butler had chosen earlier to go with their meal.

"The library once we've finished dining, I believe. We can spread your papers out on the desk if needs must and we can talk in private." Robert looked at Margaret. "Perhaps, we could even walk to the stone circle before darkness closes in."

"A splendid idea, Robert," Professor Ross replied. He shoved a forkful of potato into his mouth.

After they finished their meals, Robert and his guest returned to the library. Ian went upstairs and returned with his briefcase. He rummaged through it and pulled out an ordnance survey map. "It's from 1867 but the stone circle is right here." He peered at the map until he found the location and put his right index finger on the spot. "And Weetshill is here." The professor marked the mansion's location with his other hand. "Mark these two spots for me, will you? There's a good lad."

He then took a straight edge and lined it up so both locations were on it. "Now if you continue beyond your mansion you pass through the Strichen Circle. So, if there is something to these lines, then the stone circle and Weetshill are on one. Now if you follow on a different orientation." He moved the stick as he spoke. "The stone circle is in direct alignment with Deer Abbey and the Old Kirk over at Old Deer."

Robert took in a deep breath and exhaled. "Ian, promise me you won't think I'm mad. I've had strange things happen when I've been at the stone circle. Sometimes when I was a wee boy and since Sarah's return home and between here and there."

"I want to see this stone circle. You can tell me of your experiences along the way. Perhaps the Kendonald area is a hub of mystic powers. Not that I'm a believer in hocus pocus but I am fascinated with time and all things old. That's why I studied archaeology."

Robert summoned the butler who retrieved their outerwear. "There be quite the nip in the air, sir. Dinnae stay out too long. You'll catch your death," Archibald declared helping his employer into his overcoat.

Outside the mansion, the men strode up the laneway to the gates. Robert related some of his recent experiences to his companion. At the Kendonald Road, he pointed out the tree that appeared different. He tried to describe what he had seen crashed into it. "It was in this location wee Jenny found something and brought it back to me. It had to have been from the future. I've never seen the like of it before or since."

"Most interesting, my friend," Ian mused stroking his chin. He walked to the tree and examined the trunk. It was pristine. "And do you still have this object? I'm interested in seeing it."

"No, I'm afraid I don't."

The men continued towards the stone circle. When they passed the Free Church and manse, Robert paused. "It's no use, Ian. I can't lie any longer. I can't explain how or why but somehow Sarah has gone into the future. She told me these places don't exist in her time. She'd never heard of them before."

"I believe there was a church indicated on the map I brought," Ian replied. "You say the stone circle is just ahead." He turned back to look at Weetshill. We're most definitely on one of these straight lines. I believe your wife called them Ley Lines?"

"I think you're right. Shall we carry on?" Robert extended his arm beckoning the professor to continue.

The tops of the upright stones poked up above the hill and Robert quickened his pace. Would Sarah be there waiting for him? Wondering where he was? He hoped so but kept his hopes tempered to avoid disappointment when the place was void of life.

Once they reached their destination, Robert collapsed onto the boulder lying on the ground. He had seen Sarah sit on it many times. Ian, standing nearby, leaned against one of the upright stones gasping for breath.

"This is quite the place you've brought me to, Robert," the professor wheezed. "So you say you've seen strange things here?"

"Yes, from the time I was a young lad and Margaret and I used to play here. Actually, I've seen Sarah as a young lassie with an elderly woman. They sat in this exact place. She told me the woman was her grandmother."

"Most interesting," Ian replied walking around the stones. "But didn't you say your wife was from Edinburgh?"

"I did. It was a lie. It was the only way we could marry. My Sarah lives right here on this land … in the future."

"What else can you tell me about the place?"

Robert stood and joined his companion. He had been honest with the professor but the man hadn't paid any attention to him it seemed. "The day Jenny found the object by the tree we were on the path as well. When we started for home, one minute we were here and the next we were in a strange place. Sarah was there and connected to all sorts of bizarre machines. We were there for such a short time and the next thing we knew we were back on the path. Margaret's children saw us fade away and it terrified them."

"No doubt. Where was the farmhouse located you told me about?"

"Down there at the foot of the hill," Robert replied, his attention still on the track they had walked. "The barn was across the road."

"Was the house a one and a half story, two dormer windows on the upper level on the façade perpendicular to the road? Drystane dykes around it?"

"Why yes," Robert cried. "You can see it?"

"Aye. Right there, as plain as the nose …," the professor declared.

Robert spun around and like his companion said, the house was there.

"Let's go speak to the occupants. Perhaps they can shed some light on things for us." Ian trotted down the hill.

Robert blinked a few times to ensure he wasn't seeing things then ran to catch up with Ian. "Surely, you can't be serious. We can't walk up and knock on the front door," Robert puffed when he caught up with the man. His protests were in vain.

Mrs. Shand walked into the vestibule to open the outer door. When she pulled it back, a strange man brought his hand up as if to knock on it. She jumped. "You scared the life out of me. I didn't hear your car pull in," she babbled.

"My good woman, I am so sorry to frighten you." He bowed and extended his hand to her.

"Who are you?"

"I am Mr. Ian Ross, Professor of Archaeology at the University of Aberdeen."

Was this guy for real? At first she thought she was seeing things. This man wore clothing which seemed to be over one hundred years out of date but in excellent condition. She knew some people in this field were eccentric, and maybe the man standing in front of her was one of them.

"Mrs. Shand," Robert stated and stepped forward to stand beside his companion. "Do you remember me?"

Staggering back into the hall table in the vestibule, she clutched her chest. "I-it's y-you," she sputtered."

"You would be Sarah's mother?" the professor inquired.

"Yes. Is something wrong with her? Do I need to go to the hospital?"

"Not that I am aware of. Robert told me she had to come home for a family emergency. I find it odd if she was staying this close to Weetshill, she wouldn't come here to see her family."

"Mrs. Shand. Are you quite all right? You've grown quite pale."

The woman started to collapse and Robert lunged to catch her before she fell and hurt herself. "I think you could do with a cup of tea, Mrs. Shand. I'll take you inside, get you settled then I'll make some tea for you."

Sarah's mother stared into Robert's golden-brown eyes. "I-I've met you before, haven't I?"

"Yes, you have. Sarah and I came here with our adopted daughter Jenny the day after our wedding."

"B-but our Sarah has been in hospital since August."

Following the woman's instructions, Robert carried her to the family dining room. After putting her down on the sofa, he entered the galley kitchen. Shocked by all the knobs, dials and shiny surfaces everywhere, he blinked. He always thought the kitchen at Weetshill was modern. This was something far beyond anything he'd ever seen, even at the Edinburgh Exhibition.

Befuddled, Robert returned to Mrs. Shand's side. "I'm sorry, but I'm afraid I don't know my way about in there."

Sarah's mother smiled.

"I'm not sure how to say this, but Sarah has been at Weetshill since August."

"The kettle is on the worktop. Make sure there is water in it and plug it in," she instructed.

"However, I have seen some strange things. Whilst walking from Weetshill to the stone circle, I saw Sarah lying in the road. Some strange sort of carriage crashed into a tree."

"There's a switch on the outlet you have to push. The teabags are in a box in the corner by the cooker."

"When I saw her on the road, she wore the same clothes as when I found her collapsed outside our front entrance."

"Milk is in the fridge and the sugar is ...,"

"Mrs. Shand, I need you to help me understand what is going on," Robert implored. He took the woman's upper arms in his hands. "I've seen Sarah where she is now and she has all manner of things connected to her body. I don't understand."

"You don't understand? How on earth could she end up back in the past? She got hit by a car. She's in Aberdeen Royal Infirmary and has been since that awful night. And besides, Weetshill mansion is a ruin."

"Ian, do you have any explanation?" Robert asked.

"I'm afraid I don't. My specialty is archaeology. I know nothing of what could only be explained as time travel?"

15

Jimmy Shand stepped through the back door of the farmhouse. He heard voices coming from the family dining room. He hadn't seen any cars other than Moira's in the driveway. It didn't sound like the radio and she never turned the telly on during the day. Two men stood with their backs to him in centuries' old-style clothing. Maybe they were Jehovah's Witnesses? Under normal circumstances, his wife didn't let them past the threshold.

"Moira?" he called out.

The men turned.

Straight away, he recognized the one. Scrubbing his hands down his face, Jimmy looked again. It couldn't be. This was like something out of a science-fiction movie. There was no way it could be happening. "I thought you swore to me you would take care of my daughter," he bellowed at Robert.

"Mr. Shand, I have taken care of Sarah. Excellent care."

"If you have, then why is she lying in hospital?" He rolled up his sleeves. "I could throttle you," Mr. Shand snarled.

Moira sprang from the couch and grabbed his arm. "Please, Jimmy, don't. I don't know what's happening any more than you but settling it with your fists isn't the answer." She turned to the visitors. "You better leave."

"We're sorry to cause you both such vexation. I know you want answers. So do I," Robert commented. "Come Ian, we'll take our leave now."

Tipping their hats to Mrs. Shand, they brushed past her husband and into the hallway. Jimmy followed with his wife still clinging to his arm. When the men reached the front door, they vanished.

"Get off me, woman," Mr. Shand yelled, shaking her grip from his arm. He rushed to the door and looked towards the road. Turned in the opposite direction, and up the hill in the direction of the stone circle. His feet clad only in white socks, he ran outside. He checked around the corners of the house but there was no trace of the strangers from the past.

Within seconds, Moira stood at his side.

"What the …?" Jimmy started. "What happened here?"

"I-I don't know."

"It's like something out of a science-fiction film. Those ones where they get talking about rifts in the space-time continuum. I don't get it. Those things don't happen in real life, do they?"

"Come back in the house, Jimmy. You'll catch your death out here with no boots on."

Robert and Ian stared at each other. What happened? When Robert turned, the house had vanished. The surrounding landscape was the way he always knew it. No Gordonsfield farm. No house. No barn. No explanation. Only the remains of the ruin's gable end below the hill visible from this vantage point. He rubbed his temples with his index and middle fingers to quell the throbbing but it was no use. If anything, the action made his head hurt even more.

"That was the most fascinating event, don't you think?"

His friend sounded gleeful. "Not quite the turn of phrase, I would choose. My head is aching. We should go back to Weetshill."

"Very well, as I wish to get this phenomenon documented on our return."

The men walked back up the hill in companionable silence to the laneway leading them back to the mansion.

Archibald met them at the front door on their return. "You look like you's seen a ghost, sir," he observed helping Robert shrug out of his overcoat. "Go in the library, I'll see you gets a drink."

Whisky wasn't what Robert wanted. He wanted something which would take his headache away, not add to it. What was it Sarah talked about? Oh yes, Paracetamol but it wasn't yet invented. He could have Doctor Burnett prescribe morphine or some other opiate but that was more than he needed. Besides, he was sure he had read or heard those drugs were addictive.

"If you'll excuse me, Robert, I'm going to my room so I can get this written down whilst it remains fresh in my mind. A most extraordinary experience," he rambled walking to the stairs.

The butler followed Robert into the library and poured him a dram before leaving.

Drink in hand; he stared out the window over the grounds towards the stone circle. How could he get Sarah back to Weetshill? He knew he and Jenny got to her in whatever time and place she was.

Regardless who went when or where, was there any guarantee they would stay? With Sarah swept back to *her time* and he and Jenny materializing there, he concluded staying in the other's time forever was impossible.

"Here you are, Robert. I saw Ian rushing down the corridor to his room. I thought you might be in here. He seemed to be quite excited. Nothing at all like you."

"Sit down, Margaret."

She slipped into Sarah's favorite chair. "Go on," she urged making herself comfortable.

Robert sat his drink on the table beside the wingback. He related the events he and the professor had experienced. The expressions on his sister's face as he spoke told him she didn't believe a word. He knew she wouldn't before he even started but getting it off his chest was paramount.

"Oh poor, Robert. You poor dear," Margaret comforted standing and hugging him. "Losing Sarah like this has been so, *so* difficult for you. You need to face the fact she's not coming back to you and Jenny."

"I'll do no such thing," he hissed. "Sarah is coming back. If I have to move heaven and earth to make it happen, then so be it. I will."

Robert stormed out of the library. Shrugging into his overcoat, he grabbed his bowler and gloves from the rack. He slammed the front door behind him. The fresh air did nothing to appease him. If anything, it made him angrier.

He had no particular destination in mind. He needed to get away from Weetshill and his sister's biting tongue. That's all that mattered. Picking up a windfall, he juggled it then heaved it with all of his might.

Before he knew it, Robert stood outside the gate at the Old Kirkyard. Maybe some quiet contemplation here was what he needed. With luck, his grandfather would bestow some words of wisdom on him. Help him through this difficult time, or better still tell him how to get Sarah home where she belonged.

Robert lifted the latch on the gate and started through. A flash of color appeared from the middle of the churchyard near his grandparents' grave. Did Sarah come back to him? Did she come here rather than the mansion because she didn't know what kind of welcome she'd receive? Racing to the spot where he'd seen the movement, Robert crept around the headstone. A figure in a black velvet cloak and royal blue gown knelt there, its face obscured by the outer garment. Unable to contain himself any longer, he reached down and pulled the person up. "Sarah," he stated. "You've come back."

The person pulled the hood down with their free hand and shook their head. Blonde tresses spilled out. The head tipped up to face him – the corners of the mouth curling into a smile.

"Letitia," he yelled. "What on earth are you doing back here?"

"I came for Jenny."

"What do you mean, you came for Jenny?" he asked, tightening his grip on her arm.

"I want her to live with father and me. She is our child."

"Never," Robert yelled, grabbing her other arm and shaking her. "You'll never get her back. I swear."

"I wouldn't be so sure," she sneered.

"She's mine and Sarah's now. We've taken her in, given her the Robertson name. And we have the legal documents to prove it."

"I-I gave birth to her," Letitia yelled.

"And your father, the other person you want to take Jenny to live with, threatened to kill her. She was a disgrace to the Christie name. If he didn't want her then, I don't believe he'd want her now."

"Father has changed, Robert. He's much kinder now."

"Horatio Christie kind? I don't believe it." Robert let go of Letitia's arms and pushed her away from him.

"He's dying. He wants to make amends for the things he's done," she sniffled.

"Oh please," Robert drawled. He moved closer and waggled his finger in her face. "I'm warning you right now, Letitia Christie. You or your father come anywhere near Weetshill and my family. I'll see you're prosecuted to the full extent of the law. Do you understand?"

Turning on his heel, Robert stamped off. Having the Christies back in Kendonald was the last thing he needed. Compounded now with the threat of taking Jenny away from him. He must keep her safe and out of Horatio's and his demented daughter's clutches. That was his number one priority. It even ranked higher than getting Sarah back to this time.

"Mr. Robertson, what brings you here today?" Police Constable Skinner asked, looking up from his desk.

"I don't believe it. The nerve of those people," Robert mumbled.

"What people?"

"I've seen Letitia Christie in the Old Kirkyard. She says she and her father are back."

"After the ruckus they caused before you and Miss Shand wed? I best pay them a visit."

"There's more. She says they've come for Jenny. Sarah and I have adopted her. They can't take her away from us. You remember the information Jean MacDonald gave us that day."

"Aye," the policeman mused, standing up and straightening the papers on his desk. "You go home to your family Mr. Robertson. I'll come and see you after I've talked to Horatio."

"Can't you do more than that?" Robert asked, pounding his fist on the desk.

"Calm yourself. Getting worked up won't solve anything."

"Arrest him then."

"I cannae. Not for this 'cause it hasnae happened yet. Could it be Miss Letitia wants to cause you grief since you dinnae marry her?"

"Possibly," Robert murmured. It sounded logical. Letitia Christie getting revenge for him buying his way out of their arranged marriage. Maybe that's all it was. She wanted to get her own back on him and the easiest way to accomplish that was to threaten to take Jenny away from him.

Drifting towards the door, Robert paused and turned. Rubbing the back of his head, he glared at Police Constable Skinner. "What about the attack on my wife? Horatio Christie was behind it. You wanted to arrest him then but he and Letitia had already disappeared."

"Please, Mr. Robertson, I am the one appointed by Her Majesty the Queen to uphold the law. Let me worry about Horatio Christie. Now go home."

16

Slamming the front door of Weetshill mansion behind him, Robert rushed into the library. He pushed the door crashing shut. Go home. Don't worry. How could he not worry? He took the stopper out of the whisky decanter. He poured himself a large glass, downed it in one gulp and poured another.

The door latch clicked followed by creaking hinges and swishing skirts. "Robert, whatever is going on?"

He ignored his sister and paced about the room, muttering to himself. Standing behind the desk, he took a few deep breaths. Robert leaned forward and swept everything off the surface with his arm. When the ink well hit the floor, it shattered. A spray of droplets cascaded into the air and onto the walls, bookcases and other furnishings. A puddle of black pooled around the remains of the glass object. It was soon followed by the paraffin desk lamp. The oil lay on top of the spilled ink and being thinner spread faster.

"Dammit, dammit, dammit." Robert pounded his fists on the desk in unison with his curses.

Margaret rushed to his side. "Please tell me what has you so vexed."

The butler and housekeeper charged into the room.

"It's all right. Go now. Let me speak with my brother alone and then you can clean up this mess," she instructed.

When the servants retreated, she took Robert by the arm and led him to the sofa. "Tell me, please."

"Letitia and Horatio Christie are back."

"They can't be."

"They are, trust me."

"How do you know?"

"After I left here earlier, I went to the Old Kirkyard and Letitia was there," Robert replied.

"I can't believe they would be so stupid. I mean after all the uproar they caused before your wedding?"

"Letitia said they had come back to take Jenny to live with them."

"Oh dear God, no," Margaret lamented collapsing on the sofa beside her brother.

Constable Skinner locked the police house. In the small livery in the back, he hitched his horse to the constabulary's Black Maria. This was a visit he dreaded. Horatio Christie, the overbearing, overweight, pompous Laird had many questionable dealings over the years. He had always managed to stay on the right side of the law – just. That was until he paid Hamish MacMillan to attack Sarah Shand – now Mrs. Robert Robertson.

When he reached Gleanstane, the place looked deserted. A twitch of a curtain in an upstairs window said otherwise. Gripping the doorknocker, he rapped on the brass plate.

After a brief wait, metal hasps scraping echoed through the heavy wood, and the door creaked open.

"I'm looking for Horatio Christie. Word has it he and Letitia are back in the area."

"Aye," the elderly butler invited, "This way."

The old man shuffled ahead of him to a doorway off to the left of the corridor. When the servant turned the knob, it creaked open. "Police Constable Skinner to see you, sir."

"Show him in, Carlyle. Show him in."

Any hopes Horatio Christie squirmed at the announcement dashed. The man appeared as cool and untouchable as ever.

"Good to see you, Skinner. Good to see you. Sit down. Carlyle, get the man a whisky."

"No thank you," the policeman replied. Keeping a clear head while speaking with the man was imperative. One drink could lead to more and he'd lose any chance of getting any useful information.

"What brings you here today? I say ..."

"I spoke with Mr. Robertson, the Laird over to Weetshill", he interrupted. "He told me he saw Miss Letitia in the Old Kirkyard. The two of you plan on taking the wee lassie, Jenny, away to live with you."

"Nonsense, utter nonsense," Horatio bellowed.

"Well, your daughter certainly has Mr. Robertson vexed."

"First thing I hear when we return is his new bride has run off and left him. Run off and left him. He broke the arranged marriage agreement. Had he not, he would remain wed to my beautiful, Letitia. She would never do such a ruthless thing."

It didn't sound like a fair trade for Robert. But that wasn't why he came. He had to get straight to the point and keep Horatio onside. "I'm sorry to hear about your ill health and impending demise."

"Ill health? Impending demise? I'm healthy as an ox. Healthy as an ox, I say. Where did you hear such poppycock?"

"I'd like you to come with me back to the station. We can have a proper chat without the distractions of Gleanstane."

Noting, Mr. Christie's puzzled expression, Skinner took a deep breath. This had to work. It couldn't blow up in his face. An arrest of this nature was new to him and he had to tread with caution. The first step was getting Horatio outside the mansion.

"Carlyle, fetch my overcoat, hat and gloves," he bellowed.

Outside, Horatio started to climb up into the driver's seat of the Black Maria.

"Ahem, Mr. Christie, back here please."

"What? Why are you treating me like a common criminal? Why?"

"Because Horatio Christie, I am arresting you. The charges are incest, forgery, and paying Hamish MacMillan to attack Sarah Shand. Said attack caused the effusion of blood, broken bones and danger to her life."

"You'll not take me, I say. You'll not," he snarled and lumbered away from the horse-drawn vehicle.

The next thing Horatio knew, he lay face down in the gravel. Police Constable Skinner sat on the small of his back, twisting his arm up behind him.

"Stand up," he ordered and gave his prisoner's arm another jerk.

"Letitia," Horatio called out. "Get word to my solicitor I need him urgently. He needs to come to the Police Station in Kendonald – now."

Bundled and locked into the back of the paddy wagon, Horatio pounded on the front wall. "You'll not get away with this," Mr. Christie roared.

He didn't receive a verbal reply. The carriage lurched into motion propelling him against the wall. He hoped Letitia heard his plea to get his solicitor. He knew he'd gone too far in his attempt to get Sarah Shand out of Robert's life once and for all. His darling Letitia deserved to get the man she loved. Now he had to get himself out of the mess. Why had he buckled to his daughter's pleas to return home so she could get her daughter back? He should have stuck to his story the child died soon after its birth. That's why Jean MacDonald whisked it away. He remembered the night the wee lassie was born. Banished from Letitia's room during her labor, he still had the scars on his left index finger. He'd chomped down on it every time he heard her scream in pain. But he had such a soft spot for his daughter, he had to come clean and tell the truth. Now because of the things he had done in the name of love for Letitia, he risked spending time in prison.

The Black Maria groaned to a stop. Moments later, Police Constable Skinner opened the door. "Inside." It wasn't an invitation but an order.

Horatio descended from the paddy wagon. Pushed forward by the lawman, he stumbled. When the prodding got to be too much he whirled around and bellowed, "I'm going, I say. I'm going."

"Careful Mr. Christie. I dinnae take kindly to threats."

Inside the police station, Skinner shoved Horatio into a cell and slammed the door shut. The scrape of metal on the hasp and click of the padlock told him any escape attempt would be in vain.

The accommodations were far from opulent. There was a chamber pot in the far corner. A narrow bed stood along the opposite wall. The sight of chains and shackles bolted into the stone horrified him. Metal clanked from the other cell indicating its occupant was fighting the restraints. Frustrated, Horatio kicked the chamber pot. He dropped onto the bed and buried his face in his hands. How had it come to this? What would the people of Kendonald think? If anyone saw him wrestled to the ground and shoved into the Black Maria, his reputation would be in tatters. Horatio yelled through the small barred window. "Skinner, can I have a word? A chat like two civilized gentlemen?"

He heard the scrape of wood against wood from the main part of the police station. Footfalls coming in his direction followed the noise. "What do you want?"

"Why don't we come to some kind of agreement? I recently came into a large sum of money. Two thousand, five hundred pounds. It's yours if you let me go and never speak a word of this to anyone."

"If it was something minor like not adhering to the regulations for keeping animals. Allowing too much filth to accumulate on your lands, I might be able to look the other way. But when it's related to such a number of serious incidents, I cannae. I'm sorry, but you'll be standing trial right along with your henchman."

Niamh crept down the corridor towards Sarah's room. She'd tied her bright red hair into a ponytail, and hid it under a ball cap. Her large Oakley sunglasses, obscured most of her face. She hoped no one recognized her. She had slipped past security downstairs. Now so close to her destination, she couldn't get caught. What she had to tell Sarah was so important she had to get it off her chest.

She paused in front of the corridor window opening into Sarah's room and saw Sarah in a chair with her back to the door.

Taking a deep breath to summon her courage, Niamh stepped through the door and into the quiet room. But it wouldn't remain silent for long. She stepped closer, her trainers muffling the sounds of her footsteps. When she reached Sarah's chair, she touched her on the shoulder.

Sarah jumped and turned around. "Who are you?" she demanded.

Niamh removed her ball cap and took her hair out of the ponytail. She shook her head releasing her tresses from the shape from being bound. She grabbed the arm of her sunglasses and removed them.

"You," Sarah seethed. "You're barred from here. How did you get past security and the nurses' desk? I don't want to see you. Don't want any more to do with you – you boyfriend stealing cow!"

"Please Sarah, listen to me."

"Why should I?"

"I know Blair and I hurt you and I am *so* sorry. You know how charming he can be."

"I do," Sarah snapped.

"I bumped into him at the railway station in Aberdeen after a day out. He was whingeing about how you never satisfied him. He wanted more from you than you were willing to give."

"What are you getting at?" Sarah demanded, gripping the arms of her chair.

"You were off in Glasgow, at college. I never intended for it to go anywhere."

"Anywhere?"

"We started hanging out together. Going to the cinema, bowling, out for a burger, the kinds of things mates do."

"What are you getting at?"

"I-I'm so sorry, Sarah. When you caught us snogging that day, I wanted to end it right then so you two could get back together. Blair wanted no part of it. He said he loved me. And I loved him. But I was willing to give him up for you. It was never meant to go any further."

"Obviously, it did," Sarah hissed.

Niamh bowed her head. "I am so, *so* sorry. It wasn't right to steal Blair away from you, but maybe if he was happy with you, he wouldn't have asked me to marry him."

"I could slap you silly, you know that. But you've got me at a disadvantage. I hate you Niamh MacIsaac."

Niamh tried to gather what bit of dignity she had left along with her ball cap and Oakleys. She stopped at the door. "Just for the record, I'll never forgive myself for what I've done to you, Sarah. I know you'll never forgive me. But at one time we were best friends and could tell each other anything. Guess I was hoping to get some of that back."

The next day the head of the physiotherapy department visited Sarah. "I'm to assess your ability to begin treatment," the woman stated, pulling a chair over.

Sarah smiled, hoping things would soon start moving and then she could get out of the hospital. The name tag read Jean Webb. She leaned over Sarah and manipulated her arms. Her white shirt covered chest lingered under Sarah's nose. The clothing reeked of bleach, making Sarah choke.

"So sorry," Jean apologized sitting beside Sarah. She pulled a small notebook out of one of her front pockets and a ballpoint pen out of the other.

Sarah watched the woman write. Her short, brown hair was spiky and streaked with grey. What Sarah wouldn't give to have her long hair washed and brushed again. She'd not seen the student nurse who gave her the bed shampoo since that day. But it wasn't all that important. Getting out of this chair and this place was.

Jean crossed and uncrossed her legs. The fabric on her pant legs scraped. She raised her head and scowled at Sarah then went back to her notebook. A few minutes later, she clicked her biro shut and jammed it back in her pocket along with the notebook.

"Well?" Sarah asked.

"We can't do anything until the surgeon removes the external fixator from your leg. At least not properly."

Sarah bowed her head in disappointment and buried her face in her hands.

"That's not to say we can't do anything," Jean went on.

The news perked Sarah up and she looked straight into the woman's dull, grey eyes.

"I'll get some weights brought up so you can start working on your arm muscles. We'll start you on that. You'll need upper body strength before you'll be able to come down to the physio suite."

"So when will I be able to do more?"

"That will be up to your surgeon," Jean said, pausing at the door.

"Are you going to talk to him?" Sarah called after her but it was too late. The woman had disappeared into the corridor.

Later that day, Jill put a sign on the wall above the bed. "What does that mean?" Sarah asked.

"You're scheduled for theatre tomorrow to have the external fixator removed," she answered.

Mrs. Shand arrived at the hospital about nine-thirty the following morning. She wanted to be there before Sarah went for her operation.

The theatre team came for Sarah and her mother walked with her as far as allowed. "I'll be waiting for you. I'll be here when you wake up." She leaned over the gurney and kissed her daughter's forehead. She held Sarah's hand until they wheeled her through the huge double doors.

Waking up in recovery, Sarah thought she was in a long tunnel. The far side of the room appeared to be miles away. The walls on each side of her seemed to close in. A nurse stopped and checked on her, took her blood pressure and checked the surgical site. "You'll be able to go back to your room in another hour," she whispered, adjusting an IV drip.

The walls on either side of her bed turned out to be curtains. The nurse left but opened them more allowing Sarah to see around the room. There was at least one bed on her right and it looked like three or four on her left. Now the opposite side of the room didn't seem so far away.

When they wheeled Sarah back to her room, Mrs. Shand met her and walked with her. Mr. Youssef was there, too, and he talked to both of them about the surgery. Sarah was too groggy to comprehend much of the conversation. The rest of the day, she dozed off in the middle of words. Finally, her mother kissed her goodbye promising she'd be back soon.

About ten o'clock that night, Sarah pulled the blankets away from her leg. The cage was gone. The leg brace her orthopedic surgeon told her she would need would soon take its place.

17

The next time David stopped in to check on her progress, Sarah thought he seemed evasive. On his previous official visits, they chatted while he conducted his examination. All he'd said to her was the usual greeting she got from everyone. "How are you doing today?"

Today was no different from any other day, although she had used the weighted wristbands a few times to exercise her arms. She was so tired of people asking the same question day in and day out. At least the conversations progressed from that point but not today. Unable to remain quiet any longer, she broke the awkward silence. "What's wrong? You're not yourself today."

"Huh? Oh nothing."

"You can't fool me ... uh ... what's your name?"

"David Robb. Don't you remember?"

"No, I guess I forgot it." Sarah, alarmed she'd forgotten his name, tried to get her previous train of thought back. When it returned, after another awkward silence, she continued. "We've spent enough time together I know something is up."

David looked at his watch. "Dammit. Is that the time? I've got to go."

"Will I see you later?"

"Aye. I'll stop in after my shift. Oh and here are the earbuds I promised you," he answered digging them out of his tunic pocket.

Sarah found David's behavior unnerving. He'd been open and kind to her and today he couldn't get out of her room fast enough. Had he found a girlfriend or did he already have one and didn't know how to tell her? Had management reprimanded him for spending too much time with her? Or worse, did he know something about her condition she didn't?

At the usual time for David to drop in after his shift, there was no sign of him. Supper time came and went and still no David.

Sarah's dismay turned to anger. Eleven o'clock arrived without a hint of him showing up. She rolled over and pulled the covers up around her ears.

Since she came out of the coma, Sarah experienced many personality changes. She'd always been stubborn and had a temper much like her father. Her irritability was far worse and far more frequent than it had ever been.

18

Days later, the Justiciary Court judge arrived at the Police Station. "Tell me what you have here," he stated.

"Well, Hamish MacMillan for criminal assault. It caused the effusion of blood, broken bones and danger to life of a Miss Sarah Shand. He's already at the East Prison awaiting trial."

"Anything else?"

"Horatio Christie, Laird of Gleanstane. He's charged with incest, forgery, and paying Hamish MacMillan to assault Miss Shand. I've now added bribery to the list of charges."

"Do we have witnesses?" the court official asked.

"Yes," replied Police Constable Skinner. "Mr. Robert Robertson, Laird of Weetshill, and now husband of the victim. He came along in the middle of the attack."

"And the victim?"

"I'm afraid she's had to go away and we dinnae ken when she'll be back in the area."

"Hmm, I see. And the charges brought against Horatio Christie. Do you have witnesses for that case as well?"

"I can assemble them given a few days; a week at the most."

"Very well. I suggest you get Horatio Christie moved to the East Prison, too. Given the severity of the charges, these are both High Court cases. These men will have their trials at the Sheriff Court in Aberdeen."

"I'll take Horatio there myself first thing in the morning."

"Thank you, Constable Skinner. I'll send word when the Circuit Court judge will be in Aberdeen next and the date will be set for then."

Police Constable Skinner thanked the man for stopping in and passing on the information. He escorted him to the station door and bade him farewell.

Loud pounding jerked Horatio awake. Disoriented at first, he didn't know where he was. When the haze cleared, it became apparent. He was in the cell at the Kendonald Police Station. It wasn't a bad dream after all.

"Up 'n' at 'em', Christie. Big day for you. You're going on a train ride to Aberdeen ... to the East Prison."

"What about my solicitor? I need to see him, I say, I need to see him," he bellowed.

"You'll see him at the prison," Police Constable Skinner replied, "if you're lucky. Now get a move on. The goods train will be stopping at the station within the hour."

A small hatch at floor level in the cell door opened. A board with a plate of what looked like an inedible meal and a teapot and cup on it materialized.

"I'm told I have to feed you."

"You call this food?" Horatio roared and kicked the tray sending the food and drink across the room.

"Suit yourself but it will be a long time before you get anything else to eat."

The cell door opened in front of him and the policeman stood in the opening holding a pair of leg irons. Skinner shackled and handcuffed Horatio, before he had a chance to react. Any escape attempts by the pompous laird were now rendered impossible. The constable then escorted his prisoner to the Black Maria behind the police station.

At least Skinner had the courtesy to take him out the back door so the nosey villagers wouldn't see. By now, everyone in Kendonald and beyond would know of his incarceration.

The paddy wagon stopped and the door opened. Seeing the crowd waiting at the platform mortified Horatio. Skinner helped him down and dragged him by the jeering and taunting gathering. But there was no sign of Letitia. Not even Carlyle or his ghillie, Thomas Sievewright. Horatio thought for sure they would be there to show support for him.

Something cracked when it struck the back of his head. Wet ran down towards his collar. At first Mr. Christie thought it was blood but it wasn't the right consistency. This felt too slimy for that. Someone had thrown an egg at him.

The goods train pulled in and one of the wagon doors slid open. It was too high for Horatio to step into so someone placed a small stool on the platform for him to use.

The policeman climbed in at the same time. He pushed his

prisoner onto a wooden crate before fastening his leg iron to a metal ring attached to the floor. "Keeps the cargo secure, so it should work for prisoners."

"Damn you, Skinner. Damn you. You're no better than that crowd out there," Horatio growled.

A signal from the constable and the door slid shut plunging the wagon into darkness.

When the door opened at the joint station in Aberdeen, the bright light was blinding. Horatio raised his arms in front of his face to shield his eyes.

Two Aberdeen constables approached. With the help of Police Constable Skinner they got Horatio off the train. A struggle ensued but they bundled him into the waiting Black Maria.

Horatio's treatment at the East Prison shocked him. He had his fingermarks taken; his possessions stripped. They dumped him into a cell smaller than the one at the Kendonald Police Station.

"Hey guard, when you lettin' me out?" a man's voice yelled from someplace nearby in the jail.

It took a moment, but Horatio soon recognized it. That voice — that man – was Hamish MacMillan.

"Hush MacMillan. Told you before. Next time the Circuit court is in Aberdeen. You'll be here until they pronounce sentence. If I'm lucky, you'll get out and I won't have to listen to you and your constant moaning.

19

On the appointed day, the judge arrived in Aberdeen and the trials against the two men commenced. Hamish sat shackled in irons. His jet black hair he always wore tied in a thong at the nape of his neck hung loose over his collar. Horatio, seated beside him, hung his head, humiliated. Held in restraints in full view of everyone from his community and many others. Reporters and photographers jockeyed for position.

Looking over his shoulder at the crowd, he whispered to his solicitor, "You have to get me out of this."

"Quiet in the court room, please," the judge announced. When a hush fell over the room, he began. "Very well, we'll start with the charges against Mr. MacMillan. How do you plead to the charge of criminal assault? The assault that caused the effusion of blood, broken bones and danger to Miss Shand's life?"

Standing to face the court official, Hamish replied, "Guilty."

"And the charge of accepting payment in order to carry out said assault?"

"Guilty, but I wouldnae done it if Mr. Christie hadnae paid me. It was more money than I ever seen."

"I see. You've pleaded guilty to the charges. Given the bribe you've accepted, you should have more than enough money to pay a fine." The judge paused. "Instead, I'm sentencing you to five months penal servitude. You'll spend your first month in solitary confinement followed by four months' hard labor. Sentence is to begin at once and be served at the East Prison, in Lodge Walk, Aberdeen. You may take Mr. MacMillan away."

Horatio swallowed hard. He would be safe. He had every confidence his solicitor could get the charges dropped. At the very least, reduced to a fine – even if it meant a substantial one.

"Please rise, Mr. Christie. How do you plead to the charges brought against you?"

"Not guilty, I say. Not guilty."

"To all of them?"

"Yes."

"We'll begin with the matter of the charge of incest."

Jean MacDonald testified first. She told of the night the Christie's butler summoned her to Gleanstane to deliver a baby. She said when Horatio found out she'd placed the infant in the parish poor house, he had threatened to kill it.

Margaret spoke next. She told of how Letitia had seemed off on their recent visit. "Letitia told me her father had prepared her for marriage. It wasn't until we gathered at Weetshill much later I realized what she meant," she concluded.

Doctor Burnett related what he knew about the matter. He knew very little – other than what he'd been party to at Weetshill.

Police Constable Skinner concurred with the previous testimony.

The judge ordered Letitia to take the stand.

"D-do I have to?" she hesitated. "He is my father."

"Yes, my dear. That's why you have to do it."

Margaret squeezed her hand and Letitia made her way to the witness box and was sworn in. She turned to face her father. "After mother died, father was so lonely. He came to my room one night, crying for her. He really loved her, you see."

Horatio watched his daughter, nodding his approval.

"Another night when he came to me, he slipped under the covers and cuddled me. He was wearing his nightshirt and me my nightgown." Letitia began to cry.

"Go on my dear."

"Well, could I have a glass of water, please?" After taking a sip of the refreshing liquid, she continued. "Well, this night, he pushed my nightgown up and … oh father, I'm sorry. He whispered in my ear 'this is what married people do'. I didn't like it that first time. It hurt and I told him so. He came to me over and over again and each time it was a bit better. He told me I would be prepared for marriage and know what to do when my husband had needs. And then I fell pregnant."

Shattered by his daughter's betrayal of their confidence, Horatio leapt to his feet. "You traitorous, deceitful child," he bellowed.

"Sit down, Mr. Christie," the judge ordered. He looked at Letitia and in a softer voice, asked, "Was everything you told us now the truth, Miss Christie."

She nodded, tears streaming down her face.

"This is a most heinous act, Mr. Christie. Unthinkable, depraved. And to do it under the pretense of preparing your daughter for marriage. That is despicable. For this charge alone, I am sentencing you to twenty years penal servitude in the East Prison. You will spend a period of no less than six months in solitary confinement."

"Twenty years," Horatio blustered. "Why that's ludicrous. You can't do that to me. I'm an influential landowner."

"Sit down, Mr. Christie or I'll add another twenty years to your sentence," the judge countered. "You're also charged with forging Doctor Burnett's signature on commitment documents. Documents resulting in having Miss Sarah Shand confined at the Ladysbridge Asylum. Do you still want to plead not guilty to this charge, too?"

Horatio nodded.

The matron and superintendent of Ladysbridge, Mr. and Mrs. Nelson, were in the court. Other asylum workers who knew Sarah well during her confinement attended the trial, too.

"Superintendent Nelson, please tell us how you came to be in receipt of the forged documents."

"Police Constable Skinner," he conceded pointing to the officer. "He handed them to me after we secured Miss Shand on her arrival."

"And at the time, you had no reason to suspect the document was a forgery."

"No, sir."

"And have you since seen Doctor Burnett's signature?"

"Yes, and it looked nothing like the one on the papers given me at Ladysbridge."

"Thank you. That will be all," the judge replied, looking out over the courtroom. "Now for the charges of bribery. We'll begin with you paying Mr. MacMillan to dispose of Miss Shand by whatever means necessary. And conclude with your attempted coercion of Police Constable Skinner."

A hush fell over the spectators. Horatio mopped his brow. Things had gone wrong. His solicitor should have been able to get the charges dropped. After all, he had paid him good money to get the unpleasantness swept under the carpet.

"Mr. Christie, will you please rise again?"

Struggling to his feet, Horatio faced the judge.

"I'm further sentencing you to ten years for the charge of forgery. Another ten for *each* charge of bribery. In other words, Mr. Christie, you will be in prison for a total of fifty years. Sentence is to commence immediately, and will continue until you serve your full terms."

"Wh-what have I done," cried Letitia. "Father please forgive me.

I'm sorry. I never meant it to come to this." She collapsed in front of Horatio and laid her head on his thigh.

"I no longer have a daughter – or any children or grandchildren for that matter. You have humiliated me in front of everyone with this damning testimony and I will never forgive you, I say. Never forgive you," he blustered. "Someone get her off of me."

The police in attendance led Horatio down the steps into the tunnel leading to the East Prison.

Before he disappeared from the courtroom, Horatio scowled at the gathered throng. Letitia, Margaret, Robert, Doctor Burnett, the matron, and the superintendent watched his descent. His world crashed down.

20

When David returned to his rotation in the ICU, he huffed, "I'm sorry, Sarah." He jogged to her bedside. "Been working A&E these past few days and haven't had a chance to get up to see you."

"I thought you worked in this department?"

"I do, and A&E and anywhere else they tell me. I'm a medical student. I have to work in almost every department here in the hospital."

"So where have you been? There are hours after your shifts," she snapped, her eyes shooting daggers at him.

"I'm sorry, Sarah. This last rotation has been brutal. I'm so knackered at the end of my shifts all I've wanted to do was go home and sleep. Last night, a bunch of us who'd been working A&E these past few days went to The Lemon Tree after work. We ended up staying until closing."

"And being with your mates was more important than spending time with me?"

"Sometimes it is."

"Then why bother spending any time here with me?"

"Because I enjoy it, or at least I did." David started to leave.

"Wait," Sarah called. "Please don't go. I'm sorry."

He faced Sarah but didn't venture any closer. Instead he held his ground by the door.

"Did your trip to The Lemon Tree have anything to do with the way you were acting in here the last time you stopped in?"

"Yes."

"Why don't you tell me about it?"

"You wouldn't be interested."

"And how do you know? There was definitely something bothering you."

"What do you care? You only think of yourself." He turned his back to her and left. David knew that mood swings and personality changes occurred after a head injury. He didn't know her before the accident so he had nothing to compare. When he was on duty, spending time with her, maybe a bit too much, had been enjoyable. He liked dropping in on her at the ends of his shifts, too. Maybe her mood tonight was down to boredom. He'd suggested magazines and tabloids – and even asked the nurses to share theirs with Sarah. There was no sign of reading material of any kind in her room.

David stabbed the button for the lift. When the doors opened, he returned to Sarah's room but stayed near the door. "I'm sorry. I shouldn't have walked out on you like that."

Sarah looked up at him from her bed, her bright emerald-green eyes filled with tears. "I'm glad you came back. I'm sorry I snapped at you. I can't explain it."

"Perhaps …," David stopped. Should he suggest she talk to a psychiatrist? Who knew what sort of a reaction that would elicit.

"Perhaps what?" she asked.

"This is better coming from your consultant. People with severe head injuries like you have mood swings and personality changes. Did Compton ever suggest the neurosurgeon coming to talk to you? He could explain the extent of your injury. Maybe help you come to terms with some of the changes you're experiencing." David swallowed and continued. "It might even help if you talked to a psychiatrist."

"You think I'm crazy, don't you."

By now, David stood near the foot of Sarah's bed. He didn't think she was crazy, did he? Okay, her stories about going back to 1886 and marrying the Laird of Weetshill were weird. What if there were something to it? He'd had a few odd experiences after meeting Sarah. "No, you're not crazy. I thought it would help you to talk to someone."

"I've always been stubborn and had a bad temper. I know that. But now, I'm more like Jekyll and Hyde."

"Talking to someone might help you control your outbursts." David pulled a chair over to Sarah's bedside and hugged her before sitting down.

"Besides what you already know," she started. "I'm jealous, too. I'm stuck in here day after day. You get to leave at the end of your shift." She grabbed his hand in an effort to keep him from getting up and leaving. "I have no idea how long I'll be here. I want to be able to go out and go shopping, go to a club, go out for a meal – things people my age do."

"There you go thinking of yourself again. You haven't got a clue, have you? You have no idea what it's like to work in a hospital, especially in A&E or the ICU."

"But that was your choice."

"Yes, it was, but there is only so much you can do for these people. Sometimes you're lucky and you see them go home. Other times, you don't. If we didn't go out for a pint now and then we would go crazy."

"But you promised you would come and see me after work. I was looking forward to it. I like spending time with you. It helps me forget I'm in here." Sarah shifted and turned so her legs dangled off the side of the bed.

"I shouldn't have stayed away like I did," David apologized. "I'm sorry."

"You're not the one who needs to apologize. It's me. Me and my temper. Will you tell me now what was bothering you so much the other night?"

"It was a terrible day. A&E was insane and we were running about like mad. A young girl got hit by a car on Great Northern Road. I met the paramedics at the doors when they brought her in. I didn't look closely at her until we got her into the treatment room. She was about your age with injuries similar to yours. She looked very much like you, too. The resemblance was uncanny. But this girl wasn't lucky like you. We were unable to stabilize her condition and we lost her."

"She died?"

"Yes."

"David, you should have said. If I'd known, I wouldn't have carried on about my problems." Sarah reached out and put her hand on the back of his.

"The whole thing shook me up. I guess I was afraid you might die, too."

"But I'm fine now. Why would you think I would die?

"I don't know. Being daft, I guess."

"Oh David," Sarah cried, leaning over and hugging him before pulling back.

"Are you all right?" he asked.

She nodded.

"So how did you come to be out on the Kendonald Road to get yourself hit by the car?"

"Where?"

"You don't remember?"

"No."

"I worked A&E the day they brought you in. I guess that's why I took losing this other girl so hard. Do you remember anything?"

"I remember finding out my boyfriend cheated on me with my best friend, Niamh."

"Ah, the couple I had barred from here so they didn't upset you."

"She managed to get back in past security and the desk on this floor."

"How?" David asked leaning forward.

"Amazing what you can hide under a ball cap and a huge pair of Oakleys," Sarah replied. She shifted into a comfortable position. "Anyway, she and he ... they're engaged. It should have been Blair asking *me* to marry him. Not her." Upset from recalling the incident, Sarah pounded her fist on the bed.

"I know they hurt you but let's get back to the night you got hit by the car," David prodded.

"Oh yeah. Okay, I had taken a bottle of sleeping tablets out of the medicine chest and then went to the stone circle. I don't know how many pills were in it, but I took all of them. I wanted to die because of what Blair and Niamh had done to me. Then I changed my mind and I thought I was going back to the farmhouse. I ended up at Weetshill mansion. I don't remember getting hit by a car."

"What all have the Doctors told you?"

Sarah related what the consultant and surgeons told her to the best of her recollection. They'd all been good with their explanations. Not so technical she couldn't understand any of it. Comprehending was a whole different thing. But Doctor Compton's words 'arrested three times' haunted her the most.

"So no one mentioned when you crashed the last time they wanted to call it and almost did. Then your heart started back into a normal rhythm. It was like you weren't ready to go yet."

Sarah, stunned by the additional details, couldn't believe how close to death she'd come.

21

Rachel burst in to Sarah's hospital room. "You won't believe what I found at the library. It's so cool. I couldn't believe it. Oh yeah, and I saw Niamh and Blair there, too – well they were outside and didn't see me. You should see the size of the diamond she's wearing. I bet it cost at least ten grand. Any bets they're engaged?" she chattered.

"I know Blair asked Niamh to marry him," Sarah sighed. "She came and told me, the gloating cow."

"I'm really sorry," Rachel comforted kneeling by her sister's chair. "But here, this will cheer you up." She handed the printout from the old newspaper to Sarah. "They have a book there with Robertson information in it, but they couldn't find it. They've left a note at the Local Studies reception to have someone let me know when it's found."

Rachel's hairstyle had changed again. She changed the color often so it was no surprise but now she had it cut short and dyed blue underneath. The top layer was longer and so blonde it was almost white and styled in a spiky, messy way that suited her.

Sarah skimmed over the article. She looked up at her younger sister. "I have to find a way back to Weetshill so I can save Robert from the fire. I need your help."

"That crack your head took has sent you doolally, sis."

"You saw Robert and Jenny and me. You made a comment about our clothing. Please don't tell me you didn't."

Just then, the air in the corner of the room shimmered. A few minutes later Robert materialized.

Rachel's eyes grew wide as saucers. "I-I-I …," she stammered.

"Lovely to see you again, Miss Shand," he acknowledged. Robert bowed and kissed the back of her hand before walking over to Sarah and kissing the top of her head. "Sarah, you must get well and come back to Jenny and me. We miss you so much." He looked at Rachel. "You can help her find her way. I know you can."

Sarah took Robert's hand and held it against her cheek hoping it would keep him there with her. But it was to no avail. Footsteps in the corridor became louder and Robert faded away.

David appeared in the doorway. "I thought I heard a man's voice in here."

Rachel looked at him, her mouth still gaping open.

"No, just us," Sarah replied. "Rach here has a bit of a chest cold and her voice sometimes sounds like a man's," she lied.

"If she has a cold, she shouldn't be visiting you here and spreading her germs," David answered. He turned to Rachel and continued, "I'm afraid I'm going to have to ask you to leave. Your sister is still weak and if she were to catch your chest cold, it could develop into pneumonia."

"Okay. Okay. I get the picture. I'll try to get to the Family History Centre at the weekend, Sarah," Rachel sighed, reaching out to her. Their fingers didn't touch and it turned into a feeble wave.

"And how are we feeling today, Miss Shand?" Doctor Compton asked entering the room. "Off you go now, Mr. Robb," he ordered nodding his head in the direction of the door.

Once David had gone, the consultant pulled a chair over and sat down next to Sarah. "You're doing so well we're going to transfer you to Woodend Hospital. They specialize in rehabilitation and orthopedics."

"B-but isn't it a hospital for old people?"

"Yes, there are *old* people there. Anyone who needs rehabilitation from stroke or accident, or whatever, they help."

Sarah bowed her head. If the doctor transferred her out of ARI, Robert and Jenny would never find her. She wouldn't be able to see David as often. She'd be all alone in a strange place.

"Well my girl, I'll get the paperwork done up and we'll get you moved," Doctor Compton promised as he stood.

"Do I have to go? Can't I stay here?"

"We need to free up this room. You're well enough you don't need to be here."

He wasn't listening. Sarah didn't want to leave ICU. She couldn't leave. She balled her hands into fists and punched the arms of her chair in anger.

David returned a few hours later. "Can only stay a mo. Wondered what Compton wanted."

Sarah looked up at him, her eyes red and puffy from crying.

"Hey, what's wrong?" he asked.

When he got next to Sarah's chair, she grabbed his jacket and buried her face against him. "Th-they're tr-transfer-fering me to-to Woodend," she sobbed.

David knelt beside her chair and put his arms around her. "It's not that bad. I've never been but I hear it's a nice place. The staff is great and it's what you need to get back on your feet."

"B-but, I-I don't w-want to g-go," she wailed.

"I'll still come and see you. Just won't be as often as it is now."

"Y-you will?" Sarah asked. She leaned back and looked into his eyes. "I'd like that."

"Did he say when you'd be getting moved?"

"N-no. Could you find out for me?"

"You bet," David answered. He hugged her. "Now you cheer up. It's not going to be the end of the world."

Inside his flat, David dropped his keys and the mail on the table by the door. He turned on the light on his way to the kitchen. He needed a drink. He took a glass out of the upper cabinet to the right of the sink. Reaching into the cabinet on the other side, he took out his bottle of Ardmore. Less than half of it remained. This was his special occasion whisky and today's events didn't quite fit the bill. He put it back and took out the bottle of Glen Garioch instead. David poured a glass and took it through to the lounge. He picked up his mail, sat his glass down and dropped into the easy chair. He flipped through the bundle of envelopes – junk, electric, more junk, phone, and gas. He tossed them aside and took a drink.

David had feelings for Sarah. Until he found out about her upcoming transfer to a rehab unit, hadn't admitted them to himself. He took another drink. What could he do about Sarah? Could he persuade Doctor Compton not to transfer her out of ARI? They could find a bed on another unit until she could resume her physio as an outpatient, couldn't they? He sensed she felt something for him, too. After all, why would she have been so upset the night he went to The Lemon Tree with some of his work-mates? Her reaction to the news of her discharge from ARI to Woodend. What could he do? As much as he had feelings for Sarah, he couldn't start seeing her while she was a patient. At least not boyfriend/girlfriend type seeing her while she was still at ARI. The rules of conduct stated that. The occasional kiss he'd planted on her cheek or forehead pushed the limits. They could be no more than good friends until her discharge. But if she went to another hospital, things could be different.

David slugged down the last dregs of his drink and took his glass to the kitchen. Leaning against the counter, he wanted to be with Sarah. He wasn't sure what he could do for her, even if he could reassure her things would work out. He showered then fell into his bed, exhausted.

22

When David arrived at the hospital the following morning, he sought out Doctor Compton. He found him in the staff lounge. "Could I have a word?" he asked.

"Of course, Mr. Robb."

"Not here. I'd prefer it to be in private."

"All right then, let's go to my office. It must be something serious." The consultant led the way down the corridor and up a flight of steps. "After you," he invited, opening the door.

David stepped through and walked to the window. Staring out at the cityscape, he started. "It's about the Shand patient in ICU."

"Ah, the one you spend so much time visiting. You're walking a fine line there, my boy. I've not said anything yet, because you've managed to stay on it. But carry on," Doctor Compton continued easing himself into his chair.

"Well, she doesn't want to go to Woodend for rehabilitation." David turned to face his superior.

"She doesn't or you don't want her to?"

"No, it's her. She cried for an hour when she told me of the situation."

"We need the bed. Did you explain it to her?"

"I tried. I told her Woodend wasn't so bad even but she still wasn't buying in." David leaned back and stared at the ceiling. "Okay, we need to free up ICU beds. Couldn't we transfer her to another floor here at ARI while she undergoes physiotherapy? At least until she's well enough to continue in an outpatient capacity?"

"And you can assure me this has nothing to do with any feelings you might have for the young lady."

"Yes, sir. I'm asking on her behalf is all."

"Well, let me see what I can do. If there's nothing else, I have paperwork that needs attending to." Doctor Compton stood and shook David's hand.

"Thank you. Sarah … I mean Miss Shand will be thrilled with your decision."

When David stepped into the corridor and the door clicked shut behind him, he breathed a sigh of relief. He hadn't realized the staff at the consultant level noticed how much of his free time he spent with Sarah. He would have to be more careful from now on. Walking through the crowded halls, David headed to A&E. He could keep his mind occupied there. One thing in particular – his feelings for Sarah.

23

After the outcome of the trial, Margaret couldn't bear to send Letitia back to Gleanstane on her own. "You'll stay with us at Weetshill. I'll come with you and we'll gather some of your things." She looked at Robert for his consent.

"This is until we arrange something more permanent and suitable," he replied.

Margaret bundled Letitia into her cloak. Putting her arm around the young woman's shoulders, she said, "Come along. We'll get you away from here."

They rode to Gleanstane without speaking. Letitia hunched forward in the seat, crying and dabbing her eyes with her handkerchief. Margaret patted her leg or rubbed her back attempting to soothe her but to no avail. When the carriage stopped outside the front door, Letitia broke the silence. "I-I can't go in there."

"Very well, you stay with Robert and I'll go gather enough of your belongings to get you through the night."

Inside the mansion, Margaret relayed the results of the trial to Carlyle. She then went to Letitia's room. With military precision, she went from wardrobe to chest of drawers to dressing table. She picked out things she thought her friend would like to have and placed them on the bed. When she pulled out a nightgown and laid it with the other items, a wave of nausea struck her followed by rage. How could any father do the horrible things to his daughter Horatio had done to Letitia? Hanging was too good for the man. Besides, it was far too quick and easy. Perhaps the lengthy prison sentence was better in the end. At least then, he'd have a good long time to think about the damage he'd done.

Margaret found a carpet bag and stuffed Letitia's things into it. Sweeping out of the bedroom, she slammed the door shut behind her.

Downstairs, the elderly butler took the luggage from her and shuffled towards the carriage. Callum clambered down from the driver's seat and placed it in the box on the rear then helped Margaret climb in.

"We'll have a guest for a day or two, Archibald. Can you take her bag upstairs and put it in one of the rooms in the same wing as Margaret's room, please? But not Sarah's. And not too close to Jenny's either," Robert instructed.

"Aye, sir. The room on the far side o' Mrs. Esslemont's then?"

"That will be fine," he replied ushering his sister and Letitia into the library.

The housekeeper joined them in the great hall. "Aye, the poor wee hen," she sympathized after Robert had reported Horatio's sentence. "I'll sees that the room gets aired and clean linens brought in."

His employees went off to follow his instructions. Robert recalled Letitia's threat in the kirkyard. "Wait," he called out striding to the foot of the staircase. "At any time, and I repeat any time, I do not want Letitia and Jenny left alone together. It is imperative this never happens. The day I bumped into Miss Christie at the kirkyard, she told me she and her father had come back to take Jenny. We don't have to worry about Horatio, but Letitia is in a state. Whilst I don't want to believe what she told me then, I can't rule it out now."

"Aye, sir, I'll sees wee Jenny isnae left wi' her an' I'll talks to the others so they kens, too."

"Thank you, Mrs. MacEwen.

"You dinnae think Miss Christie would take the wee lassie away, do you, sir?"

"Right now, Archibald, I don't know what to think. I really don't."

"I'll keep a close watch whilst Miss Christie is here, sir."

"Thank you," Robert answered, returning to the library. He paused with his hand on the knob. Given the choice, he didn't want Letitia and Jenny together even if there were others present. He couldn't keep watch over them twenty-four hours a day, nor could he expect his employees to do it either. But that would most apt to be the time Letitia would try to steal Jenny if she were serious and not toying with him.

Turning the handle, Robert joined his sister and houseguest in the library. They were on the sofa, Letitia still crying, and Margaret trying to comfort her. He walked to the small table and poured three glasses of whisky from the decanter.

"Here, Letitia. Drink this," Robert offered. He held glasses out to her and his sister before retrieving his.

"Th-thank, you," she replied drawing a ragged breath.

Seated in the armchair at the end of the sofa, he asked, "Do you have any family elsewhere we can contact for you?"

Letitia wailed.

"Well done, Robert. I was just getting her calmed down. The poor girl has been through too much today to be thinking so far ahead," Margaret scolded.

"Mrs. MacEwen is preparing a room for you. When you're ready to retire for the night, she'll show you to it. Archibald has taken your bag up for you.

Nodding through red, tear-filled eyes, Letitia murmured, "Thank you."

The butler announced the evening meal. Robert stood and waited for the women by the library door before escorting them to the dining room. The housekeeper met them in the great hall outside the door. "Miss Margaret, sir, I's had Morag feed the bairns and they's upstairs. Janet be wi' the 'em. I promised wee Jenny you'd be up to see her afore she goes to bed, sir."

"Thank you Mrs. MacEwen."

Grabbing his sleeve she whispered, "I thought you wouldnae want Jenny an' Miss Letitia wi' each other e'en with you an' Miss Margaret bein' there. Did I do right?"

"You did fine," he reassured. He turned to his sister. "You and Letitia go on in and get settled. I'll go say goodnight to Jenny then join you."

When he reached his daughter's bedroom, he heard Janet's voice. She was reading *Snow White and Rose Red* from *Grimm's Fairy Tales*. Robert waited in the hall for her to finish.

"F-father," Jenny called scrambling off the bed. She rushed to him with outstretched arms and hugged him.

Janet sidestepped past them and disappeared into the corridor.

"Wh-when is S-Sarah c-c-coming b-back?"

"I wish I knew, sweetie. I wish I knew," Robert sighed and sat on the bed. He patted the mattress beside him and Jenny climbed up into his lap. "I'm sorry I'm not spending much time with you of late. I've had many things on my mind and have been trying to determine solutions to them."

"L-like b-bringing S-Sarah home?"

"Yes, like bringing Sarah home," he reassured the little girl. "But there's another problem. I don't want you to be by yourself. Anytime," Robert stressed.

"N-never?"

"For the time being. Something is happening and I need to know you're safe."

"Y-you're sc-scaring me," Jenny stammered.

"I don't mean to. Would you like it if Mary Elizabeth spent the night in here with you?"

"C-can she? R-really?"

Robert got off the bed and went into the hall where Janet waited nearby. He relayed his request to her and she brought the other young girl back to Jenny's room.

"Now, I want you to both get some sleep. No lying awake half the night giggling."

"We won't Uncle Robert," his niece assured him.

Hugging them both goodnight and tucking them in to bed, he returned to the dining room and his meal.

"Is everything all right?" Margaret asked as he walked to his place at the table.

"Fine, now. Mary Elizabeth is sleeping in Jenny's room with her tonight."

"Is that wise? You know what they're like," she answered, laying her cutlery on her plate.

"Can I go up and say goodnight?" Letitia asked.

"No," Robert blurted. He felt bad. He hadn't meant it to come out in such a harsh tone. "I'm sorry. I didn't mean to say it quite that way. I think it is best if we leave things as is for the time being. We're all fraught over today's events."

They finished their meal then returned to the library. The butler followed and stoked the fire before leaving. The housekeeper entered a short time later with a tray of cheese and oatcakes and an enormous pot of tea.

"Hot, sweet tea, wi' do you the world, Miss Letitia, an' a good night's sleep," Mrs. MacEwen claimed. She placed a filled cup and saucer on the coffee table in front of the girl. "When you's ready to go to bed, lets me ken an' I takes you to your room."

Robert plucked a piece of cheese off the tray and poured himself a cup. He stood near the window and stared off towards Gordonsfield. Hoping any minute he'd see Sarah rushing up the laneway and into his arms. "Sarah, please, *please* come back to me," he whispered.

Letitia moved to his side. "I would never have left you the way she did, Robert," she cooed and stroked his hair starting at his temples. "I would be a good wife to you and always be by your side. I still can be. After all, I'm prepared."

Putting his tea on the table, he snatched Letitia by the wrists and yanked her hands away from him. "Get off, you stupid girl. I could never take you for my wife," he snarled, squeezing her wrists tighter. Before he could let go and push her away from him, an orange glow became visible on the horizon. It expanded and contracted, grew brighter and faded.

Robert turned to the fireplace and back to the window. "Fire," he yelled.

Margaret joined him. "It looks like it's coming from your house, Letitia. I think Gleanstane is on fire."

Bursting into the great hall, Robert shouted, "There's a fire. Archibald, get Angus, Callum and wee James. We need the carriage made ready straight away."

In the following moments of organized confusion, everything Robert requested was prepared. His sister and Letitia stood next to him in their warm, outdoor clothing. He shrugged into his overcoat and raced out the door with the women close behind matching him stride for stride.

Callum brought the carriage to a stop in the driveway to Gleanstane. Letitia leapt out and ran for the house. About halfway there, a pair of strong hands grabbed her and restrained her. She looked over her shoulder to see who it was, hoping it was Robert. Instead she saw Tommy Sievewright, their ghillie.

"You cannae go no further, Miss Letitia. It isnae safe."

Robert's men, along with Robert, joined the brigade and passed buckets of water to those at the front. No matter how fast they worked, they could not quell the fire.

Tommy handed Letitia over to Margaret and joined the others. Over the crackling of the flames, they heard the sound of creaking timber. "Gets back. E'erybody gets back," Tommy roared. As the men retreated to the area where Letitia and Margaret stood, the roof caved in. Sparks flew into the air.

The Christie's ghillie pushed everyone back even further. One of the sparks landed on his coat sleeve and set it alight. Angus threw a bucket of water on it dousing the flames before it set Tommy on fire.

Letitia collapsed. "Why?" she repeated over and over.

"I don't know," Margaret soothed. "Let's go sit in the carriage. It's more comfortable in there than out here on the stones."

"Who did this, Tommy?" she cried.

"I dinnae ken, Miss Letitia. Why dinnae you do 'at Miss Margaret said. Sit in the carriage."

"I'm not leaving this spot until I know what happened."

Police Constable Skinner appeared from the darkness. "It's most apt to be accidental. A spark from one of the grates catching the carpet on fire. We don't know yet."

"I don't want you anywhere near my house," Letitia screeched, scrambling to her feet. "It's bad enough you've taken my dear father away from me. I don't want you on Gleanstane lands."

"Letitia, those things your father did were wrong. Very wrong," Margaret murmured rubbing her friend's arms. "Come, we'll go sit in the carriage."

Looking back over her shoulder at the remains of her home, Letitia followed her friend. Inside, she rested her forehead against the window in the door. She stared at the silhouettes of the men still hard at work trying to put the rest of the fire out. Tears burned her cheeks and she wiped them away with her fingertips and swallowed hard and sighed.

Since the police took her father away, Letitia had been living in a nightmare she wished she could wake up from. Why had she asked him to bring her back? They were quite happy where they'd gone after Robert bought his way out of the marriage contract. Did she want Jenny to live with her and her father? A child she knew suffered from fits and stuttered. No. It was more to make Robert and Sarah suffer. Most of all Sarah since it was down to her that Robert wanted out of the arranged marriage in the first place. At this moment, her life was in shambles. Even more so than it was when she tried to take her life at the stone circle.

"Who will look after mother's roses?" she asked. "Now that father is gone and I'll be going away, there's no one to look after them."

"Your mother's roses will be fine," Margaret assured. "Someone has been looking after them all this time, and I daresay whoever it is will continue. No one holds a grudge against your mother. She was well liked in and around Kendonald."

The first traces of morning light appeared over the hilltops. Steam hissed as the men threw the last buckets of water onto the blackened timbers. Letitia wrapped her cloak around her and shivered. The smell of burnt, wet wood and upholstery permeated the air. Standing by the carriage, she spotted Carlyle with Tommy Sievewright. "You stupid old man," she yelled, pushing the palms of her hands into his chest. "How could you let this happen? You've destroyed my home. It's all your fault. You were likely supping whisky in your pantry. You knew father wasn't around to catch you, and I was staying at Weetshill. Father's best whisky, too, no doubt. You drank too much and fell asleep. I know you, Carlyle. You've done it before."

The aged butler staggered from the force of her jabs. "Aye, I has. But it wasnae like 'at this time. Aye, I was in me pantry but I heard a window break and came out to see. You ken I cannae move very fast. By the time I got here, and opened the door to your father's drawing room, it were on fire and the front window busted."

"Trying to save your own skin, more like," Letitia ridiculed. "Here's the man who destroyed my home," she yelled and pointed at him. "Got inebriated and wasn't tending the fires as he should."

"Letitia, stop," Margaret demanded, grabbing her by her upper arms and shaking her.

"Miss Letitia, I swear, I's tellin' you the truth. It wasnae me," Carlyle pleaded.

Sticking her nose in the air, Letitia turned on her heel and marched back to the carriage.

Margaret pondered the exchange between Letitia and the butler. Yes, it was a well-known fact around Kendonald that Carlyle had a problem with the drink. But to set the house ablaze? It made no sense at all. With Horatio being in prison for the rest of his life, the running of Gleanstane would fall to Letitia. If she couldn't bear that she could sell up and provide the staff with references. The next thought that entered her mind terrified her. What if someone else set the fire on purpose? What if she hadn't insisted Letitia come back to Weetshill? Her friend could well have perished in the blaze.

Taking her place by her brother's side, she whispered her fears in his ear.

"You're over-reacting, Margaret. You're tired – we all are. Let's go back to Weetshill. There's nothing more to do here."

"I'll keep wee James here wi' me," Angus commented. "The fire might flare up again."

Margaret smiled and the young boy beamed.

"Oh you poor wee hen," Mrs. MacEwen clucked putting her arm around Letitia. "You needs sleep. Come I'll take you to your room. You's welcome here at Weetshill as long as you like."

Letitia managed a weak smile.

"Here you be. Get yoursel' cleaned up and into your bed. I'll keep the curtains closed so it be dark for you," the housekeeper declared. She closed the bedroom door behind her.

Alone in the room, Letitia washed her face. Even though she hadn't been all that close to the blaze at Gleanstane, she was grimy with soot. Maybe Carlyle hadn't set the fire after all. Maybe it was a chimney fire. She couldn't remember the last time her father had brought a sweep in to clean the flues or maybe it was a spark from the grate.

She did her best to rinse her hair but with only the pitcher and bowl on a washstand, it was almost impossible. The worst of the smell was gone at least. She put her clothes out in the hall so she wouldn't smell them, pulled her nightgown on and crawled into the bed and tugged the covers into place.

Sleep didn't come easy. She tossed and turned as visions of her father's hatred filled face glared at her. The judge's verdict echoed in her head. What was she to do on her own? She couldn't stay here at Weetshill forever. Robert had made his feelings towards her well known. It would only be a matter of time before he would be asking her to leave. The last place she wanted to go was back to her auntie's in Polperro. She and her father went after things had begun to unravel before Robert married Sarah. Auntie Millicent, her mother's youngest sister, was nice enough and didn't ask awkward questions. Living near the English Channel was much too far away from her life in Aberdeenshire and Robert.

She had to find a way to change Robert's mind. Let her stay at Weetshill. Ask her to become his wife. She already had something Sarah didn't in the beginning. Robert and Sarah would have had those relations at least once. She could hope her rival didn't like them. Her father prepared her for marriage and she knew what to do when a man had needs of that kind.

Maybe she would have to demonstrate her knowledge to Robert. By the time Letitia fell pregnant, she enjoyed the way it made her feel. She became responsive to the advances and eager to please. Happy she had a plan, Letitia snuggled down under the covers. She readied herself to dream of making love with Robert. Soon she would have her husband and the daughter taken away from her all those years ago.

Robert thrashed about in bed, unable to sleep. He had a woman in his house he didn't trust, never loved, nor would ever love. The fire at Gleanstane on the heels of Horatio's trial seemed too coincidental for his liking. But who in or near the village of Kendonald would do such a thing? And what was most important, why?

Unable to doze off, he climbed out of bed and went to the window. Snow covered the ground. Huge, white flakes fell, sometimes whipped around by gusts of wind. When that happened it was impossible to see outside. Exhaustion from working alongside the men in the bucket brigade had set in. Robert thought he'd fall asleep the instant his head touched the pillow. The longer it snowed, the better it was for keeping the fire extinguished. His employees could come home for some much needed rest.

He knew Philomena Christie had one sister but he didn't know where she lived. He hadn't seen her since the woman's funeral about ten years ago and was she still alive? With Letitia determined to become the next Mrs. Robertson, he knew she would never tell him. But perhaps Margaret could. After all, she and Letitia were friends and had been for many years. He would ask her after they'd all had some sleep.

Margaret worried about the fire and what it would do to Letitia. The poor girl was fragile enough before this. What would the toll on her be in the coming days? Seeing your childhood home destroyed in flames would push anyone to the brink. Letitia, she thought, would fall over the edge.

Right now, Margaret wanted to hug her children and never let go of them. She needed George, too. With him trying to run the shop in Edinburgh and find a buyer for it at the same time, it was impossible. The governess would come soon. Margaret needed to make sure the household was running like clockwork for her arrival.

Sarah had to come back – for her sake as much as Robert's. Jenny had declined health-wise and her stuttering increased. The wee child missed her adoptive mother. Margaret understood Robert's fears of leaving Letitia alone with Jenny. Now with everything else happening, keeping them apart without supervision was paramount. But they needed to do it in a subtle manner and now, more so than before, given Letitia's state.

Margaret crept down the hall to John Bryce's room. She opened the door and watched him sleeping before closing it and continuing to Jenny's.

When she looked in her daughter stirred, opened her eyes and whispered, "Mama?"

"Shh ... you don't want to wake Jenny."

"Is everything all right?"

"Yes dear. Go back to sleep. It's almost morning."

Assured the children were all safe, Margaret returned to her room and collapsed onto her bed.

A feeling of unease niggled at Sarah. Unsure of the reason, she pulled out her iPhone and called her mum to see if everyone was all right. Despite hearing everyone, including her grandparents, was fine, she couldn't dismiss the fact. She felt like something was going to happen or had happened to someone close to her. Since her present-day family was okay, then it had to have something to do with Robert or Jenny. But what? Being stuck in the hospital and in a different time, she was powerless to do anything to help. Or was it to do with David? She'd not seen him yet today so that was possible.

Whatever it was and whoever it involved haunted her.

The mantle clock in his room chimed twice waking Robert. He grabbed his pocket watch from his bedside table and consulted it. The silver, half-hunter confirmed it was, indeed, early afternoon. Still tired from being up all night at the Gleanstane fire, he knew if he didn't get up now, he would never sleep that night.

Pulling his dressing gown on, he padded into the hall looking for his valet. "Will you draw me a bath, please, Dougal? And let me know when it's ready."

"Aye, sir. I'll tend to the clothes you had on, too. They's in a awful state."

Robert had to agree with the man. Even having washed up a bit last night, he still smelled of smoke.

"Thank you. And can you arrange to have my bedding laundered, too?"

"Aye, sir," the valet answered before leaving to follow his employer's instructions.

Returning to his room, Robert pulled the drapes open and threw up the sash. He leaned out and breathed in the fresh air but even it remained tinged with the stench from the blaze.

Bath prepared, he went off to the room where the copper tub sat in front of a crackling wood fire. He stripped down and stepped into the hot water before sitting and submerging himself.

Scrubbed from head to toe, Robert emerged from the bath and

wrapped himself in a towel.

Once dressed, he sought out his sister and found her and the children in his and Margaret's late brother's room. He walked to the window and motioned for Margaret to join him there. "Do you know where Letitia's auntie lives? I think we should get her to come here and take Letitia to live with her."

"It's Millicent and she lives in Polperro but that's all I know – and she was a maternal aunt who remained a spinster. That's where Letitia and Horatio went when they vanished before your wedding. Letitia told me about it in the carriage during the fire at Gleanstane."

"Do you recall her last name?"

"No, but isn't Mrs. Christie buried in the Old Kirkyard?"

"Yes, the Christie vault is there, why?"

"Her maiden surname might be carved on the monument, as our mother's is on father's stone."

"You're a genius. I can find out without Letitia suspecting a thing," he replied grasping her hands in his. "I'm going there now. The sooner Letitia Christie is out from under Weetshill's roof and ensconced with her own family far from here, the better I will sleep."

"So will the rest of us." Margaret rejoined the children. "Best of luck," she called as he left the room.

Robert stood in front of the Christie family vault in the Old Kirkyard. Only the surname appeared over the door and the first names on the monuments in front. Except Mrs. Christie's had 1835-1875, the years of her birth and death, engraved. To his dismay, the woman's maiden surname wasn't included. He was no closer to sending Letitia back to her aunt's in Polperro than before.

Dejected, Robert started back to Weetshill. He paused outside the manse. He didn't know if Reverend Mitchell could help him or not, but he wouldn't be any worse off than he now was. He lifted the latch on the gate and stepped through.

"I thought I saw you out here, Robert. Horrible business this is with Horatio Christie. His poor daughter must be terribly distraught what with the trial and then her home burning down. Perhaps I should pray for her or visit her and give her spiritual guidance. You don't happen to know where she's staying, do you?

"She's at Weetshill. My sister insisted she stay with us."

"That's very kind of her, I'm sure. Come in and we'll have a cup of tea. It's cold and damp out here," the short white haired man invited.

The minister ushered Robert into his office. Soon afterwards, the maid brought in a steaming teapot, cups, saucers and a plate of oatcakes.

"Letitia was staying with an aunt on her mother's side in England along with her father. When they left Gleanstane, they went there." Robert shifted in his chair then continued. "I'd prefer to have her as far from here as possible. I don't trust her and I fear for Jenny."

"Perhaps you should write this aunt and ask her if she'll have Miss Christie stay with her again?"

"I would except I don't know her last name. I went to the kirkyard to see if Mrs. Christie's maiden surname appeared on her monument. I'm vexed to say, it doesn't."

"No fear, dear fellow. What year did Mrs. Christie die?"

"It says 1875 on the stone."

Reverend Mitchell stood and walked to his bookcase. "This one here should be the one we need." He returned to his desk with a large ledger. "Civil registration began in 1855 but I still maintain the parish records for Kendonald. Call me old fashioned if you like. Come around. Two heads are better than one. And with any luck, we'll find the information you seek faster."

Robert moved around the desk. He stood behind the minister who was opening the book to the first page of the 1875 deaths and burials.

"Oh dear, this isn't going to be as easy as I thought. I've listed the women by their maiden surnames and their spouses in parentheses."

Crestfallen, Robert vowed to carry on, no matter how daunting the task.

About four pages into the book, Robert pointed to an entry. "That's it. I'm certain of it. Philomena Coles married to Horatio Christie. Thank you for your help." He shook the man's hand. "I must return to Weetshill and relate our findings to Margaret."

Reverend Mitchell escorted Robert to the door and saw him off.

Robert couldn't believe his luck. If he'd gone to the manse in the first place, it would have saved the long, cold walk to the kirkyard.

When he entered the mansion's front door, Margaret rushed into the great hall to meet him. "Did you succeed?"

"Where are the children?"

"With Mrs. MacEwen and Morag."

Breathing a sigh of relief, Robert entered the library with his sister close behind.

"You didn't answer my question. Did you succeed?"

"Yes. Will you join me in a dram?" he asked pulling the stopper out of the decanter.

"Very well, but please tell me what you discovered. I'm on tenterhooks."

Handing her a drink, Robert began. "My trip to the kirkyard was to no avail. However, I stopped at the manse on my return. Reverend Mitchell keeps the parish records still. We found Mrs. Christie's maiden surname in the 1875 Deaths and Burials."

"And?"

"Coles. Before she married Horatio, she was a Coles. And you believe this aunt was Mrs. Christie's sister so that would be her surname, too."

"Millicent Coles in Polperro," Margaret mused then took a sip of her whisky.

"Would you write to her? Letitia was your friend and you're so much better at these things."

Margaret sat at the desk. This would be a difficult letter to write. What should she include? What sort of terms did Letitia and Horatio leave Polperro under? How much of the trial would the woman already know about from the papers? And of most importance, how much did she know of the relationship between Horatio and her niece. Despite the nature of the letter, the sooner she wrote it and sent it, the sooner Letitia would be far away. Jenny and her own two children would be safe.

11th November, 1886

Miss Millicent Coles
Polperro, Cornwall
England

Dear Miss Coles,

I'm a friend of your niece, Letitia Christie, and I'm writing to you hoping you should remember me. I'm Margaret Esslemont, maiden surname Robertson.

I'm writing to you of a matter that is causing me much vexation.

Letitia isn't well, I'm afraid, and recent events lead me

to think she might try to harm herself. You see, Horatio is serving a lengthy prison term. The reasons for which would be best discussed in person. To make things worse, Gleanstane has burned down.

Letitia is currently staying at Weetshill with my brother Robert and me. Given her delicate situation, we both think she would be better off (and happier) with family. I believe she and her father spent some time with you last month.

If you would agree to take Letitia back to Polperro, I would cover the expenses you incur on your journey.

Please let me know by return post if you are agreeable.

Yours sincerely,

Mrs. George Esslemont
(Margaret Robertson)

"What do you think?" she asked, handing Robert the letter.

"I'm pleased you've left out the details. If it's deemed she needs to know, we can tell her should she come for Letitia."

"Who's coming for me, Robert?"

Letitia stood in the doorway. Her complexion was sallow and her eyes red and puffy. She looked unwell. Recent events would tax a healthy person's intestinal fortitude to the limit. But what of a fragile one?

"Do you want me to have Doctor Burnett summoned for you?" Robert asked.

She shook her head.

"Let's you and I go have a chat like we used to up in my room," Margaret offered. She stopped and whispered to her brother. "Will you address the envelope for me and please see the doctor comes to look at Letitia."

Robert's handwriting was almost identical to his sister's. Should he add a postscript to the letter? Say he feared for his daughter's safety while Letitia was under his roof? No, that would bring undue attention to Jenny and could make things worse.

Not one to ring for the servants, but rather seek them out, something niggled at Robert. He pulled the cord in the corner behind the desk.

"This isnae like you, sir. You come find us," the butler remarked.

"Yes. Please come in and close the door behind you, Archibald."

"Has I done something wrong, sir?"

"Nothing of the sort. I need this letter sent by special messenger. I'm worried if it goes in the bag with the normal post, someone might remove it." Robert handed the envelope to his servant.

The butler looked at the letter then at Robert. "Miss Christie, you mean."

"Yes, Archibald, Miss Christie. She's of weak mind these days. And would you get word to Doctor Burnett. I'd like him to come examine her. Perhaps he has some wonder drug in that black bag of his that can help her."

"Aye, sir. Is that all, sir?"

"Yes, Archibald. Thank you."

24

Sarah looked up when she heard Doctor Compton's familiar whistling get louder.

"Good morning, young lady," he greeted, taking her chart and checking it. "I've got some rather good news for you."

"What?"

"You won't be going to Woodend after all."

Finding it hard to contain her excitement, Sarah prodded the consultant for more information.

"It seems you have someone here who has gone to bat for you, so to speak. Convinced me you would be served as well staying here at ARI."

Sarah knew who he referred to. It was David and he had succeeded.

"You're well enough now you don't need to be taking up a bed here in ICU. We're stepping you down to the High Dependency Unit. From there, it will be a regular ward or if you're well enough on out the door and home."

"Thank you," she exclaimed. "That's brilliant news. When will I get moved?"

"I should think you'll be having your lunch in your new room. Does that suit?"

"Oh yes."

Doctor Compton made a note in her chart and left.

Taking her iPhone out of the drawer, Sarah phoned home and relayed the good news. "I don't know what room I'll be in yet, mum, but I'll call you from there and let you know."

Gathering up her belongings, she piled them on the bed and sat back and waited for someone to come for her.

About forty-five minutes later, Jill arrived pushing a wheelchair. "I hear you're leaving us."

"Yup."

"This all your stuff?"

Sarah nodded.

"In you get," Jill instructed.

Once Sarah settled into the seat, the nurse placed her duvet and pillow on her lap. She then swung Sarah's bag onto her shoulder.

"Let's go."

Once outside the ICU, Sarah watched the passing warren of rooms and corridors change. Patients and visitors wandered to and fro. It seemed they had gone in a circle and were back where they started. Jill pushed the button to open the doors to the new unit Sarah would call home for the next while.

"You want me to stay and help you get sorted?" the nurse asked.

"No thanks. I have to call my mum and tell her my new room number and she can help me when she gets here."

"Bye, Sarah. Best of luck," Jill said before she disappeared out the door.

It took some time but Sarah found her iPhone and called her mother with the information. Now, sit back and wait for her to come.

When Robert entered the breakfast room, Margaret and the children were already there. "Can we go with you to pick up the governess, Uncle Robert?" Mary Elizabeth asked at breakfast.

"P-p-please?" Jenny piped up.

"Let us go," John Bryce echoed.

"You'll meet her soon enough, children," Margaret declared.

"F-father, c-can't I go?"

Robert looked at his little girl. It broke his heart to have to say no to her but it wouldn't be fair to the others if he said yes. "Not this time. We shan't be long and we don't need you three overwhelming the poor woman straight away. We'll be gone a short time and you'll meet her on our return."

"Aw, we never get to do anything fun," John Bryce pouted.

"Enough, young man," his mother snapped and smacked her hand on the table. "Finish your breakfast and go to your room. I don't want to hear another peep out of you. Do I make myself clear?"

"Y-yes, mother," he whimpered.

Jenny and Mary Elizabeth looked at each other and giggled.

"That will be quite enough or you'll both be suffering the same fate as John Bryce." Margaret looked to Robert for his support.

"You heard your auntie, Jenny," he responded.

The girls settled down and John Bryce slunk out of the room. He almost crashed into Mrs. MacEwen as she entered with more bacon to put in the chafing dish.

"What time did you say Miss Balfour's train arrives at Weetshill?" Robert asked.

"About nine-forty-five."

"Early to say she came up from Edinburgh."

"I think she came to Aberdeen yesterday. She spent the night there before continuing her journey this morning."

Robert finished the coffee in his cup and within seconds the butler was there to top it up. "No thank you, Archibald," he answered holding his hand over his cup. "Callum knows to have the horse and carriage ready to take Margaret and me to the railway station?"

"Aye, sir. E'erything is looked after."

Pulling his pocket watch out, Robert checked the time. "We must be going. We don't want to make a bad impression by being late."

Before leaving the breakfast room, he reiterated his instructions regarding Letitia and the children.

The ground was still snow covered. "I cannae drive too fast, sir," Callum stated. He helped Margaret and Robert into the carriage. "It's slippery and we dinnae want the mare to hurt herself."

"That's fine. We have plenty of time to get to the railway station," Robert answered, closing the door.

The carriage lurched with the coachman's movements as he climbed into the driver's seat.

"Do you know anything about this governess, Margaret? Anything that will help with introductions and small talk on the journey back to Weetshill?" Robert inquired.

"Not a thing, other than she comes highly recommended."

Robert looked out the window. The carriage bounced and swayed over the rough road. He didn't want to think how rough the ride would be had the horse been moving at speed. Great drifts of snow almost buried the drystane dykes separating the fields. Other places on the ground remained completely bare. "I wonder if the train will be late?" he pondered.

"I shouldn't think so."

"The railway line does travel through at least one deep ravine. The snow could have drifted in to it."

"Don't be such a pessimist," Margaret murmured putting her hands into her fur-lined muff. "My, but it is cold in here."

Robert covered his sister's lap with the horsehair blanket lying on the seat beside him. She was right, it was cold in the carriage but it was only a short ride to the railway station, he hoped. If he was right and the snow blocked the line, they might have to travel further to meet the train. In that case, they would have to light the brazier for warmth. On a rough ride, it could tip over and start a fire. He peered out the frosted over window making it difficult to see the station.

Callum brought the carriage to a stop. When he returned a few minutes later and opened the door, he let in a gust of cold wind and swirling snow. "The Aberdeen train willnae be coming, sir. Snow has blocked the line the other side o' Inverurie. The train cannae get through."

"What of the passengers? Are they getting them off?"

"I doesnae ken, sir. Stationmaster dinnae say."

Robert climbed out of the carriage. The weather had deteriorated since they left Weetshill. Now with the icy wind whipping the snow, it felt at least ten degrees colder. He needed to speak with the stationmaster to see what their alternatives were, if any. He returned to the vehicle a few moments later. At least in here, even though it wasn't warm, it was out of the wind and made a huge difference. "They're not letting passengers off the train. They have dispatched a crew to clear the snow that's blocking the line. When that's done the train will continue its journey."

"At least they have woodstoves in the carriages so they'll be warm," Margaret replied. "So what do we do? We can't stay here. We'll catch our deaths."

"Don't worry. We'll go home and when the time comes, we'll come back to meet Miss Balfour."

"How will we know the train has arrived?"

"Callum and Angus will hear the whistle and see the smoke from the stack. When they do, we'll make the trip again," Robert replied, motioning to his coachman to turn the carriage around and return to the mansion.

Archibald met them at the front door. "Aye, get you in and in front of the fire. You must be half froze."

Before Robert and Margaret had a chance to remove their heavy outer clothes, the children charged downstairs into the great hall.

"Where is she?" John Bryce asked.

"You said we would meet her when you got back," Mary Elizabeth pointed out.

"F-father d-did y-you f-fib?" Jenny asked.

His daughter's statement made Robert chuckle. "No. I didn't fib. The snow has blocked the railway line and until they clear it, the train is stuck. Once they get it free and it gets to Weetshill station, we'll go back and get Miss Balfour. Off you go now and play."

The rest of the day dragged. The wind howled around the windows rattling the panes. Snow blew into the glass. It sounded like thousands of needles each time it hit.

About seven o'clock that evening, word reached the mansion the train approached Weetshill station. Robert and Margaret bundled themselves up again for the trip to uplift the new governess. They arrived at their destination at the same time the train chugged into the platform.

"You wait here, Margaret. I'll escort Miss Balfour back to the carriage whilst Callum attends to her belongings." Robert clambered out into the cold night. Some of the passengers were still de-training and a few already had. A woman, who appeared to be in her thirties, huddled next to the building. "Are you Miss Balfour, Miss Constance Balfour?" he inquired.

"Yes. And you would be Mr. Robertson?"

"Aye. Come with me. The carriage is this way," Robert invited, extending his arm. "Did you have a pleasant journey?"

"Until the train got stuck, it was rather nice. The scenery is so pleasing, until we couldn't see it anymore for snow," she replied taking his arm.

"Callum," Robert called to his coachman. "Miss Balfour's belongings are next to the building to the right of the door."

"Aye, sir. I'll fetch 'em."

When they reached the end of the platform, Robert turned. Callum struggled with a huge trunk and two enormous carpet bags. "You get in out of the cold, Miss Balfour," he insisted opening the door. "I'll make the introductions on my return. I must help my coachman."

Callum had stopped on the platform. "I dinnae ken what she has in these, sir, but they's terrible heavy," he huffed, in an attempt to catch his breath.

"If I take the two bags, can you manage the trunk?"

"Aye, sir. That is very kind o' you." He swung the carpet bags down onto the platform and sighed.

Robert picked up the bags and stumbled because of the weight. On his second attempt, he succeeded and staggered to the carriage. He put the bags inside and boarded. What in the world had the woman brought with her that was so heavy? He sat across from his sister and prospective governess.

"Miss Balfour and I have already introduced ourselves," Margaret stated shifting in the seat.

"Callum is bringing the trunk. He'll be along in a moment."

He had no sooner uttered the words when the carriage jerked. The coachman loaded the last unwieldy piece of the governess's luggage onto the back. Soon they were back at Weetshill and the groom had the carriage unloaded.

When he escorted them inside, the butler stated, "Your meal is ready, sir, ladies. The bairns be in the dining room."

"Thank you, Archibald."

"I'll get Dougal to help wi' the bags. Shall we puts them in Mrs. Robertson's old room?"

"No," Robert said louder and harsher than he intended. "I'm sorry, Archibald. I didn't mean to snap. No, Miss Balfour's belongings will go to the second floor where the rest of the servants' accommodations are located." That room had to stay as it was. It was Sarah's room. He had only spent one night with her as husband and wife. That was in a different bed chamber. One prepared for their wedding night.

"Aye, sir," the butler answered. He turned to help Margaret and the new governess out of their coats and other paraphernalia.

"Any trouble with Miss Letitia?" Robert whispered.

"Nae, sir. Mrs. MacEwen took her meal to her room. Miss Christie was sittin' and just starin' at the fire, so she said when she came back."

The adults entered the dining room and the children became silent. Robert seated his sister in her usual place. He then settled Miss Balfour in Sarah's vacant chair before taking his own.

"Your home is lovely," she stated, her blue eyes sparkling.

Robert smiled. Now he'd had a chance to see the woman in proper lighting, she was attractive in a stern sort of way. She pulled her corn-silk blonde hair parted in the middle and pulled into a bun at the nape of her neck. Only a tiny bit of her earlobes showed. In them, she wore delicate gold cross earrings. He thought she would be perfect for the position.

Soon, the maids brought in and served a piping hot meal of roast beef, potatoes, turnip, and carrots.

"Let me introduce you to the children you'll be teaching. This is my sister's boy, John Bryce Esslemont and across from him is his sister, Mary Elizabeth."

"Hello children."

"And next to you, is my daughter, Jenny."

"Hello Jenny. My, aren't you a pretty girl."

"A-are y-you g-going t-to b-be m-my n-new m-mummy?" she asked, bursting into tears. "I-I d-don't w-want a n-new m-mummy. I w-want S-Sarah b-back," Jenny wailed then charged out of the room.

"Would you like me to go after her, sir?" Miss Balfour asked.

"No, I will. Excuse me," Robert sprang to his feet and went after his adopted daughter.

Perhaps having Jenny meet Miss Balfour the way she did wasn't such a good idea. Going forward, the governess would take her meals with the rest of the servants. The woman had a horrendous journey from Aberdeen to Weetshill. He thought it right to show her some extra kindness on her first night there. Having the children in the dining room seemed to be the perfect way to introduce everyone. That way, they could get down to business the following morning.

A loud crash from the first floor sent Robert up the stairs, two at a time. He found Jenny in her room. The items from her table lay scattered on the floor, some broken. She sat in the midst of the destruction, head on her knees, sobbing.

"Hey, what's gotten in to you?" Robert inquired. He found a spot on the floor that was safe to sit on. "Come here, you daft wee thing."

Jenny lifted her head and glared at him. "J-jenny n-not d-daft," she retorted, crossing her arms and pouting.

"I'm sorry. You're not. You're a very bright lassie." He patted the floor beside him beckoning her to come closer.

Eventually, Jenny worked her way to his side. Robert scooped her up onto his lap and wrapped his arms around her. "Miss Balfour isn't going to be your new mummy. She's the lady we talked about who is going to teach you and your cousins. That's all. Sarah will *always* be your mummy. Don't ever forget that."

"B-but sh-she s-sat in S-Sarah's ch-chair."

"It's my fault. I shouldn't have seated her there. I didn't realize it would upset you so. I am so sorry." He kissed the top of her head.

"Wh-when S-Sarah c-come b-back?"

"I don't know. I honestly don't know. But she will. And you don't want a new mummy? Well, I don't want a new wife. I'm like you, I want Sarah."

Jenny threw her arms around Robert's neck and squeezed.

"Shall we go back down and have our meal now?"

The little girl didn't answer but hopped off Robert's lap. It took him a few minutes to struggle to his feet, no longer accustomed to sitting on the floor. He held out his hand and Jenny slipped hers into it and they stepped into the corridor.

Janet appeared from the servants' staircase. Robert explained the noise to her. "I'll tidy up straight away, sir." She turned to Jenny, smiled and mouthed that everything would be all right.

25

Robert materialized in Sarah's hospital room but it was empty. No trace of occupation. Had she found her way back to Weetshill and somehow they passed each other without knowing?

Seized by panic at not finding her, he took the chance of others seeing him and stepped into the corridor. Voices drifted towards him from his right. He strode in that direction, pausing at the end of the wall. Peering around the corner, he saw a group of women gathered around a table.

Should he approach them? He had to find Sarah. No doubt about it. He had no choice. Taking a deep breath, he stepped forward. By now only one person remained at this place. Taking off his bowler and fidgeting with the brim, he cleared his throat and croaked, "Excuse me. I'm looking for Mrs. Robertson – I mean Miss Shand. What has happened to her? She used to be in the second room on the left down the corridor."

Jill looked up. "Very funny, David," she replied. "Where did you get the clothes? The Oxfam shop?" The man in front of her looked like he'd come from a fancy dress function somewhere in the city. His brown, wool suit well pressed but looked old fashioned like from the late 1800s or early 1900s.

"I assure you, madam, I do not know who this David is you speak of. And what's wrong with my attire?"

Standing and leaning back against the photocopier, Jill folded her arms across her chest. David was a joker and had played numerous pranks on her and the other nurses in the ICU in the past. She had no reason to believe this was anything different.

"Come on, David. Enough is enough, give it up. I know it's you. And you know full well we transferred Sarah to the High Dependency Unit."

"I know nothing of the sort. And I am not this person you keep referring to."

This prank had gone too far. Jill came around the desk, grabbed David by the arm and shoved him towards the exit. "Go get into your proper work clothes," she ordered, pushing the door open and him through it.

At the same time, the clatter of a chart on the countertop echoed through the quiet unit. She turned in the direction of the noise. David stood there. She wheeled back around. The other person vanished in the corridor through the window in the closing door. "Wh-what the …?" Jill leaned against the wall, shaken by what she had seen. "Y-you just left here."

"What are you talking about?" he asked, approaching her.

"You, you smartie pants. I watched you leave. You were wearing a vintage suit and carrying a bowler hat."

"I have no clue what you're on about, Jill."

"Don't lie to me, David Robb. You were in here dressed in a centuries old suit looking for Mrs. Robertson."

"Who?"

"I mean Miss Shand – Sarah."

"Come sit down," he ordered, walking her to the nurses' station and helping her into a chair. "You look like you've seen a ghost."

There was no explanation now to what she saw. Who was the man she was so determined was David in fancy dress? She had to have been seeing things. Overworked of late, it seemed to be the most logical reason behind the vision.

"Can I get you some water?"

Jill nodded and pointed to a BPA-free plastic bottle on the counter.

Once he had seen to Jill, David raced out of the ICU bound for the High Dependency Unit. He had to ensure Sarah was safe. When he reached her room, he paused outside the door. Had Jill seen Robert, the man Sarah had been so adamant about marrying? If so, then other than Sarah she was the only one. He'd never seen him and he spent more time with Sarah than any of the other staff in ICU. He'd had a few strange experiences since meeting her he couldn't explain. He figured if anyone would have seen this man from the past, it would have been him. Stepping through the doorway, he looked around the entire room. Sarah was alone. No sign of this mysterious man who looked so much like him.

"Hi David, I wasn't expecting to see you today. I'm glad you stopped by."

"Just checking on my favorite patient," he replied smiling.

The shrill, electronic sound of the alarm going off jolted Rachel out of her sound sleep. Saturday morning when she could lie-in and today, she was up at six o'clock. She hit the snooze button and yanked the duvet up over her head. A few more minutes was all she wanted. A few more hours, was more like it. But she had promised Sarah she would go back to the library and maybe the Family History Centre today. Since the latter closed at one o'clock, she had to go to Aberdeen in the morning. She hoped she wouldn't have to go to both.

Rachel threw the covers aside, sat up and stretched. The wool socks she wore to bed were now twisted so the heels were on top of her feet. She straightened them and headed to the bathroom to get ready to face the day.

When she returned to her room after showering, Rachel flipped on the radio. Lady Gaga's *Poker Face* came on the air. She cranked up the volume, picked up her hairbrush and using it as a microphone, sang and danced to the music. While she cavorted around the room, she laid out her clothes. That way, when the song finished she could dress and finish getting ready.

Hair dried and styled, makeup applied, and outfitted she went downstairs. It didn't matter what day it was, her father was always up early. He was in the barn or taking hay to the cows and sheep in the fields. Rachel headed to the kitchen. Her mother sat at the dining room table with a pot of tea.

"What has you up at this hour?" Mrs. Shand asked.

"Off in to Aberdeen. Have to do some stuff for Sarah," Rachel answered. She knew if she went into the details of her mission, her family would thwart her efforts at every turn.

"That's nice of you. How are you getting there?"

"Catching the bus to Duninsch then taking the train."

"You'll need some money," her mother commented. The woman opened her handbag slung over the back of her chair. "Forty pounds be enough?"

"More than. Thanks, Mum," Rachel said pocketing the cash before her mother changed her mind. She glanced up at the clock over the door. She still had an hour to go before the bus would arrive in Kendonald.

"What are you doing for your sister?"

"Just stuff," Rachel answered. She walked to the galley kitchen and put two slices of bread in the toaster. "Then I'm going to go see her for a bit."

Her toast popped while she searched in the fridge for the butter and she jumped, hitting the back of her head. A basket on the counter contained individual servings of jams, marmalades and peanut butter. None of them appealed to her.

Rachel returned to the family dining room and fixed herself a cup of tea. She took her breakfast into the lounge and flopped on the sofa. Picking up the remote, she flipped the TV on and scanned through the on-screen guide. Nothing piqued her interest. She turned the television off and went back to her magazine but clock watching distracted her.

Just past seven-thirty, Rachel returned to her room. She grabbed her iPhone off the dresser, wrapped the scarf her gran knit for her around her neck. Pulling on her down-filled bomber jacket, she bounded down the stairs and out the front door.

The wind howled around the house whipping up the skiff of snow and swirling it in the air. Rachel dug in her pockets, pulled out her matching gloves and shoved her hands into them.

She reached the stop at the end of the road about five minutes before the bus should arrive. Rachel bounced up and down to try to keep warm. She wished she'd put her warm winter boots on rather than wear her high-top tartan trainers. But that wouldn't be cool. She'd put up with the cold. It would be warm on the bus.

The diesel engine's rumble grew louder and the bus rounded the corner. It stopped a few short feet away from where Rachel stood.

After paying her fare, she dropped into a window seat on the left side of the bus. Once settled the driver accelerated and they were moving.

Rachel watched the scenery. First the trees and the stone wall, which gave way to a laneway and a wooden man-gate. Her father's fields on the opposite side of the road. The lodge and footpath to Leith Hall on her side. A few minutes later, the chimney for the distillery appeared in the distance.

As they drew closer to Weetshill, Rachel pressed her forehead against the window. She wanted to get a good look at the mansion. When it came into view, it was the same hulking ruin she knew. Still, something about Sarah's story about living there bothered her. Loathe to admit it, she had seen her sister, Robert and Jenny at the farm on Halloween. She had made a smart comment about Sarah's clothing.

The bus approached the Duninsch level crossing. Rachel pulled the cord and stood. The driver turned onto Commercial Road. She hoped he'd stop around the corner but he didn't pull over to let her off until he reached the bus stop. She had plenty of time to traverse the short distance to the unmanned railway station. She had pored over bus and train schedules and this was the best combination. At the self-serve ticket machine, Rachel purchased her same day return fare.

At least the building sheltered her somewhat from the biting wind. Still, the damp chilled her to the bone. Rachel paced back and forth on the platform rubbing her arms but it was of little help. In the one direction, past the signal box and the main road, Dunnideer loomed in the distance. The hillfort on top looked like a mere pimple. In the other, the platform bridge over the tracks dominated the landscape. The lone bench was snow-covered and even if she wiped it away, she would still get wet should she sit.

Pulling out her iPhone, Rachel texted a couple of her girlfriends but had to keep the messages short. Her fingers went numb from the cold. She shoved it back in her pocket and continued to pace. Today's weather forecast said nothing about this cold, biting wind off the North Sea. And now, it had started to snow making things worse.

The whistle sounded and the barricades went down across the Kendonald Road. By this time, Rachel had given up on the train ever arriving. Hopping from one foot to the other in anticipation of getting into the warm carriage, she waited.

When the train came to a stop and the doors opened, Rachel scrambled aboard. She selected a seat in the row right behind one of the floor heaters so her feet would warm up.

About five minutes after the train left, the conductor came through. He checked tickets and sold to folks who had boarded at the last stop. Rachel handed her ticket over and settled back for the ride.

The train arrived at the Aberdeen station about ten minutes late. There had been a delay between Inverurie and Dyce but Rachel didn't know the cause. She put her coat back on, left the warm carriage and sprinted across the car park to Guild Street.

It was colder here in the city than back home. The wind coming in off the harbor carried moisture from the North Sea with it. The lamp posts and building fronts wore coats of frost.

At Bridge Street, Rachel turned right. She hoped the buildings would shelter her from the frigid wind blowing in off the water. She wasn't so lucky. It didn't work. Instead, they funneled the cold, moist air and intensified it.

Rachel ran most of the way from the railway station to the Central Library. By the time she reached Local Studies, she was out of breath.

When she entered the department, no one was at the desk. A cursory glance over the top didn't reveal anything. Spotting a member of the staff, Rachel approached. "Do you know if anyone left a book or anything on the Robertsons of Weetshill here at the desk for me?"

"I'll take a look."

Rachel followed and watched her rummage through the papers. It took a while but she came up with something. "Here you go. There's this," she said, handing over the sheet of paper.

Scanning over it, disappointment hung over Rachel like a low hanging, black cloud. The book on the Robertsons wasn't available. When it was, the library staff would contact her if she wanted to leave her details.

"Unavailable?" she asked.

"We had some books water damaged a while back. It's one of them so it's off for repair. Sorry we can't be of more help right now, but if you're willing to wait ..."

"No, you're all right. My sister is anxious to get it so that's not an option."

Dejected by the news, Rachel left the library. Not knowing her next destination's exact location, she walked back to Union Street. She turned in the direction of the Castlegate and rounded the corner onto King Street.

The Family History Research Centre was about two and a half blocks past the intersection of East North Street. Rachel stood in front of the building for a few minutes. She stamped her feet on the pavement removing the excess snow and slush she had picked up from walking and entered.

An older woman with black hair, streaked with grey stood at the cash register checking out a customer. Bookshelves filled the room holding maps, books and other material they had for sale.

After the customer left, the woman approached her. "Can I help you? You're looking a bit lost."

"I-I am," Rachel said.

"Well let's see if we can get you un-lost. Are you here to research your family tree? Buy one of our publications?"

Now to phrase it so she or Sarah didn't come off sounding like a right numptie. "Um, well, my sister … Sarah … she's in hospital right now so I'm doing her a favor. She's obsessed with Weetshill mansion. We live not far from there and can see it from the top of the hill on our farm. She asked me to come and find out everything I can about the place and the people who lived there."

"That's a pretty tall order for someone your age but come with me, dear. We're the people to help," the woman offered taking Rachel's arm and leading her to the stairs. "Did she give you a starting point?"

"Starting point?" Rachel asked.

"What year? A name; anything to help us get you to the right place and not waste precious time."

"Well, she did mention 1886 and the fire the following year."

"Excellent. I know just the person to help you and she's here today volunteering. You go first. These stairs aren't wide enough for us to go side by side."

At the bottom, the narrow passage opened into a small room. Its walls lined with shelves filled to capacity bowed under the weight. A couple of tables stood in the middle.

"Peryl, can you help this young lady? She's interested in the Weetshill and the Robertsons who lived there."

A short, plump woman looked up from what she was working on and came over. She had curly, grey hair and wore black-framed, horn-rimmed glasses. "Be happy to help you, pet. I'm rather fond of that auld place, myself."

Rachel breathed a sigh of relief. They didn't think she was crazy. But calling her pet she could do without.

"So what time and people do you want in particular?"

"1886 and through to 1887 or later. I know there was a fire there in 1887. According to what I saw recently in the *P&J*, they claimed the Laird died of smoke inhalation."

As Rachel spoke, Peryl flitted from one side of the room to the other. She pulled out binders and other documents and laid them out on the table. "Sit down," the woman instructed as she assembled a huge stack of paperwork. "Let's start here." She pushed her glasses up her nose and flipped through a binder until she found the page she wanted. "The Laird at the time was Robert Andrew Robertson. He succeeded his grandfather – poor boy lost his own father at a young age."

"What do you know about who he married?" Rachel asked.

Peryl flipped through the pages until she came up with a chart. "You're in luck. Someone else has provided a pedigree chart. Robert married an Anna Sarah Shand from Musselburgh on 30 October, 1886."

"Can I get copies of this?"

"Yes, pet. Of course. If you need copies of the actual documents, we'll have to go online."

"Scotland's People site, right?"

"Why yes."

"They mentioned it at the library. Can I also get a copy of the Laird's death documents?"

"They'll also be available at the same place. Why don't I leave you to look over this material? If there's anything you want copies of, the copier is there so you can make them. It is twenty-five pence per copy, so you know. And for the other things, we'll go upstairs to use the computer." Peryl gave Rachel's shoulder a squeeze.

Not wanting to miss a single detail, she took her time. Rachel pored over each page, chuffed her mother had insisted she take the forty pounds. She could spend that much on photocopying alone.

Finding pages she thought Sarah would find interesting, Rachel opened the binders and copied the pages. She amassed a huge stack of papers. When Peryl flitted past her, Rachel asked, "Is there any way of tracing an adoption from back then?"

"Some are easier than others. Who are you interested in?"

"The girl, Jenny. Supposedly, Robert and his wife adopted her."

Peryl leaned over Rachel's shoulder and inspected the documents. "You know, pet, I seem to remember there being a scandal back then. Now, let me see ...," she paused tapping her fingers on her chin. "Right here." The woman pulled another binder off the shelf and flipped through the pages. "Here you go."

Rachel skimmed over the document. "I definitely need a copy of this," she gasped springing to her feet and dashing to the photocopier. In her eyes, she had hit the motherlode. Her mind raced as the machine made a copy of the document. "Is there more about this?" The discovery of these snippets swept Rachel up in excitement. Tidbits of what folks back then wanted to remain secret. Until today, she never thought history could be so interesting. That was the one thing, she and Sarah had in common. They both found history boring in secondary school.

As Rachel photocopied pages from the binders, Peryl found more on the overloaded shelves. Her resources limited, Rachel had to put a stop to it. "I've only got forty pounds. I need to pay bus fare to see my sister in hospital and get back to the train station so I can go home. She is going to be so thrilled. Maybe the next time, she'll be able to visit here, herself."

"Before you leave, we'll get the marriage and death certificates from online. Or would you rather wait and let your sister come for those."

"Let's do it now. That way I can take everything to her at once."

Peryl escorted Rachel upstairs to the small room in the back where the computers were located. They downloaded and printed copies of the Laird's marriage and death registrations.

"But how did they know for sure it was the Laird's body they found in the room after the fire?" Rachel asked.

"I think you watch too much *CSI* and *Silent Witness*, pet. They didn't have the forensic techniques they do nowadays back then."

"So it could have been anyone then. Because they found the body in that room, they assumed it was the Laird," Rachel mused. "The newspaper article I read said the local police constable was mounting an investigation. I didn't even know Kendonald had a police station at one time. Would those documents be available?"

"They've not got everything digitized yet. For some of these things, you need to go to the New Register House in Edinburgh and see the actual documents. You're apt to find more information in the newspapers in the months after the fire at Weetshill."

"Maybe. I went to the end of the reel I found the article in. I didn't go any further."

"I'm intrigued, too, pet. When I've got some free time, I'll keep looking at the newspapers. Leave me your phone number or your e-mail address and I'll let you know if I find anything."

"That would be brill. Thanks so much." She scribbled her mobile number and e-mail address on the paper Peryl provided and handed it to her.

The one thing Rachel hadn't come away with was a copy of Jenny's adoption. It was quite possible it was done privately and didn't go through the courts.

Rachel paid for the photocopies and the computer searches and left. The bus stop was in the next block. By now, the weather had improved and the sun had popped out, burning off the dampness from earlier.

Boarding the number forty, Rachel thought about things Sarah had told her about being in the past at Weetshill. Now her research corroborated the events. Well, all but Jenny's adoption. She knew Sarah would be thrilled to get the information. Rachel still wondered what had happened. The vigils at the hospital while Sarah lie unconscious. The family wondering if she would ever come out of the coma. Her confusion compounded. She'd seen her sister with a man and a little girl at the house at Halloween when Rachel knew Sarah was elsewhere. It made no sense whatsoever. It was the basis for science fiction movies – not reality.

The bus pulled to a stop at the west end of the Aberdeen Royal Infirmary complex near Forresterhill Road. Rachel got off and made her way to the entrance.

26

"M-miss," Jenny stammered. "I-I m-made s-something for you. C-can I g-go get it, p-please?"

"I'm certain you are quite able to go get it, but *may* you have permission, is the proper way to say it."

Tears filled Jenny's eyes and one burned its way down her cheek.

"Very well, but straight there and back. Don't dawdle."

"J-Jenny w-will run," the little girl stumbled. In her rush to get the gift she'd made, she tipped her chair over. It clattered onto the oak floor.

She skipped out of the room and into the corridor pulling the door closed as she went.

"Do you want to go on an adventure, Jenny?" Letitia whispered from her vantage point pressed against the corridor wall next to the classroom door.

The little girl nodded.

"Okay, but we have to be very quiet. No one can see us, and we can't tell anyone we're going. It wouldn't be an adventure if we did," Letitia cajoled, extending her hand.

Jenny slipped her small hand into the woman's and they sneaked down the corridor. At the main staircase, they stopped. When no one was there, they continued to the servants' stairs.

Letitia forced Jenny in front of her. "Don't make a sound," she ordered, pushing the little girl as they went.

The adventure was getting scary. Stifling a sob, she crept down each step in silence until she stepped on the last one and it creaked.

"Stupid child," Letitia snarled. "Stand still."

The normal household sounds from the kitchen and laundry filled the air. They listened to make sure no one was nearby.

Snatching her hand, Letitia jerked the door open and dragged Jenny to the back door and outside.

The little girl couldn't keep up with the pace the woman set. "O-ow," she cried out. "Y-you're h-hurting J-Jenny."

"Stop whining."

Frightened more than she was before, Jenny wrestled her hand free from the woman's. She tried to escape to the mansion but Letitia's hand gripped her shoulder.

"You are coming with me. Remember we're on an adventure," she jerked Jenny to her feet.

"J-J-Jenny d-doesn't w-want to g-go. J-Jenny w-wants to g-go home," she whimpered but the woman ignored her pleas and kept walking.

Jenny did her best to keep up but stumbled and fell. Letitia yanked on her arm again. "Don't be so clumsy," she scolded. "We'll never get to ... our destination ... if you keep this up."

She scowled at the woman. "J-J-Jenny d-d-doesn't l-like you. J-J-Jenny wants S-Sarah."

"Too bad. Sarah is gone and she's never coming back. She told me raising you and marrying Robert were the two biggest mistakes she ever made."

"D-d-did n-not," Jenny retorted. "I-I-I want t-t-to g-go home. N-now."

The slap across her face stung like she'd been stuck with thousands, no millions, of needles. Then it burned. Letitia dragged her into the forest. Jenny bit her bottom lip to keep from crying because she knew it angered the woman. She recalled her time in the asylum before Sarah's arrival and decided to go along with this great adventure plan without a fuss. If she did, then maybe Letitia wouldn't be so mean to her. Maybe she could get away from her and back to Weetshill.

The entrance to the cave reminded Jenny of the crypt she and Sarah used to get away. It was hard to see for all the tree branches hanging in front of the opening. But this wasn't the place she took Sarah to escape. This place was scary. Dead people couldn't hurt you. They just smelled bad. When Letitia pulled the boughs aside, bats flew from the darkness. Frightened by the onslaught of flying mammals, Jenny squealed.

"Get inside," Letitia ordered.

Swallowing hard, Jenny tiptoed through the entrance. She couldn't see anything at first. As her eyes became accustomed to the dark, she was able to make out shadows. She sought out a corner where she could hide from the Christie woman.

Letitia smirked as she entered the cave. Revenge was sweet. Robert would pay a King's ransom to get Jenny back. She would make sure of that. With Sarah out of the picture, he would be free to marry her. Truth was, she didn't care about the little girl. She was just a pawn in her game of chess with the man she loved. Revenge of this magnitude on Robert was so satisfying. She licked her lips savoring the moment.

Sitting in the cave's entrance to prevent Jenny's escape, Letitia shivered. The ground was cold and damp. The rock she leaned against was freezing cold. She should have taken the time to at least put her cloak on. Jenny could go back to the asylum for all she cared. The child was a brat. Letitia rubbed her arms to create some heat in an effort to warm herself, but it was to no avail. Her teeth chattered and she vibrated. They would stay here as long as possible then move on to another place – one much warmer.

"This letter arrived now by special messenger, Mrs. Esslemont," Archibald announced. He placed the silver tray bearing the envelope on the coffee table in the library.

"Thank you."

"Is it from Letitia's auntie?" Robert asked, peering over the top of his newspaper.

Margaret examined the post for a return address. "Yes, it is."

"What does it say? Will she come for her niece?"

Skimming over the letter for the answer, she found it about halfway through. "Yes. She says she'll be here within the week." She handed the letter to Robert. "You can read it if you'd like."

17th November, 1886

Mrs. Esslemont
Weetshill, Duninsch
Aberdeenshire, Scotland

Dear Mrs. Esslemont,

I remember you well as I do your brother. I always knew Horatio would bring shame on the family and so hoped Philomena would see sense and not marry him. I am relieved my cherished sister isn't alive to hear of these revelations you write of.

I understand your vexation and am prepared to help in

*any way I can. To that end, expect my arrival within the week.
I'll persuade my poor niece to come back to Polperro with me.
The salt air will do her the world, I'm sure.*

*I am pleased to know she has a good friend such as
yourself.*

Yours truly,

Miss Millicent Coles

Margaret sensed her brother's relief when he read the letter. She, too, would be glad once Letitia was far away from Weetshill. The strain with the woman under the same roof had pushed everyone to the breaking point.

Employing the governess had worked out well thus far. She kept the children occupied with their lessons and ensured the Christie woman never got near them. The children did most of their learning in hers and Robert's late brother's room. Miss Balfour had everything there she required for teaching. Mary Elizabeth, John Bryce and Jenny all seemed to like her, too.

The library door flew open. "Mrs. Esslemont, Mr. Robertson, I can't find Jenny. She's not in her room. I've checked there. She wanted to get something and I saw no harm in letting her go on her own since things have been running so well. I was hoping she was with you," the governess babbled. "Miss Christie's gone missing, too. I've done my best to keep them apart ...." Constance broke down in tears. "Oh, I've done a terrible thing," she wailed.

Robert sprang from the sofa as if shot from a rifle and out of the room. His newspaper spilled onto the floor. A lump formed in his throat and his mouth went dry. "Archibald, Mrs. MacEwen, come immediately," Robert yelled. He dashed to the foot of the massive staircase. "Janet, I need you, too."

The butler arrived, still polishing a piece of silver. The housekeeper entered from the ballroom. Robert paced back and forth the length of the room.

"What has you so vexed, sir," Mrs. MacEwen asked.

"Sir, I came as quick as I could," Janet cried running down the stairs.

"We need to search the house – the grounds – everywhere,"

Robert instructed. "Letitia and Jenny have disappeared. She's taken my daughter away like she threatened that day at the kirkyard." He clutched his chest and slumped against the wall, frightened for Jenny's well-being. The wee lassie being alone with a mentally weak Letitia Christie scared him to death. Who knew what the woman was capable of?

"I'll see 'at Angus kens what's happened. If anyone can find 'em, it will be him," Archibald declared. "Come, Mrs. MacEwen, Janet. We'll start here in the house – one room at a time. Get e'eryone lookin'.

Margaret stepped out of the library. She hugged Robert. "They'll find Jenny. She'll be fine."

"I'm not so sure," Robert snapped, shrugging off his sister's embrace, and storming out the front door.

"Your overcoat," Margaret cried. "You'll catch your death."

Unconcerned for his own welfare, Robert continued to the gate. Secured. He started to the stables. When he was near the halfway point, he met Angus.

After relating Letitia's abduction of Jenny to his ghillie, the man's ruddy complexion went ashen.

"Get out of my way. I must find her," Robert demanded and attempted to sidestep the man.

Angus grabbed him by the upper arms. "Get hold o' yourself. You isnae dressed to be out here searchin' for the wee lassie. I'll gets Callum an' James to help. You go back inside."

"I can't. I have to find my daughter." Robert jerked his arms free and ran off. Jenny had to be safe. He couldn't bear to think of anything bad happening to her. Sarah was gone. He couldn't lose his little girl, too, and he couldn't sit inside and do nothing.

Margaret approached carrying a bundle in her arms. "Put your overcoat on. You won't be any good to Jenny if you get sick from being out in this state."

"Don't pretend you know what I need or want," Robert growled. "Finding my daughter and that crazy woman who has taken her are far more important than putting on a coat."

He sped off to the stables. They weren't in the paddock. He checked the barn, even climbed into the hayloft and searched it but there was no sign of them. They had disappeared without a trace. How long had Jenny been missing when Miss Balfour burst into the library? Letitia and Jenny could be miles away by now.

"I's sent Callum to get us some help lookin' for them," Angus stated standing in the doorway.

The man's shadow was long so it would be dark soon. "Thank you," he called down from above then descended to the floor.

Robert stepped out of the barn. The sun was setting fast. If they didn't find the missing pair soon, they might not find them at all.

"'Xcuse me, Mr. Robertson."

"What is it, James?"

"Who are you lookin' for?"

"Miss Christie and my daughter, Jenny. Do you know where they are?"

The scrawny, freckle-faced stable boy took off his cap revealing his ginger hair. He bowed his head and shuffled his feet. "I saw them headin' into the forest."

"How long ago?" Robert urged.

"I cannae say."

"Think lad, think. This is extremely important. It could be a matter of life or death."

"I think I kens where they are," James whispered.

"Well where, then. Tell me."

"Angus and me – we found a cave when he was teachin' me how to track game."

"Can you find your way back there?" Robert squatted to eye level with the boy.

James nodded.

Orbs of light from oil lamps held in the air by phantom-like bearers approached the barn. Callum had succeeded in raising a search party. "James thinks he knows where they are. Follow us," he instructed, waving his arm to beckon the others.

The ghillie grabbed a lantern from one of the other men. "Here you be, sir," he answered handing it off to his employer.

Robert hoped Letitia and Jenny were in the cave James spoke of and the lad remembered its location. After they passed the tree line, their pace slowed. Tree roots and low hanging branches created numerous obstacles, impeding their progress.

"It's just ahead," James stated.

"Where, lad? There's nothing here but trees."

"Here," he replied and pulled some low hanging branches aside.

A woman sat across the entrance. Even by lantern light, Robert recognized her. It was Letitia. Her face had no color. Her lips were blue. She looked like a corpse. He lifted her arm and when he let go, it fell back limp. He didn't care if Letitia lived or died. If it meant peace of mind for himself and his family, he preferred the latter. Stepping over her lifeless form, Robert shone the light around the rest of the hollow. Its beam caught Jenny in the furthest corner. The little girl wasn't moving. She was still as death. Robert placed the lantern on the ground and rushed to her side. He knelt and scooped her up into his arms.

"You wait here until the rest of the search party arrives. I've got to get Jenny to Doctor Burnett, if it's not too late."

The child wasn't breathing; at least that's how it appeared to him. Robert agonized over his daughter's fate at the hands of Letitia Christie. Jenny had never done anything to the woman. She didn't deserve this. But he did. He refused to marry Letitia and went so far as to buy his way out of the marriage contract so he could wed Sarah. Now she was missing and if anything happened to his daughter, he would be alone.

The physician's carriage pulled up in front of Weetshill mansion at the same time Robert arrived from the forest carrying Jenny. Margaret, Mrs. MacEwen, Archibald and the governess rushed out of the mansion. Miss Balfour buried her face in the butler's chest wailing and bawling.

"Brings her in here, sir. Straight through to the kitchen. It be lovely and warm in there," the housekeeper jabbered.

"No, take her to her room, Robert. Mrs. MacEwen you go along, too. She needs those damp clothes taken off. Get her into a flannel nightgown and into bed and under the covers."

"Aye, Doctor."

Once Jenny was under the housekeeper's care, Robert leaned against the corridor wall. "Is she alive? Please tell me she's alive," he moaned.

"I'll know more once I've examined her," Doctor Burnett answered. "Let Mrs. MacEwen get the wee lassie settled first."

The door opened. Robert rushed to his daughter's side and took her small hand in his. It was freezing.

The physician examined Jenny. "She's alive but just. Her pulse is very weak. We need to warm her but we need to do it with caution. We'll start with lots of blankets and a hat. Can you see to that Mrs. MacEwen?"

"Aye," she replied. The housekeeper scurried around the room and retrieved the requested items."

It was difficult to see Jenny with the covers piled on her so high. Mrs. MacEwen tied the straps of the fur hat under the little girl's chin.

"Thank you. That will do nicely."

"Now what do we do, Doctor?" Robert asked.

"We wait. It will take time for her body temperature to rise." He listened to her chest before placing his fingers on the child's neck. "That's better. It's a bit stronger now. Still far from robust. Mrs. MacEwen, can you get us some towels, please? Hang them in front of the fire to warm them. We'll roll them up and place them under Jenny's arms and down along her sides. Don't let them get hot, though. We don't want to burn her."

Once the towels warmed to the proper temperature, the doctor removed them from the quilt rack. He slipped them into position with little disruption to the covers over the small girl.

She looked so small and helpless under all the blankets and quilts. Robert begged for her to wake but so far nothing was happening.

"It will be a long night, Robert. Why don't you get some sleep? I'll be with Jenny."

"Excuse me, Doctor Burnett, sir, Angus has brought Miss Christie back."

"I don't care about her. It's her fault my wee girl is in this situation," Robert bellowed.

"You sit here with your daughter. I'll take a moment to check on Miss Christie."

Robert placed his hand on Jenny's forehead. It remained cold but not to the same extent when he brought her home. The housekeeper placed her hand on his shoulder. He reached up and patted it in acknowledgement of her help and support. He would maintain his bedside vigil until Jenny woke … if she woke.

When the doctor returned, he commented, "Miss Christie is in front of the fire in her room. Your maid, the one with the red hair, Janet I think is her name, has seen to her needs. Your ghillie is standing guard outside her door. She's not as bad off as wee Jenny here."

The sooner Letitia's aunt arrived and took her niece back to the south of England, the better off everyone at Weetshill would be.

Mrs. MacEwen prepared a bowl of tepid water to wash Jenny's dirty, tear streaked face. She wiped her left cheek and a hand-shaped bruise became visible.

Horrified by the sight, Robert leapt off the bed. He wanted to throttle Letitia Christie for laying her hands on his little girl. "I'll kill that woman," Robert snarled.

"Sir, please, you cannae be doin' 'at. You'd be leavin' the wee lassie wi' no father and mother at all." The housekeeper stood blocking the door.

"Ah, you're right, but that Christie woman is so infuriating. I don't know why I let my sister persuade me into letting her stay here. Paying for her accommodations in a hotel would have been far less costly."

"Jenny's pulse is becoming stronger," Doctor Burnett interrupted. "I think she'll make a complete recovery. I'll spend the rest of the night here with her if you'd like to get off now, Mrs. MacEwen. Robert, you should get some rest, too." The physician got comfortable in one of the wingback chairs.

"No, I'll not leave her." Robert returned to his place on Jenny's bed. He stroked her forehead and cheeks. When he touched the blackened spot on her face, the little girl flinched. "She moved," Robert exclaimed. "I touched her and she moved."

The doctor strode to the bed and examined Jenny again. He replaced the towels next to her body with warm ones from the quilt rack. "Please don't get your hopes raised. It could just be a reflex."

Margaret poked her head into the room. "I couldn't sleep so I thought I would see how she's doing," she whispered coming in the rest of the way.

Robert told her of Jenny's reaction to his touch. "She's getting better. I know she is."

"Doctor Burnett, sir, I's brought you coffee," Archibald announced from the corridor.

Pulling the door open, Margaret stood aside. The butler deposited the tray on the table before retreating.

The adults stood huddled on the far side of the room. They spoke in whispers so they didn't disturb the little girl. Robert's eyes remained fixed on his daughter watching for any sign of wakefulness. Unable to stand back any longer, he sat his coffee on the table and returned to Jenny's bedside. When he brushed a lock of her hair away from her face, she stirred then shivered violently.

"Is she having a seizure?" Margaret asked.

"I don't believe so," the doctor replied, rushing to the child. He lifted her eyelids. "As I suspected. She's using her own body's healing power to warm her. I think she'll be fine. I'll check on Miss Christie one last time then I'm going to get off. I'll come back later in the day and check on the lassie again."

"Thank you for everything," Robert sighed, shaking the man's hand.

"Go get some rest. You heard what he said. He thinks Jenny will be fine." Margaret placed her hand on his forearm.

Shaking her off, he sputtered, "So long as that lunatic is under my roof, I'll not leave my daughter. The woman's not trustworthy."

"But Angus is outside her room. Surely, he wouldn't let Letitia anywhere near Jenny."

Robert strode to the window and tied the curtains back. The morning light was soft; the colors muted by the mist. He knew his ghillie would give his own life to save the family but still, he didn't feel any better.

The outdoor scene in front of him soothed his shattered nerves. The Aberdeenshire countryside was beautiful. Its length and breadth filled with lush farmland, forests, streams and rolling hills. Dunnideer, Bennachie and Tap O'Noth were the highest peaks in the area.

A soft moan reached his ears. He rushed to his little girl's bedside. "Jenny, it's Robert – father – can you hear me?" he whispered.

Her eyes flickered open. "B-bright,"

"Turn the lamps down and close the curtains, please, Margaret."

Once his sister dimmed the light in the room, Robert looked at Jenny. "You frightened us all to death. Why would you go off with Miss Christie when I told you to never be alone with the woman? We did everything in our power to keep you apart."

Tears formed in her eyes. "Ad-adventure," she answered. "I-I d-don't l-like her. Sh-she m-mean t-to J-Jenny. H-hit ..."

The little girl's arm moved under the covers and Robert stopped it. "You have to stay covered. I know Letitia hit you. You have a bruise on your face."

"J-Jenny w-wants S-S-Sarah. J-Jenny l-loves S-Sarah," she whimpered.

Margaret stifled a sob and fled from the room.

Robert gathered up Jenny, blankets and all, and carried her to the wingback chair by the fireplace. He settled in and held her. She would not get away from him again.

"I love Sarah, too, and I want her to come back," he soothed. Uneasy over Letitia Christie staying a few doors away, holding his daughter in his arms relaxed him. He dozed off.

27

When she heard squeaking footfalls on the tile floor, Sarah glanced in their direction. Her sister appeared in the doorway.

"You won't believe the stuff I got today. It matches with the things you've told me," Rachel gushed.

"Let's see then," Sarah urged, not wanting to wait a moment longer than necessary for vindication.

Rachel pulled the papers out of the plastic carrier bag Peryl had put everything in. "The lady at the Family History Society told me there was a scandal back then," she jabbered and handed the documents to Sarah. She pulled the other chair over so she could sit next to her sister.

"That's for sure. Jenny was conceived in an incestuous relationship between Horatio Christie and his daughter, Letitia."

"Was her birth ever registered, sis?"

"I don't think so. At least not the way Jean MacDonald spoke. She's the midwife who delivered the wee girl and whisked her off to the poorhouse in Kendonald."

"There was a poorhouse in Kendonald?" Rachel interrupted, staring at her sister in disbelief.

"Yes. It was news to me, too. When Horatio found out, he threatened to go there, take Jenny away and kill her. Well, Jean – strange old bird she was – would have no part of that and got Jenny out of there and out of the parish. She took her to the asylum at Ladysbridge and that's where I met her."

"I thought you were at Weetshill, not the looney bin."

Sarah ignored her sister and pored over the other documents. She had to have been there. How else would she have known all this information from the past otherwise?

Rachel's iPhone chirped its distinctive ringtone making both girls jump. "Wow," she chattered. "Peryl mentioned there had been a scandal around that time. Well, she's been looking through the microfilms of the old newspapers. Guess what? They jailed a prominent solicitor in Aberdeen for falsifying documents."

"Would the solicitor be Kenneth McIntosh?" Sarah asked.

"Yes. And the minister in Kendonald was disgraced for going along with it. No mention of charges against him but they sacked him from his position and chucked him out of the church."

"Can you ask Peryl to print those articles for me? I *told* Kenneth stealing a dead woman's identity would end in tears. I didn't want to do it at first but he convinced me it would be the only way I would be able to marry Robert. After all, my birth registration wouldn't exist for another hundred years plus."

Rachel gawped at her older sister, her mouth hanging open. "So, you *really* were back in the past," she whispered.

"Yes. And now that I know about this, I have to get back there to save Robert from going to prison, too. Or worse still, dying in that damn fire."

"What if it was someone else in the room? What if it wasn't Robert who died but whoever set the fire?"

Sarah's mind raced. Was it possible the fire had been set on purpose so Robert could get out of the country? Avoid prosecution for going along with the solicitor's plan? No. That wasn't possible. Who would be daft enough to set a fire then stay in the room until they were dead? Even Kenneth couldn't find anyone that stupid or desperate, could he?

"Okay, I asked her to print them. I should hear back from her soon."

28

Sarah dreaded the time after her visitors left the most because it was so quiet and empty. She picked at her meal. It didn't matter what they brought her, everything tasted the same. She was only allowed to eat real food in the last few days, if you could call it that, and it tasted disgusting.

When Sarah finished, she wheeled to the lounge. She found it empty giving her the choice of programs to watch on the television. That was one advantage to being in the High Dependency Unit, she had a bit more freedom. She picked up the remote control and flicked through the channels. A news broadcast program caught her eye. The reporter stood outside the Weetshill ruins. Sarah listened to the remaining segment.

"... now that redevelopment plans have received the go-ahead. On a happy note, the child severely injured here in the recent accident continues to make remarkable progress in Royal Aberdeen Children's Hospital."

Sarah dropped the remote and wheeled to the nurses' station. "Today's *Press and Journal*. Do you have it?" she asked between breaths. The head nurse of the unit worked the desk. Sarah didn't care for her. She found her strict and overbearing.

"Is everything all right, Sarah?"

"Yes but I need today's *P&J*. Please tell me you have it here."

The woman looked under the counter and came up with the paper.

Sarah snatched it out of her hands, placed it on her lap, and wheeled back to her room. She laid the paper on her bed and gleaned each page looking for anything related to the news segment she'd stumbled onto. Tucked away near the back of the local section, she found the article she sought.

HISTORIC WEETSHILL RUINS TO BE RESTORED

Life will once again be breathed into historic Weetshill. Built in 1757, the B-listed mansion has sat in ruins since owners gutted it and removed the roof in 1952 to avoid heavy taxes.

Ownership of the mansion has remained in the family over the years. The last known occupants were Mr. and Mrs. George Esslemont.

The mansion's condition has deteriorated over the years, most of all in the last fifteen.

The plans include luxury flats within the mansion, and the conversion of outbuildings.

The current owners, Arthur and Isabella Robb of Williamsmuir, were not available for comment.

Sarah didn't bother with the rest of the article. She couldn't believe what she'd read. Were her eyes and brain playing tricks on her? Robert's sister was Mrs. George Esslemont. She'd met the woman. David said his mother stayed in Williamsmuir. Was she the Mrs. Robb in the article? She dismissed the thought since Robb was a common name.

David had to see this and the sooner the better. The same with everything Rachel had brought to her from the family history place.

When he stopped in later in the evening, Sarah retrieved the copy of *The Press and Journal.* She'd left it open at the page containing the Weetshill article. "You have to see this," she chattered. "You wouldn't believe how hard it's been to keep them from throwing this newspaper in the bin." Sarah placed the paper in his lap. "Is that your parents mentioned in it?"

"Hang on. Give me a chance. I've not read it yet." David skimmed over the article. "Yes, they're my mum and dad. I knew dad inherited a substantial piece of property, but I never knew its location. They never mentioned it to me. Mind, with the accident in the earlier paper you showed me, I'm not surprised. It explains why when I went home mum was too busy to look anything up."

"Why wouldn't they have told you about Weetshill?"

"I figure they didn't think they needed to go into detail."

"Are you not close to your parents?"

"Not so much since I moved to Aberdeen after I started training to be a doctor."

"I think I know what you mean. You've got your own life now and it's up to you what you do with it. I know I felt so free when I first went to Uni. I could make my own rules – stay out late, ditch class, eat lots of junk food, go to clubs every night. After a few weeks, I settled down to my studies."

The shimmering light in the corner appeared and the strange buzzing sound started in her ears. She clapped her hands over them hoping it would stop. Sitting here with David like this made her feel like she was cheating on Robert. The noise and light were things she experienced whenever Robert was nearby. This time he didn't materialize. Was it because David was with her?

"You look like you've seen a ghost. Let's see what we can do to get you cheered up. You said you wanted a junk food fix. Do you want me to get you a takeaway?"

"Would you?"

"Tell me what you want."

"A big, greasy burger with cheese, bacon; the works, and chips."

"Your wish is my command, me lady." David extended his left arm, folded his right one over his stomach, clicked his heels, and bent over in a deep bow.

Sarah burst into laughter.

"Much better. I'll try not to be too long."

A few moments later, the head nurse of the unit, Sister Longmuir, brought in Sarah's supper tray.

"You can take that tasteless slop away. I won't be needing it tonight. David has gone to get me a burger and chips."

"You won't be able to eat it. Mark my words. David should know better. He's a medical student, for pity's sake."

"David asked me what I wanted and I told him. He's trying to make me happy."

"You might be happy for the first little while after you indulge in your meal. But you'll be sorry afterwards. Don't say I didn't warn you." The nurse turned on her heel and left the room.

"Bitch," Sarah mouthed.

David returned about forty-five minutes later. "Here you are. Sorry it took me so long. The queue was longer than I expected."

Sarah opened the bag. "Where's yours? Did you get something for yourself?"

"No. I'll eat your leftovers. I'm quite sure you won't be able to eat it all."

"You don't know me very well, David Robb. I used to be able to eat this much and more."

"Piggy."

"Yup, and I had the weight on me to prove it." Sarah tucked into the food David had brought to her. About halfway through the burger she stopped. "I'm stuffed. I can't eat another bite. Here you go. You can have the rest."

"I knew you wouldn't be able to eat it."

"But it tasted so good. I would have loved to be able to eat more."

"Leaves more for me." David chuckled and finished the rest of Sarah's meal. "I have to go. I'm on early tomorrow so I best get home and get my head down for a couple of hours."

"Do you have to?"

"Yes, I'm afraid so. I'll come see you tomorrow."

"Good night, David."

"Tomorrow."

"The swelling in my hands has gone down. Can you bring my rings back?"

"Sure."

Sarah, contented after her visit with David and junk food fix, got into bed and settled in.

About midnight, Sarah woke up in extreme pain. She pushed the call button for the nurse. Much to her chagrin, Sister Longmuir came. "My stomach hurts something awful. I feel like I'm going to be sick."

Instead of saying I told you so, Sister Longmuir helped Sarah out of bed and to the bathroom. She stayed with her the entire time. Wave upon wave of nausea came over Sarah. When she finished vomiting, she was exhausted.

The nurse handed Sarah her toothbrush and toothpaste. "Here clean your teeth before I take you back to bed. Get the awful taste out of your mouth."

Sarah accepted the offering and scrubbed her teeth and her tongue. She would have done her throat could she have reached any further back with the toothbrush. "You were right. It was too soon to eat junk food."

Sister Longmuir smiled. She took Sarah back to her room and tucked her into bed. Sarah realized the head nurse wasn't so bad after all. She was much like the housekeeper, Mrs. MacEwen, at Weetshill.

29

A black carriage stopped in front of the mansion. Robert didn't recognize it or the driver who was helping someone alight. Margaret joined him at the window. "I wonder if that's Letitia's auntie," she mused, tapping her right index finger on her lips.

"Miss Millicent Coles," Archibald announced, ushering the woman into the library.

She took her hands out of the white fur muff and unfastened the clasp at the neck of her cloak. Letitia's aunt handed the items to the butler. The woman was stocky but looked impeccable in a blue satin gown. Her hair, visible beneath her hat was the color of snow.

"Could you get us some tea, please?" Robert asked.

"Aye, sir."

The woman wore an enormous, dark blue, sapphire ring on her right pinkie finger. It made it difficult to grasp her hand in a proper greeting. "Robert Andrew Robertson, Miss Coles. I'm pleased you could make the journey."

"You're the gentleman, although you don't deserve that distinction," she sneered. "You broke my niece's heart when you jilted her for another."

Stepping forward, Margaret greeted the woman. "It's lovely to see you again. It's been such a long time. I think the last time I saw you was at your dear sister's funeral."

Millicent lifted a jewel-encrusted Lorgnette to her face and peered through the oval lenses. "You've grown into a fine woman." She let her eyeglasses fall to her chest, held around her neck by a delicate chain.

Robert guided the women to the sofa near the fireplace. "Sit down," he invited. Once they were comfortable, he sat in the armchair closest to his sister. "Since we first wrote you, we've had some trouble here at Weetshill," he began. The butler returned with the silver tea service, interrupting the conversation. "On the coffee table will be fine, Archibald. That will be all." Dismissing the butler, Robert picked up where he left off. "Letitia hasn't been herself since the fire at Gleanstane. She recently caused much distress by taking my daughter away. I'm pleased to say, we found them both alive. Still your niece is of weak mind."

"Oh, I think her state of mind goes well past the fire. She's not been herself since before she and her father came to stay at Polperro. You've been the undoing of her."

"I beg to differ, madam, but Horatio holds that honor," Robert declared.

"After what she's done, Letitia can't stay here anymore," Margaret commented, pouring. "She needs to be with family."

Millicent's eyes grew wider. "You mentioned in your letter Horatio is in jail. I always knew he would be the ruin of the family. That man is ruthless."

"Did you know Letitia had a daughter?" Robert asked.

The woman paled so her complexion and hair color were almost the identical shade of white. "N-no," she replied, fanning herself with her hand.

"It's true," Margaret confessed. "My brother and his wife adopted her. Given the circumstances it was the best thing for the child."

"What do you mean?"

Margaret told Letitia's aunt of Sarah finding Jenny in the asylum and why she was there. "But, the story Horatio told of the parentage of the wee girl is a blatant lie. You see, one of the charges against him was incest."

Robert leaped out of his chair and snatched the cup and saucer from Millicent as she slumped back on the sofa in a faint. He and his sister patted the backs of the woman's hands attempting to revive her. The last thing Robert needed was two mentally weak women under his roof. One was already more than enough.

When Letitia's aunt came to, Robert held the tea cup to her mouth. "Drink this," he said.

She took a sip. "Oh dear. Oh my." Flustered she fanned herself more. "I had no idea. You said one of the charges, what were the others?"

"Forgery and bribery."

The woman looked about to faint again. Margaret persuaded Millicent to take another sip.

Robert motioned to his sister to join him near the desk away from their guest. "Bring Letitia down here. Tell her she has a caller," he whispered.

Margaret nodded to Angus who maintained his post outside the door. She wondered if the man had slept since the night they rescued Jenny and Letitia. Tapping on the door, she pushed it open.

Letitia rocked back and forth in a wingback chair staring into the fire. Still dressed in the same clothes she wore when she took Jenny, and a wool blanket around her shoulders. She looked disheveled and dirty.

"You have a caller," Margaret stated before crossing the room.

She received no reply.

Placing her hand on Letitia's shoulder, she repeated, "You have a caller."

The woman recoiled at the touch. Her piercing blue eyes were wide and wild as if she were a caged animal.

"Please Letitia, let me help you. We'll get you washed and into some clean clothes. You have things here. Remember after the trial, we went to Gleanstane and I gathered some of your belongings? Things I thought you would like?"

Again no response.

Margaret flitted about the room retrieving clean clothes for her friend. She laid out a white satin chemise trimmed with lace, clean drawers and stockings. She chose a green chintz gown which was also adorned with similar threadwork.

Task completed, she poured water from the ewer into the bowl on the washstand. Margaret then topped it up with hot from the black iron kettle near the fire. "Come, let's get you washed up. You'll feel better, I'm sure. And you want to look your best for your visitor."

"Is it the police?" Letitia whispered.

"No."

"Do you hate me for what I've done?"

Margaret swallowed; her mouth dry. "No, I don't hate you. I'm upset with you for torturing Robert and everyone here at Weetshill," she lamented. She then helped her friend out of the chair and onto the stool at the dressing table. "What you did was thoughtless and inconsiderate. Jenny could have died," she continued watching their reflection in the mirror.

Tears formed in Letitia's eyes. "I only wanted us to hide in the cave for a short time, but it was so cold and dark."

Wringing out the cloth, Margaret washed her friend's face. "There. That's better, now isn't it? I'll leave you to complete your ablutions and change and I'll come and fix your hair. If you need anything, I'll be right outside your door."

The latch clicked shut and Letitia turned verifying Margaret left the room. She had done a bad thing taking Jenny away from where people loved and wanted her. No one had to remind her. Relieved the little girl was still alive, well she was, wasn't she? Why else would Margaret have said 'could have died'? Now Letitia wished she had died. With her father in prison, Robert married to another, and her home destroyed what did she have to live for? She rested her chin on her hands and stared at her reflection in the mirror.

Still angry with Robert for jilting her and bent on revenge, an evil thought entered her mind. Dropping the wool blanket from around her shoulders, she gripped the front of her dress. She pulled, ripping the fabric. Buttons flew into the air. They bounced off the wooden surface of the dressing table, the mirror and other hard furnishings. She tore her chemise and petticoat, too, and threw her drawers into the fire.

Satisfied her underwear had burned, leaving no trace, she called Margaret back into the room. "Your brother did this to me," she sobbed.

"Oh, Letitia, you know perfectly well he did no such thing."

"He did. I swear," she claimed.

"I just got those things out of the wardrobe for you and have been right outside your door. No one has been in or out of here except me. And tell me, why are there buttons from your dress all over in here?" Margaret retrieved one from the dressing table. She held it next to Letitia's dress where one of the fasteners dangled by a few threads.

Her plan foiled, Letitia dropped down onto the seat. She should have known Margaret would be too clever to fall for the lie. Revenge by taking Jenny hadn't worked. Revenge by claiming Robert had attacked her hadn't worked either. There must be something else she could do, but what?

Shaking her head at the challenge ahead of her, Margaret pulled the ivory combs out of Letitia's hair. She picked out bits of grass and leaves. At first, it was difficult to run the brush through the matted mess. It took a long time before she made any headway. The woman's hair needed a good wash but there wasn't time. She couldn't keep Millicent waiting any longer.

With the task completed and Letitia dressed in fresh clothing, the women left the bedroom. Margaret nodded her head to Angus and he followed them. No one spoke. The silence disrupted by their footsteps on the bare oak floors, quieted intermittently by the Persian rugs placed at regular intervals.

The butler met them at the foot of the staircase. "You's lookin' much better today, Miss Christie," he commented extending his arm to her.

Letitia pushed Margaret away and turned to run but Angus grabbed her preventing her escape.

"Let go of me," she yelled kicking and squirming to escape the ghillie's grip.

Fighting to regain her balance, Margaret stumbled into one of the hall tables sending a vase crashing to the floor.

Robert burst from the library into the great hall. "What is all the strushan?" he asked.

"Miss Christie here, she dinnae want to come wi' us. She tried to get away," Angus replied.

"Are you all right, sister?"

Rubbing her shoulder and upper arm where she'd hit the wall, Margaret nodded.

"What is the meaning of this childish behavior, Letitia? I am appalled. You get yourself in here right this instant," Millicent ordered. She pointed to the open library door.

The ghillie deposited the woman on the sofa.

"Thank you. That will be all," Letitia's aunt insisted, dismissing the man.

"I be outside the door, if you need me," he replied.

Closing the door behind Angus, the woman turned to her niece. "It's bad enough your father has disgraced the family, but now you as well? What on earth were you thinking of abducting a child?"

"My child," Letitia cried. "I was taking her so she could live with me."

"A child born in uncleanness. One you didn't know existed until recently."

"I should have married Robert. We were arranged. We could have raised Jenny together. Been a family."

"Should have, would have, could have are all well and good. In reality, things don't always turn out that way," Millicent soothed. She sat on the sofa beside her niece and held her hands. "You and Robert weren't destined to be together."

"But we were, auntie."

"No child. I'm sorry but you weren't." She wrapped her arms

around her niece and pulled her in. "You have endured a lot, too much, in these last months for a young woman your age. You need to break the ties you have with Kendonald, Gleanstane and Weetshill and start fresh. Come back to Polperro with me."

"No," Letitia cried, wriggling out of her aunt's embrace. "I want to stay here. I want to be the Lady of Weetshill. Robert's wife has left him. I would make a wonderful one. After all, I'm prepared," she ranted, staring down at her mother's sister on the sofa.

Exasperated by her niece's stubbornness, Millicent stood and looked Letitia straight in the eye. "I'll not stand for anymore of this nonsense. Either you come with me back to the seaside or I'll have the police brought in. They'll charge you and you'll go to prison like your father. I may not condone Robert buying his way out of the marriage contract but I certainly do *not* condone your actions. Taking that poor unsuspecting child from the only loving home she's had. I think you've actually gone quite mad."

Crossing to the door, Letitia's aunt opened it a crack. "Margaret, dear, would you gather my niece's belongings. Whether she is in agreement or not, I am taking her to Polperro with me. We'll leave here within the hour."

"No, Auntie Millicent, no," Letitia moaned before throwing herself on the sofa and sobbing.

It didn't take long for Margaret to gather the few meagre things she had brought from Gleanstane for Letitia and return them to the carpet bag. She stood next to her brother outside Weetshill mansion and watched Letitia climb into the carriage followed by her aunt.

The carriage pulled away. The girl's vacant expression in the window spooked her. She and Robert waited until the vehicle disappeared from sight before going back inside.

"I'm glad that's over," he sighed, walking to the fireplace.

"She's not well. I do hope the salt air at the seaside will prove beneficial to her," Margaret sighed. She dropped in the armchair by the sofa.

"She should be incarcerated for what she's done," he countered.

"Jenny is back. She's well. Shouldn't that be what matters? Incarceration would serve no useful purpose. I don't think Letitia is well enough to understand the consequences of her actions."

"You're right. I have my daughter back and that Christie woman is out of my house. Perhaps now, we can get back to the way we were."

"I do hope so, Robert. I truly do."

30

When Jean Webb, Sarah's physiotherapist, came in Sarah's breakfast tray remained untouched.

"Not eating?"

"I can't. Too much of the wrong thing last night."

"Somebody didn't smuggle you in a bottle now, did they?"

"No, but I don't think I could feel any worse."

"This should make you feel better. You'll be going to the physio suite starting Monday. Feeling up to it?"

"Absolutely! I'm sick of either being in bed or this wheelchair."

"Good, I'll see you then."

Sarah, excited at the news, couldn't contain herself. She told everyone who entered her room. She wanted to share it with David, most of all, but he wouldn't be in to see her for a few days. She would have to settle for telling her mother and sister – and that wasn't the right way to think about it.

By the time visiting hours were over no one other than on-duty hospital staff had been in to see Sarah.

Saturday arrived and Mr. Shand visited. "How are you doing today?"

"Wonderful, I get to start therapy down in physio on Monday."

"That's my girl. You'll be out of here in no time."

"Why didn't mum come yesterday?"

"She stayed home to give your Gran a break."

"How is Grannie?"

"Tired."

"Do you think she and Grandpa Shand will come visit me?"

"I don't know. It's hard for them to sit in a car for so long."

"Grannie and Grandpa Duncan, too?"

"I'll be sure to tell them my wee girl wants to see them. They've all been very worried about you."

"Thanks, Dad."

"I brought something to show you."

"What?"

Mr. Shand took out his wallet and extracted a folded up piece of newspaper. Another piece fell to the floor. He bent and picked it up.

"What are these, Dad?"

"I want you to read them. Here, this one first." He handed it to her.

Sarah looked at it and back at him. "I don't understand."

"Read it, please, Sarah."

She took the preserved clipping with the date, 10 August 2010, in her father's handwriting and began to read.

WOMAN 'CRITICAL' AFTER BEING KNOCKED DOWN

An unidentified woman is in critical condition after being knocked down on an Aberdeenshire road near the village of Kendonald.
Believed to be in her early 20s, paramedics treated her at the scene before air-lifting her to Aberdeen Royal Infirmary.
The driver of the vehicle, 25 year-old Heather Rennie, was uninjured and treated for shock at the scene.

"And now this one." Mr. Shand handed Sarah a second clipping from a more recent edition of the newspaper.

INJURED WOMAN IDENTIFIED

The young woman injured when struck by a car near Kendonald has been identified as 19 year-old Sarah Shand of Gordonsfield. She remains in the intensive care unit at ARI with life-threatening injuries.

Sarah looked up at her father with tears in her eyes. "It really was a dream, wasn't it."

"I'm afraid so."

"But it seemed so real."

"I'm sure it did. Maybe now you'll stop all this nonsense about going back to the past and concentrate on your future?"

"All right, Dad. I promise."

The two visited until the time came for Mr. Shand to return to the farm. "Your mother is expecting me home for my supper so I best be on my way. You be good and we'll be back in to see you soon."

"Bye, Dad. Love you."

"I love you, too." Mr. Shand kissed her on the cheek and left.

Sarah wheeled her way over to the lounge and flipped on the television. She wished David would soon return. She missed his visits. She wanted – no needed – to tell him her news. Telling David was paramount.

Supper came – the usual bland fare – but after the burger experience, most welcome.

Sarah's worst enemy was boredom. There were only so many hours she could spend looking out the window at the hospital grounds. At this time of day, darkness had already fallen so there was nothing to see anyway. Sarah still had difficulty concentrating. When she flipped through magazines or the newspapers, she focused on the pictures. Although it wasn't quite six o'clock yet, Sarah climbed into bed.

"Good morning."

Sarah rolled over in the direction of the voice. "David, I'm so glad you're here," she gushed, sitting up. "I've got the most exciting news. I've wanted to tell you since Friday but you weren't here."

"What is it?"

"I start in the physio suite on Monday. Great, isn't it?"

"Brilliant, I'd say. I'm so happy for you," he congratulated and gave her a big hug.

For a moment, Sarah felt like she'd returned to the past at Weetshill. David was so like Robert. What kept her mind anchored in the present was the fact David wore a leather jacket.

"How was Glasgow?" she asked, still snuggled to him.

"Same as always."

"And the football or rugby or whatever match?"

"Football. And the match was good. So were the pints in The Scotia Bar afterwards."

"When are you back on duty?"

"Tomorrow."

"Stay with me. Tell me all about Glasgow. I miss it."

David pulled a chair up to the bed and regaled Sarah with his stories of the trip.

"The big switch-on for the Christmas lights is coming soon. Do you think they'll let me out to go to it? I've never missed it here except when I was off at Uni. I went to George Square for Glasgow's."

"I can't see it being a problem. Do you want me to take you?"

"Would you, please?"

"If it's okay with Doctor Compton, sure."

"Thank you," she gabbled unable to contain her excitement.

"Hi, Mrs. Shand, Rachel," he chatted when they walked through the door.

"Hello, David." Sarah's mother replied.

"I best go. Leave you three to it. I've not been home yet. Stopped here first. I'll see you tomorrow."

"Bye," Sarah called after him. She turned back to her mother and sister. "I start in the physio suite tomorrow," she chattered.

"That's wonderful news, Sarah."

"You bet. Glad for you, Sis."

"How's Grannie Shand? Dad told me yesterday she's not well."

"She's fine, dear. Just tired is all."

"Good. Did dad tell you I want them to come see me? Your parents, too?"

"Yes."

"It's so boring here. I watch telly, look at magazines and the newspapers."

"I brought you some new magazines, yesterday's paper and a book of word search puzzles. They might help with your concentration. And it will give you something different to do. But, with you starting therapy tomorrow, you might not have time for all these things."

"No danger there, Mum. All I've got in this place is time."

"Oh dear, speaking of time, is it that late already? I've got to go. Get supper on. Your father will be hungry and your grandparents are joining us. Come Rachel, we've got to go."

Sarah accompanied her mother and sister to the lift where they said their goodbyes. She hoped when the doors opened, David would be there but he wasn't. The elevator was empty. She watched the doors close and the lighted numbers above change until they were on the ground floor.

The commotion of a crash call drowned out the knock on the hospital room door. It wasn't until she glimpsed a shadow in the opening, Sarah looked up from her magazine. "You looking for someone?" she asked.

"I-I'm looking for Sarah Shand," the girl faltered, shuffling from one foot to the other.

"You've found her. Do I know you?" Sarah set the glossy publication in her lap.

"Y-yes and no. I'm not even sure if you'll want to see me," she croaked, inching closer to Sarah's chair.

"I appreciate the company. Why would you think I wouldn't want to see you?"

"I'm the person who hit you that night on the Kendonald Road."

Sarah stared at the girl. Her voice was familiar. Those big, fear-filled, brown eyes brought that horrible night rushing back.

"You're ... you're ... ?"

"Heather Rennie. Yes."

"How did you find me?"

"The accident was in all the papers, and on the telly. I tried to come sooner but they wouldn't let me see you. Told me it was family only. I was so afraid I had killed you. I had to see for my own eyes that I hadn't. I am *so* sorry about everything. I've never driven since then."

"As you should be. Everyone will be a lot safer with you off the roads." Sarah's recollections of that night became clearer. She remembered the frightened girl leaning over and covering her with her coat.

Sarah's father had shown her the clippings about her accident from *The Press and Journal*. A photo of the girl's car resting head-on against the tree accompanied the first one. "You're looking for forgiveness? You almost kill me and you want me to forgive you? Are you off your trolley?"

"In all fairness, you stepped out in front of my car. I didn't have time to stop or take evasive action. You popped out of the trees along the verge. Th-the next thing I knew you were in front of me," she cried, huge tears falling from her eyes. Clapping her hand over her nose and mouth, she turned and fled from Sarah's room.

Alone again, Sarah thought about her exchange with the driver of the car that mowed her down on that fateful night. Had she been too hard on the girl? It took a lot of nerve for her to come to the hospital to check on Sarah's condition. Still, she wasn't ready to forgive, much less forget.

31

Monday, in the physio suite, Jean helped Sarah position her wheelchair at one end of the parallel bars. She stood between them. "Okay, now grab both bars tight and pull yourself to a standing position."

Sarah pulled herself up with ease.

"Brilliant. Now stand there for a minute."

"Ooh, I am a bit dizzy. Guess I stood up too fast."

"You're all right. Take a few deep breaths and look at me."

Sarah nodded.

"Okay, now one foot in front of the other, start walking towards me."

Sarah struggled. She felt like a baby learning to walk. It took every bit of concentration she could muster to get her legs to move.

"You're doing great. Now keep coming." Jean backed up until she reached the other end of the bars. "Take your time. It's not a race."

One foot in front of the other, Sarah told herself with each slow, painful step. She didn't get quite halfway before she fell. "My legs. They hurt. I can't do this."

"I know they do but get up and try to get the rest of the way to me."

"I can't," Sarah screamed.

"Yes, you can. You'll never walk again if you don't work through the pain."

"Okay, okay. When I get to you, do I get to rest?"

"Maybe for a minute because once you get here, you're going to turn around and walk back to the other end. You'll keep doing it until you can walk from one end to the other and back again without falling. So, the more times you fall, the longer we'll be at it."

"Jean, are you crazy? I can't."

"Yes, you can and you will. Not because you want to be able to walk without a frame, crutches or a cane. Because you're going to be so mad at me, you'll do it just to get at me. I'm going to push you harder than you'll push yourself and I know how determined you can be."

Sarah got to her feet. After a brief pause, she tiptoed her way to the end of the bars.

"Okay, now turn around and walk back to me," Jean ordered from the other end.

Sarah changed her grip on the bars so she could turn around and walked towards Jean. This time she took only a few steps before her legs gave out and she landed unceremoniously on her bum.

"Get up. You don't walk with that part of your anatomy."

Sarah struggled to her feet. She took a few more steps and fell down again and began to cry. "I can't do this. It hurts too much. I have to stop." She punched her thighs over and over. "Damn, stupid legs. Why won't you do what I want you to? Might as well not even have legs for all the good they are to me."

"You don't mean that." Jean knelt by Sarah.

"I do mean it. I'll never be able to walk again. Who am I kidding? I'll always be stuck in that chair."

"Stop feeling sorry for yourself. You will walk again. Now, get up. I told you, we're not stopping until you can walk from one end to the other and back again without falling. The sooner you do, the sooner you can go back to your room."

On the brink of exhaustion, Sarah traversed the distance both ways. Afterwards, she collapsed into her wheelchair. Shattered she needed her feet placed on the footrests and someone to push her back to her room.

When Jean helped Sarah into bed, she broke their silence, "Same time tomorrow."

"Yeah, yeah, whatever." Sarah managed before she pulled the covers up and fell asleep. She woke much later and felt someone watching her.

"Hey there, sleepyhead. Hard day at the physio suite?"

"David, how long have you been here?" Sarah shifted into a sitting position.

"Not too long."

"Why didn't you wake me?"

"I didn't want to disturb you. Did you know you snore?"

"I do not," she retorted.

"For someone who doesn't; you were doing a fine job of it. So how did your first day go?"

"Jean is a slave driver. Even though I was tired and in pain, she made me keep going."

"Good for her."

"But there were other people in there working with their therapists. They weren't pushing them as hard."

"Don't concern yourself with the other people. Just worry about yourself and your recovery."

"Aye, aye, sir." Sarah saluted and giggled.

"I'm being serious, Sarah."

"I know you are. I promise I'll pay less attention to the others and concentrate on me."

"Good. I better go now. It's almost time for my shift," David advised, standing up to leave. He put his hands in his jacket pockets and felt the velvet bag containing the rings and pulled it out. "I almost forgot, I brought these like you asked me to." He handed the package to her. "You should be able to wear them now."

Sarah poked her left index finger into the bag stretching the opening. She extracted the precious items. Staring at the rings, they looked different. When Robert brought them to her the gold gleamed and the gemstones sparkled. Now they were lifeless and dull. Still they were hers. She slipped them onto her finger wedding band first. They fit as if they were custom made for her but knowing Robert he did that.

She removed the engagement ring and rubbed the ruby with the velvet storage bag. It began to shine. Sarah felt better knowing that ring cleaner would bring back their former luster.

"I really have to get a move on."

"Will I see you later?" she asked.

"I doubt it. Working A&E. I probably won't be able to get away."

"Tomorrow?"

"I'll come in early and see you before I have to start my shift. By the way, you still have your trainers on."

"Priorities. Sleep was higher on the list than taking off my shoes. Can you do me a favor before you leave?"

"Sure."

"Get my bag out of the closet and put it up here on the bed."

David lifted the bag off the closet floor. "What have you got in this thing? Bricks?"

"My mum packed it so I'm not sure."

"See you tomorrow, maybe later, if it's not too busy downstairs." David kissed her on the forehead and went off to work.

Sarah took the jewelry off and scoured each item with the soft, cloth bag. It took a great deal of effort but their appearance improved. She couldn't wait to get home and give them the cleaning they deserved. Placing them back on her finger, she held her hand out in front of her inspecting the job she had done to that point. The next time Robert appeared, he would be happy that her wedding and engagement rings were back on her hand where they belonged. She made a solemn vow to herself then she would never take them off again.

32

"This letter arrived in this morning's post for you, Mrs. Esslemont," Archibald said holding the envelope on a silver tray.

"Thank you. Leave it there on the end table. I'll look at it shortly," Margaret replied looking up from her mending. The stack was never-ending. John Bryce either poked holes in his socks or tore his trousers or shirt sleeves. Still, it was a relief not worrying about what Letitia might do.

Thinking the letter might be good news from George, Margaret ripped the envelope open.

20th November, 1886

Mrs. Esslemont
Weetshill, Duninsch
Aberdeenshire, Scotland

Dear Mrs. Esslemont,

I want to thank you for your kindness to my niece especially after the cruel thing she did to your family. I believe the child, Jenny, is in the proper place. I will do nothing to facilitate her removal from Weetshill. Your brother and his wife are loving parents, I'm sure. It's a shame I didn't get to meet her.

Letitia isn't at all well. I hoped being here and going for walks along the seaside, breathing in the salt air would do her the world. It has done nothing.

Numerous examinations by umpteen physicians and surgeons haven't helped. It grieves me to say, I've had Letitia committed to the Cornwall County Lunatic Asylum at Bodmin. She will spend the rest of her days there.

I visit when possible but she doesn't know me. She spends

her waking hours in a stupor. No matter what sort of treatment they administer, she doesn't come out of it.

It vexes me to see her in this way. She was always a fragile child. With the things her father did to her (he's paying for them now, thankfully) I can understand why she has gone mad.

I thought you and your brother would want to know of this news.

Yours truly,

Miss Millicent Coles

Margaret read and re-read the letter in an attempt to comprehend the written words.

When Robert joined her in the library, she thrust the correspondence at him. "You must read this. It's from Letitia's aunt."

"Now what has that crazy woman done?" he sighed walking to the window before settling into Sarah's favorite chair. "At least she can't torment us anymore."

"Robert, can't you show a little compassion? I mean after everything she's been through during her lifetime, is it any wonder?" she asked, standing in front of him.

"It still doesn't excuse her taking Jenny."

Hatred formed in her brother's eyes and it frightened her. She had never seen him so malevolent before. It had to be all Letitia's doing. No one else had ever made him so angry – not even Horatio. If only Sarah would walk through the front door. She was good for Robert in so many ways; he so besotted with her. "Go speak with Reverend Mitchell. I'm sure he can offer you guidance," Margaret suggested. "The children will be fine. Letitia Christie won't bother us ever again." She closed the library door behind her.

The next morning, before her breakfast arrived, Sarah got dressed and ready for physio. She hoped it would be a fry up but the usual poached egg and toast were on the plate.

After she finished, Sarah went to the physio suite. Besides the parallel bars she walked between the previous day, the room housed more equipment. There were exercise bicycles, a hoist, assorted walking aids. Exercise beds and mats were in the center of the room. A middle-aged man working with his therapist occupied one of them. Sarah wheeled about the room observing.

"May I help you?"

"Can I come here anytime to work out?"

"Monday to Friday between nine and five providing there's someone in here. By the way, I'm James."

"Sarah."

"So this is where you're hiding. I thought I would have to drag you down here kicking and screaming," Jean said, interrupting the conversation.

"You don't know me very well." Sarah didn't like her physiotherapist's tone. She continued around the perimeter of the room.

Jean met Sarah at the parallel bars.

"How long do I have to do this?"

"Same as yesterday. Once you can walk down and back again without falling, you're done."

"So if I do it the first time, I don't have to do it anymore?"

"Yes, but you won't be able to."

"Bet I do," A determined Sarah stood up at the end of the parallel bars. She waited a few seconds to get her balance. With dogged determination, she walked to the other end. The bands of her rings dug into her finger but she didn't care. She turned around and walked back to where she started from. "So I guess this means I'm done. You said back and forth without falling. I did it."

"Okay. You're done for now. Tomorrow it will be five times in each direction without falling before you stop. Once in the morning and again in the afternoon."

"It's a deal. You don't think I'll be able to do it."

"No, I don't."

Sarah didn't answer. She was in extreme pain but she'd shown Jean she wasn't a wimp. Her father's words *show her what you're made of* echoed through her head. With her back to Jean, she smiled and wheeled out of the room.

At the nurses' station on her floor, Sarah stopped. "I'm going back down to the physio suite after lunch so when David comes will you send him down?"

"Yes."

"Oh, and my sister is coming this afternoon so if I'm not back ..."

"We'll tell her where to go, too."

Lunch wasn't any more appealing than breakfast. A bowl of cream of something soup, with green bits in it. They could have been asparagus, leeks or broccoli, and Jell-O for after.

Rather than head straight back to the physio suite, Sarah went over to the lounge. She caught the last half of *An Affair to Remember* on television.

Determined to work out more, Sarah returned to the physio suite. She found it empty. Remembering James's words 'only when there's someone in here' echoed in her mind.

"You know you shouldn't be in here alone." David's voice startled her.

"I'm not. You're here."

"So am I to find you here until they let you go home?"

Sarah looked up. "Am I going home?"

"Not that I know of."

She continued her trek between the parallel bars. About mid-point Sarah stopped and turned to David, "Do you think I'll get out of here any time soon?"

"Can't say. That would be up to Dr. Compton."

"I mean now I've been 'uncaged' and moving around, surely they'll be showing me the door?"

"Maybe."

"When were you planning to leave for Williamsmuir?"

"First thing Saturday morning. David changed the subject. "So why the sudden interest in the physio suite?"

"Something my father said." Sarah told him about her conversation with her parents the night before.

"You don't think you're overdoing things a bit much?" He folded his arms across his chest.

"No. I'm determined to walk those bars twenty times if it means shutting Jean up and getting her off my case."

"You won't be doing yourself any favors if you burn yourself out in the first couple of days."

"I won't."

"You think you won't. Who's the one in the medical profession? Not you. So please listen to me. I know what I'm talking about."

"I promise. I'll slow down," Sarah relented.

"I'm not leaving you here on your own, so let's go. I'll take you to your room."

"Do I have to leave?"

"Afraid so."

"When will I be able to start walking besides between the bars?"

"I can't answer that. Jean's your therapist. She'll know."

"Good. I'll talk to her tomorrow about it."

"And I told you not to get carried away." David pushed the button for the lift. The door opened and they were face to face with Rachel.

"I'll leave your sister with you, shall I?"

"Hi, David. Did I interrupt something?"

"No. I have to get off to work." David pushed Sarah into the lift, gave her hand a squeeze and hopped out as the doors closed.

"I saw that. And these clothes aren't to show off for him."

"What do you think you saw, Rachel?"

"For starters, you're red as the emergency button and I saw the little hand squeeze."

"I'm warm from being in the physio suite and it's quite warm in here."

"I'll believe you because you're my sister. You're full of it."

"You brought everything I asked for?"

"And a few more things, too. You can look once we get to your room." Rachel put the lighter of the two tote bags on Sarah's lap.

When they reached her room, Sarah unzipped it and dumped the contents onto the bed. Among the tops and jeans was an assortment of fresh socks and undies.

"So what else have you brought me?"

"I loaded up your iPod with music because I know you don't have a lot on your phone. You're likely getting sick of hearing the same songs over and over."

"Brilliant. Thank you," Sarah exclaimed.

"Why'd you want the street clothes? Trying to impress someone? Some male medical student? Hmm?" Rachel goaded.

Sarah shook her head at her sister. "It's not David I wanted these clothes for. I want to dress in proper clothes for a change. Pajamas, track pants and sweatshirts get boring after a while."

"If you say so."

"What else do you have in the other bag?"

"I brought your Doc Martens. Your six-hole Docs. And something to read."

"You're the best, Sis." Sarah hugged her younger sister.

"Do us both a favor and don't cause a lot of bother like sneaking out to go clubbing or something. Mum and dad will go mental if you did."

Sarah's supper tray arriving interrupted their conversation.

"I've got to go. I didn't realize it was this late. I have to meet Jacquie and her mum at the main entrance. They were coming to Aberdeen to go shopping at the Bon Accord Centre and offered me a ride."

"But it seems like you just got here."

"We've been in town for ages. I walked from the mall over here."

"Come back soon."

"I'll try to come back on Sunday but it might not be until Monday. I've got a paper due then and I haven't even started it yet."

After Rachel left, Sarah pondered her conversation with her. She had nailed it when she said the clothes were for David's benefit. Still being able to wear normal, street clothes made her feel less like a hospital patient.

Sarah picked at the usual bland fare. Once she'd eaten her fill, she gathered her toiletries, and went to the shower room.

Back in her room, dressed in her cozy pajamas, Sarah plugged the earbuds David had brought her into her iPod. She selected Boyzone from the menu, and curled up in bed with the two magazines Rachel brought to her.

33

Sarah's daily physiotherapy regimen continued. She still walked in the gym but most of the time with the aid of a walking frame and not between the parallel bars. During this time, Sarah graduated from the frame with no wheels, to one with two, to one with four. Her biggest complaint about walking with a Zimmer was she couldn't stand up straight. Her back was sore. Whenever she could get away with it, she'd take a few steps without the aid of the device.

Jean kept a close watch on her during these visits. After one of their intensive physiotherapy sessions, she called Sarah into the office. "I think we can take the frame away from you now."

"Really? I don't have to walk with it anymore? Just my own two feet?"

"Not quite. But I do think you're ready for the next step." Jean produced a pair of forearm crutches. "You'll use these for about six to eight weeks, maybe longer ..."

"And then?" Sarah couldn't contain her excitement any longer. She was ecstatic to be getting rid of the walking .

"A cane. But ..."

"But what?"

"You've got to slow down Sarah. You're not doing yourself any favors by pushing yourself this hard. Your recovery is about six to eight weeks behind what it should be because you were in the coma."

"But I want to go home. I'm tired of being stuck in this hell hole day after day."

"I know you are. But promise me, you'll slow down. Now let's get these crutches adjusted for you. Stand up and put your arms into the cuffs and your hands on the grips." Jean passed the crutches over her desk to Sarah. She watched to see if they were the right height for her patient. "I thought as much. Not quite, but don't worry, they can be adjusted." Jean came around the desk. She shortened the crutch and adjusted the cuff and handgrip. "How does that feel?"

"I-I don't know what to say. It feels great."

"I mean the crutches. Take a few steps and tell me if they feel right. I can make more adjustments if we need to."

Sarah took a few steps under Jean's watchful eye. "They feel all right to me."

"Turn around and come back."

Sarah turned and walked back toward the physiotherapist.

"A little bit more." Jean fussed over the position of the handgrips and the cuffs. "There. Perfect. Walk across the gym and back ... slowly. I want to make sure I've got them adjusted so you're not always leaning forward."

Sarah found this more of a pain than anything else she'd endured since she came out of her coma and began therapy. But she did what Jean asked. Anything to get out of the hospital. The crutches felt fine to her. She didn't know what all the bother was about.

"Okay. Back to your room. But take your time."

"Thank you," Sarah gushed wanting to flee from the physio gym but her abilities wouldn't allow it. Instead she made her way out the door not any faster or confident than before. Outside the gym, she leaned against the wall and thrust both crutches in the air in triumph. "Yes," she yelled into the empty corridor.

Sarah wanted to see David so she could tell, no, show him she no longer needed the frame. She felt like she'd been set free. Free from the encumbrances she'd endured thus far. But it would have to wait. He had a lot of leave left he couldn't carry over to the next year, so was off on holiday.

The following day, Doctor Compton paid an early morning visit to Sarah. "Well, my dear. Things didn't look promising at the outset, but you've made the most remarkable recovery. I can't see any reason why you can't go home tomorrow."

"What? Tomorrow? You mean I'm out of here?"

"Yes. You still have to continue with your physiotherapy but you can do it on an outpatient or home-care basis. You'll have some bad, and I mean bad, days whilst you continue your recovery but we're a phone call away. Any questions, concerns – anything – you call."

"I will, I will. So I can call my mum to come collect me in the morning?"

"Yes. I'll sign the papers when I leave you."

"Thank you so much," Sarah exclaimed hugging Doctor Compton.

"You've been a handful here at ARI by times but we're going to miss you."

Sarah ignored his last comment. Instead, she focused on the words go home tomorrow. Nothing else mattered.

She had to tell David. She thought back to what he'd told her he was doing to use up the paid leave, but couldn't recall. Before the accident, she had a good memory. Since then, she could barely remember her own name at times. The question loomed, if she went home would he want to bother with her anymore?

"Ah, me lady."

David's voice. Sarah couldn't contain her excitement. She sat in the chair by the window. "Don't come any closer and close your eyes."

"All right," he replied.

Sarah left her crutches on the far side of her chair. She got to her feet and walked to where he stood.

"You can open your eyes now."

David opened his eyes and was face to face with Sarah. "Sarah, that's brilliant," he burst out. He hugged her and planted a kiss on her cheek.

"Take it easy. I'll be on the floor on my backside if you're not careful."

"I won't let you fall."

"I have great news. Doctor Compton is going to let me go home. I can't wait to get out of this place ..." Her excitement vanished. "But if I'm not here, I won't see you anymore."

"Don't talk daft. I won't let the fact you're not here stop me from seeing you."

"You really mean it?"

"Of course, I do."

"Now, when can you leave?"

"Tomorrow. I have to let my mum know so she can come get me."

David turned and started for the door.

"Bye, David. Drive carefully."

He turned back, smiled and winked. "Go on. Call her. Share your wonderful news," he insisted.

Sarah walked to her bedside table and took her iPhone out of the drawer.

"You know you're not supposed to use mobiles in here."

"I know, but I'll only be a minute." Sarah called her mother and gave her the news. She rang off and looked at David who was now standing next to her. "She'll be here tomorrow morning for me."

"Good. I'm off home until Christmas. I'm working over the holidays so the nurses who have families can spend the time at home. But I'll see you Sunday morning for the switch-on."

He hadn't forgotten. Sarah's heart felt like it skipped a beat, she was so happy.

"I'll phone you from mum's before I come. I'll need directions anyway, although I'm pretty sure I know where your parents' farm is."

"Here's my number." Sarah tore a sheet of paper from the notepad Rachel had brought her and handed it to him.

"And here's my mobile number. Just in case."

His number. He'd given her his number. Sarah clutched it in her left hand. "David, I need to sit down. Can you help me?"

"Overdid it a bit, did you?"

"Yes."

David escorted Sarah to the chair and helped her into it.

"Thank you."

"I want to get out of the city before the traffic gets heavy and I've got loads of things to do before I go. I best be off."

"Do you have to leave right now?"

"Afraid so. I'll see you soon. I'll come visit you before I come back to the city." David kissed her forehead and left.

Excited about her release the next day, time seemed to stand still. When it came time to go to bed, sleep eluded her. She stared at the large clock on the wall above the door. She swore she saw every hour on the hour tick by.

At six-thirty, Sarah couldn't stand it any longer. She got up, showered and put her cleanest clothing on. She would have preferred fresh clothes to go home in, but leaving the hospital was more important. She needed her mum to get there. Doctor Compton had assured her the day before he would sign the release papers.

Around eight o'clock, someone brought in her breakfast tray. It smelled like a fry-up. Sarah couldn't wait to have one of her mother's. They were always so good. She took the lid off the plate. No fry-up awaited – only scrambled eggs, toast, and sliced tomato. On the side of the tray sat a pot of tea and a bowl with a box of cold cereal and a glass of milk. Since she was hungry, Sarah ate the eggs, tomato and toast. It didn't taste anything like it smelled.

Sarah glanced up at the clock. Where is she? She should be here by now. Sarah phoned home to see if her mum had left Kendonald yet. No answer. She would be on her way. About an hour at the very most and Sarah would be on her way home. The hour passed followed by another thirty minutes. After two excruciating hours of waiting, there was still no sign of Mrs. Shand.

Doctor Compton stopped in. "You're discharged now but I still want to see you for regular checkups."

"Yeah, yeah. Whatever," Sarah answered staring out the window. "Where is she?"

Doctor Compton's pager went off. "I have to leave you now. I'm sure she'll be along shortly."

Sarah didn't answer him. She continued looking out the window. About another hour passed before she heard a familiar voice.

"Hi Sarah. Have you got your things packed and ready to go?"

Sarah turned around. "What took you so long?"

"There must have been an accident up ahead on the A96. By the time I got caught in the tailback from it, it was too late to get off at Inverurie and it took forever to get to Kintore. I got off the road there and came into Aberdeen across the A944."

Sarah grunted. "Let's go home. I want to get out of this place – now. I've seen enough of it to last a lifetime."

Doctor Compton returned to the ward to say his goodbyes. "Mrs. Shand; good, you're here. I've got some information I think you'll find of interest. Sarah may seem like she's fully recovered but I can promise you, she'll have many relapses. Caring for people who have suffered brain injuries is stressful to say the least. The BIG organization is available to help. They have support groups at various venues throughout the North East. You should take advantage of their services." He turned to Sarah. And you, young lady, have to ride out of here in this." He pulled the wheelchair into the room.

"You mean I can't walk even with my crutches?"

"No. Hospital policy states you have to leave the premises in a wheelchair." He turned to Mrs. Shand. "Where did you leave your car? Maybe you would like to go down and bring it round to the main entrance?"

"Thank you, Doctor."

"I'll get a nurse to take Sarah down in a few minutes." They started towards the hallway.

34

Sarah waited at the nurses' desk while Doctor Compton arranged to have someone take her down. She wanted to see David one last time before she left the hospital but he'd already left to go home. He was taking her into Aberdeen on Sunday. It was almost like going on a date. Did you call it a date if it was two friends going out? When she was out with her girlfriends she never thought of it that way. But she'd be with a guy. That *had* to make it a date … a proper date.

Mrs. Shand pulled up to the front door at the same time Sister Longmuir wheeled Sarah out. "I suppose you'll be glad to see the back of me."

"There were times when you were our problem child but we will miss you, Sarah."

Mrs. Shand loaded Sarah's bags into the boot and her crutches on the floor in the backseat. Once done, Sister Longmuir wheeled Sarah to the passenger side and she and Mrs. Shand helped her in.

Soon, they were on the road and their way back to the farm. The traffic on the A96 leaving Aberdeen was light but headed into the city was heavy. Sarah drank in the passing scenery as if she'd never seen it before. She had her driving license and wondered how long it would be before she could get behind the wheel again – not that she drove much before her accident.

The Oyne fork appeared in the distance. The main A96 trunk road curved off to the right. The Kendonald Road continued straight. Sarah relaxed and sank back into the seat. She was almost home. Despite the events she remembered before the accident, home was where she wanted to be. It meant not seeing David at all. When he was on rounds, he stopped in to see her and came more when he was off duty. She closed her eyes and remembered his face, his smile and his touch. But it wasn't David she saw and whose touch she felt. It was Robert.

Not long after they crossed over the railway line at Duninsch, Sarah became apprehensive. When they passed the derelict Weetshill railway station it worsened. She recalled being on the platform in

1886 waiting for a train to Aberdeen and again on the return trip. Back then, the windows were intact. No broken panes from rocks pelted through them. The building well cared for. There were no holes in the roof where the slates had fallen off and the wood beneath rotted away.

They approached the track where Sarah emerged from on that fateful night. She spoke for the first time since getting into the vehicle. "Please stop the car, Mum. I need you to stop."

"Whatever is wrong, Sarah?"

"Please, just pull over."

Mrs. Shand flipped the left turn indicator on and pulled her car off onto the verge. She brought it to a complete stop across the foot of the track leading up and over the hill to the road their farm was on. Turning and facing her daughter, she asked, "Tell me what is bothering you?"

Sarah ignored her and opened the car door. She undid her seatbelt, struggled to get out and affix her forearm crutches. The brisk late autumn wind rustled the few leaves remaining on the trees.

Once she got her balance, Sarah hobbled to the tree. It still bore the scar from the car coming to rest against it the night of the accident. The exposed wood had weathered and was now a dirty-grey but there was no mistaking the location.

Sarah reached for the trunk but when her hand was inches away from it, she jerked her arm back. She wanted to be back with Robert and Jenny so why was she afraid to touch the tree? With trepidation, she stretched her arm out again until her fingertips brushed it. The bark was rough and covered with moss and lichens. Sarah ran her hand down the surface and into the scar below.

The car door closed. Her mother approached wrapping the heavy knit cardigan around her. "Get back in the car, Sarah. It's freezing out here. You'll catch your death and end up back in hospital."

Touching the rough surface of the tree trunk hadn't provided the magic Sarah had hoped for. She turned and limped back to the car – entrenched in her own time.

Mrs. Shand helped Sarah back into the passenger seat. She stowed her daughter's crutches before settling in behind the wheel. Buckling her seatbelt, she looked at Sarah. "Please, no more of this nonsense about you having been back in the past."

She cast a sideways glance at her mother, the tears burning her eyes and nodded. Sarah knew her time in the past was real. She knew her mother knew it, too, even though she denied it. It took some time but her sister believed it, too. The information Rachel discovered at the library and the Family History Society proved it. Robert's appearance at the hospital in front of the two of them cemented it. Now Sarah had to convince her father.

They passed the opening in the trees along the road where Weetshill mansion was visible. Sarah closed her eyes, unable to look at the mansion in its ruined state.

A short time later, Mrs. Shand pulled the car into the driveway at the farm and stopped outside the front door. "I'll get you in and settled first, then move the car around back. It's closer for you to get in from here. I hope the step up isn't too much for you."

"I need to go to the stone circle," Sarah stated.

"Whatever for?"

"I have to know if it's real."

"It is and has been for centuries. So no more talk about it."

"You don't understand, Mum. I need to go up there."

"You'll never get there walking. Don't be so ridiculous," Mrs. Shand answered. She handed Sarah her crutches and helped her out of the car.

"I've got these."

"And the ground is half frozen and riddled with rabbit holes. You'll step in one of them and break your legs all over again."

Sarah glared at her mother. "This is something I have to do. I don't expect you to understand."

Mrs. Shand opened the door to the downstairs en-suite guest room. She stepped aside so her daughter could enter. "This will be yours for as long as you need it."

Sarah stood for a moment before taking a few steps forward. She wished this could be her permanent bedroom. The sage green on the walls matched one of the muted shades in the tartan carpet. The heavy, winter curtains matched the mauve. White, antique reproduction furniture took pride of place throughout. To her left the queen-sized bed nestled between two nightstands. Straight ahead a wall divided the en-suite bathroom from the accommodations. Against it stood a matching wardrobe and chest of drawers. The dressing table and stool were on the far side of the room near the window. "But if I'm in it, you won't have it for guests," she whispered.

"We'll still have the two rooms upstairs. They'll be plenty for now. We're not busy this time of year. Just having two rooms won't be a problem."

"Where's dad? I can't wait to see him."

"He's in the barn, I expect."

"There's my girl."

"Dad," Sarah exclaimed hobbling out into the foyer.

Murphy appeared from the back of the house. He rubbed around and between Sarah's legs in figure eight movements.

"You stupid cat, you're going to trip Sarah. Now get," Mrs. Shand ordered giving the cat a gentle nudge with her foot.

"Ah, Sarah. It's brilliant having you home. The place hasn't been the same these past months." Mr. Shand hugged her.

"Come along now, Jimmy. We'll leave Sarah to get settled in and rest." Mrs. Shand turned to her daughter. "Tomorrow if you still insist on it, you can go up to the stone circle. Your father will even drive you. You're exhausted. Why don't you lie down for a wee while?"

"I don't need to lie down. I'm not tired." Sarah walked with an awkward gait past her parents. More tired than she wanted them to know, she paused outside the lounge door. "I'm going to go watch some telly."

"That's fine, Sarah. I'll get the rest of your things out of the car."

Sarah watched her mother go out the front door. She longed to go up to the stone circle to see if the magic that would get her back to Robert existed there. It hadn't where the car had come to rest against the tree on the Kendonald Road.

She turned the knob and pushed. A *Welcome Home* banner hung over the fireplace. There were helium balloon bouquets in every corner. Floral arrangements were on all the tables. A stack of unopened mail addressed to Sarah lay on the coffee table.

A tear slid down her cheek. Settling herself at the end of the sofa closest to the lounge door, she laid her crutches on the floor. Sarah picked up the stack of envelopes. There were cards from both sets of her grandparents. Neighbors and friends from the village had sent cards, too. More came from some friends from The Gordon Schools. One was from Niamh which Sarah tore into little pieces without opening it. The last one was from David. She stuck her finger under the flap and tore it open. Sarah ran her fingers over the message and his signature. She missed him even though she had seen him the day before. Would he come and take her to the switch-on like he promised? She hoped so.

When the lounge door closed behind her, the clicking latch made Sarah jump.

"We'll have to get that lot moved out of here soon," Mrs. Shand reckoned.

"Can we put it in my room?"

"If you like. I wanted to put it there in the first place, but your father wanted it in the lounge. Thought it would be more of a welcome for you."

"Can we take a picture before we move it?"

"That's a brilliant idea. I'll get the camera, but the photo has to include you."

"All right," Sarah moaned. She hated getting her picture taken at the best of times but in this menagerie – well, it was embarrassing.

Mrs. Shand returned with the camera. "Say cheese."

"I remember my graduation from The Gordon Schools. You swore then you had a spool in the camera but you didn't. Good thing Grannie Shand was there with her camera."

"Enough cheek, young lady. This is a digital camera. I don't need to worry about spools." After Mrs. Shand took the photo, she took some of the decorations and flowers across to Sarah's room. "I'll leave you to arrange it the way you like," she commented returning for the next load.

"Thanks, Mum." Sarah gripped the bundle of cards. She didn't want to lose a one; most of all, the one from David.

The lounge appeared so empty now. Sarah sat in silence for a long time before returning to her temporary room.

When Rachel got in, she helped Sarah arrange the flowers and balloons and hung the banner on the wall for her.

35

David arrived at the farm about ten-thirty the morning of 21st November. "So what all do you want to see today?"

"Everything, I think. What all is there this year?"

"It so happens I have a copy of the Programme of Events." David handed her the brochure.

"I'd like to see the Reindeer Parade, and maybe some of the street entertainment. Not fussed about the stuff going on at the Castlegate but I don't want to miss the switch-on of the lights."

"All right then, me lady. Your wish is my command. Where would you like to watch from?"

"How about somewhere near the Trinity Mall?"

"Sounds good to me. Now, you're not going to like this but I had a word with Doctor Compton about taking you today. I mean when you first mentioned it, you were still an in-patient. He said it's all right for you to go but you've got to dress warm and you need to be in a wheelchair. I keep a heavy, wool blanket in the car so we'll have it, too."

"A wheelchair? Do I have to?"

"Yes," he replied, his voice firm. "You can take your crutches, but we'll have the chair too, so when you get tired you can sit and rest. I was able to get one from the hospital and it's in the boot of my car."

David helped Sarah into the passenger seat of his blue Renault Clio. He trotted around and slipped behind the wheel. Once he secured his seatbelt, David started the engine and they set out.

"Parking is going to be at a premium. It will make more sense to park further away and walk or in your case, ride to Union Street," David concluded. He maneuvered his car out of the driveway and onto the narrow road.

When he turned right onto the Kendonald Road water drops pelted the windscreen. "Oh no, David. It's raining."

"Are you sure you still want to go?"

"Yes."

The closer they got to Aberdeen, the heavier the traffic became. David exited the A96 at the North Anderson Drive roundabout. He wove his way via the less congested back streets to Whitehall Place where he pulled in behind a block of flats.

"Are you sure about parking here? Won't you get towed?"

"I hope not. I live here."

Sarah looked out the car window at the building and wondered which apartment was David's. She hoped he would invite her in but with the time, she couldn't see it now. Maybe later when they came back for the car.

David wrestled the wheelchair and blanket out of the car's boot. He rummaged around some more until he found an umbrella.

With reluctance, Sarah sat and allowed David to push her. Her forearm crutches rested on one of the footrests. She held them between her legs with one hand and the umbrella over their heads with the other.

As they walked, the rain came down harder. The rhythmic pelting of the drops on the nylon canopy became almost deafening.

When they reached Union Street, the parade hadn't yet started. David stood on Sarah's right. He wouldn't obstruct her view towards the Castlegate on this side of her. The Reindeer Parade originated from there.

"What time is it, David?"

"Just a bit past twelve."

"Shouldn't the parade have started by now?"

"It probably has but it will take a while for them to get down here."

Sarah strained to see around people who had stepped off the pavement onto the road. It was one o'clock by the time the parade reached their location. She shivered and patted her hands together but refused to admit she was cold.

"After this is over, we'll go and have a bite to eat and something hot to drink. Get you warmed up." David rubbed his hands up and down Sarah's arms.

Enjoying the heat created by the friction, Sarah murmured, "That feels nice."

"Glad to hear. Ready to eat?"

"Uh huh."

"Like anything in particular?"

"Hmm... maybe curry?"

"Curry it is. My favorite is down here a bit." David pointed in the opposite direction of the Castlegate.

After the parade ended, they turned towards the restaurant. "David, you're so good to me. I don't deserve it." Sarah reached up and put her hand on the back of his.

"Here we are," he declared about ten minutes later. David took the umbrella from Sarah and folded it down.

Another patron entering the restaurant at the same time held the door for David making it easier for him to get Sarah and her wheelchair inside.

"Looks like everyone else had the same idea. Oh well. The longer we're in here, the less time we'll have to kill waiting for the lights." David helped Sarah out of her coat and hung it up for her. He folded the blanket and put it on the shelf over the coat rack, removed his leather jacket and hung it beside hers.

A table for two was available. The other customers who waited were parties of four or more. A hostess guided Sarah and David to a small table in a secluded corner. It was well away from the crowd and noise of the main dining area. Once seated, a waiter in a crisp, white shirt and black trousers brought their menus and a plate of crunchy pappadums.

"I'm going to have a Vindaloo," David announced.

"I can't eat anything that hot," Sarah commented. "I tried it once and couldn't do it. Good thing I only had a taste of someone else's," she confessed perusing the menu.

"What would you like? They have plenty of milder curries."

The waiter returned to their table a short time later and asked, "Are you ready to order?"

"Are you, Sarah?" David asked.

"Yes. I'll have the chicken in cashew nut sauce."

"Good choice. And you, sir?"

"Lamb Vindaloo. And can we get an order of onion bhajias, too?"

"Certainly, sir. And would you be liking your bhajias as a starter or with your meals?"

"With our meals, I think. Is that okay, Sarah?"

"Sure."

"And to drink?"

"I'll have tea," Sarah answered.

"Make mine a Caledonian 80. No, I have to drive later. I'll just have coffee."

"Very well."

"I like this place. It's nice. Do you come here often?"

David leaned his forearms on the table. "A bunch of us from work used to come about once a month."

"What happened?"

"I don't know."

"I hope it doesn't take long for the food to get here. I'm famished."

"Here." David picked up a pappadum, broke it in half and passed the other piece to Sarah.

"Thanks." She took a bite. "Mmm. Garlic."

"Should I have asked for the bhajias as a starter?"

"No. I'll be fine. Really."

"The service and the food here is quite exceptional."

Sarah broke her piece of pappadum in two and popped the smaller piece in her mouth. Within minutes of ordering, their food arrived accompanied by a plate of warm Naan bread. Another waiter came along at the same time with their drinks.

Neither one spoke during their meal. Sarah felt David watching her and it made her feel self-conscious.

"When we're done here, what would you like to do? The switch-on doesn't start until past five."

"Could we go to your flat?"

"It's too far to walk there and be back in time for the switch-on."

"Aw." Sarah said disappointed. "I would really like to see where you live."

"Another time."

"I'm going to hold you to that, David Robb."

They finished their meal in silence. When they left the warmth of the restaurant the rain still fell, although not heavy like before. David pushed Sarah up Union Street towards the Castlegate. It was going on three o'clock and the switch on was set to start at five. In order to get a good vantage point, they would have to be back out on the street no later than four. The rain had forced the street entertainment to take refuge inside the Trinity Mall and put their shows on there. Sarah and David went in and watched and looked around in some of the shops.

When they exited the mall the Jingle Jog runners, all dressed in Santa costumes, ran by.

David chuckled. "Do you want to go up to the Castlegate to watch the switch-on?"

"Can we get that close? We're probably too late," Sarah observed. "Look at all the people up there."

"I'll do my best."

By now the rain was no more than a mist but it remained quite damp. At least there wasn't an icy wind blowing in off the North Sea. Sarah shivered.

"Are you warm enough, me lady?"

"Not too bad but I wouldn't refuse the blanket."

David covered Sarah and tucked it in around her.

When they reached Broad Street, the crowd made it impossible for David to push Sarah any further.

"Looks like this is it. Sorry I can't get you any closer."

"It's fine. Don't worry."

"Hey look. We've got a light right here above us. We don't need to be any closer. We'll have a great view."

The excitement built throughout the crowd the closer the switch-on time drew. In the minutes before the final countdown began, Sarah stood. David wrapped the blanket around her shoulders. He took her gloved hand in his. To Sarah, it seemed to take forever, but the parade started in the distance. String by string the overhead lights along Union Street came to life. Every set depicted something different. Some were children's toys, others were religious but all were bright and colorful.

"I'm so happy you brought me here today. I can't believe I could have missed it because I did something stupid." Sarah threw her arms around David's neck and hugged him.

"Well you did make it and I'm happy I could be a part of it. Now I best get you back to the car and then home."

David settled Sarah in the wheelchair and began the walk back to his flat. His original plan was to walk down Union Street to Huntly and home but the street was a sea of people. He stole a glance on Broad Street and it wasn't much better. He'd have to put up with the crowds a bit longer. Flourmill Lane looked almost deserted so he ducked in there and headed towards Upperkirkgate.

"Did you enjoy yourself, today?" he asked once the din had lessened to a point where Sarah could hear him.

Not getting a reply, David leaned over for a closer look. She'd propped her head on her hand and closed her eyes. She was asleep. He stopped and readjusted the blanket over her before resuming.

About twenty minutes later, he stopped next to his car behind the block of flats on Whitehall Place. He lifted her into the front seat and fastened her seatbelt. Sarah groaned but she didn't wake. The day had been too much for her. Exhausted from the outing, he knew her well enough now to know she was too stubborn to admit it.

Folding the wheelchair, he tried to remember how he'd put it in the car in the first place. He hoped he wouldn't wake Sarah trying to get it back in the boot. Things went better than he expected and in no time he had the chair stowed.

David slipped in behind the wheel and put the key in the ignition. He didn't start the car right away. When they first arrived Sarah had asked if she could see his flat. Now, he was glad she was asleep. It wouldn't be fair to wake her to go inside but he didn't trust himself on his own familiar turf. She was a beautiful girl. Although he might be ready to make theirs a physical relationship, he knew she wasn't.

He leaned back against the seat and sighed. Rather than torture himself with what ifs and why nots, he started the car and pulled out onto the street. In the beginning, the traffic was stop and go because of other revelers making their way home. Once David made the turn onto Great Northern Road and out of the city, it thinned.

The street lights in Aberdeen masked the fog and held it at bay. Out of the city with no illumination, it became thicker making it difficult to see. By the time he reached the fork for the Kendonald Road, visibility was almost nil. David slowed the car and crawled the remaining distance to Sarah's house. He wasn't driving back to the city in this. He'd stay at his parents' house tonight. Williamsmuir was far closer.

When he brought the car to a halt in the gravel driveway at Gordonsfield, Sarah stirred. "You're home," he whispered so he did not startle her.

"Mmm," she sighed and leaned against his shoulder.

"Let's get you inside," David fussed opening the car door. "You stay there. I'll help you out."

He leaned in the passenger side, turned Sarah so she was facing him. "Put your arms around my neck," he recommended. David wrapped his around her waist and pulled her to a standing position. Holding her this close felt good. He lifted her chin and kissed her. The taste of the curry she'd eaten earlier lingered on her lips.

David pulled her crutches out from behind the seat. He escorted her to the front door, keeping his arm around her.

36

The next morning, Sarah woke to a commotion outside her room. Opening the door and stepping into the corridor, Sarah burst out laughing. Her mother chased Murphy with the broom. She'd closed the door by the stairs and ones to the lounge and dining room to force the cat towards the front and out of the house.

"Your cat has a baby rabbit in its mouth, Sarah. Help me get him outside," Mrs. Shand panted.

Murphy cowered in the corner. The animal in his mouth lay limp. Sarah took two steps toward the cat and it scarpered between her legs and into her room.

"Great," her mother moaned. "He could be underneath almost anything in there."

"Maybe if you weren't chasing Murphy with a broom, whacking it on the floor, scaring him half to death, he'd let go of his trophy," Sarah snapped. "You wait out here. I'll try and corner him without threat of a beating."

Sarah closed the bedroom door behind her. The cat had the baby rabbit in the middle of the bed. It wasn't in his mouth anymore but he swatted at it with his front paws. Despite the limited mobility with the leg brace, she dove onto the bed and tackled Murphy. She hobbled to the door and handed the hissing feline to her mother to put outside. Once the cat was out Sarah closed her bedroom door.

Assuming the bunny was dead Sarah reached into the chest of drawers and pulled out a plastic bag. She put her hand in it so she could pick the animal up without touching it and it twitched its ears. It was alive.

She grabbed the cardboard shoe box from underneath the wardrobe and a hand towel from the quilt rack. Sarah fashioned a bed for the poor, frightened thing. Scooping it off her bed, she realized Murphy hadn't tried to kill it. The baby rabbit wasn't limp and when she laid it in the box, it snuggled into the terrycloth.

The next problem Sarah faced was what to do with it? She couldn't keep it in her room. Murphy would be in here at the first opportunity. He might even finish the poor animal off before anyone had a chance to intervene.

Watching to ensure the rabbit didn't try to get out of the box and hide, Sarah turned on her laptop. She searched for the Scottish SPCA and keyed the number for the Aberdeenshire branch into her iPhone.

"Scottish SPCA, how can I help you?"

"My cat caught a baby rabbit."

"How badly is it hurt?"

"I don't think it is."

"How old would you say it is?"

"I don't know. It's awfully tiny. Can you take it? If it's with you, it will have a chance at survival. I don't think it would here. Murphy would find him and maybe finish what he started."

"Do you know where your cat caught him?"

"No. When I got up this morning, he already had it and my mum was trying to chase him outside with it."

"Okay, we'll send one of our volunteers to come and get the wee thing. Whereabouts do you live?"

"Gordonsfield Farm, Kendonald." Sarah heard the clacking of someone typing on a computer keyboard in the background.

"Okay, someone should be there in about an hour."

"Thank you." Sarah disconnected the call. She could look after the rabbit for that length of time but what if it needed to eat? Was it old enough to eat or was it still nursing? She moved the box into the bathroom and closed the door. If it managed to escape in there, the number of hiding places were limited.

Her leg throbbed after lunging after the cat. Sarah limped to the kitchen and found some fresh salad greens in the fridge. When she got back to her room, she closed the door and picked up the rabbit and cuddled it to her. Its nose twitched tickling her neck where it nuzzled. She held out a spinach leaf hoping the tiny thing would eat but it showed no interest.

A little over an hour later, she saw the SPCA van pull into the driveway. The exchange was quick; from Sarah's hands into a small cat carrier. She watched it get loaded and the vehicle drive away. She felt good she had managed to save the wee animal's life.

After lunch, David rang inviting her to his parents' house in Williamsmuir for supper. The day had gone from the worst possible to almost the best.

"Rachel, I need your help," Sarah yelled up to her sister from the foot of the stairs.

"What?" she asked, leaning over the handrail.

"I need help figuring out what I'm going to wear."

"Meeting royalty are you?"

"Might as well be. David's parents."

Rachel bounded down the stairs into Sarah's bedroom and flung open the wardrobe. "I see what you mean. Wait here."

Sarah dropped onto the bed, awaiting her sister's return.

"You can borrow these," she invited holding up her black leather trousers. "And, I know the top you can wear with them." Rachel fumbled through the chest of drawers looking for Sarah's pink, off the shoulder jumper. "Black and pink look fab together."

"Will they fit over my leg brace?"

"Doubt it. You'll have to wear it over top of them."

"Don't you think it's a bit much?"

"Not at all. David will love you in it. I'll be back to see how you look before you leave."

It wasn't him Sarah wanted to impress. It was Mr. and Mrs. Robb who, by now thought she was a head case with her talk of living at Weetshill in 1886. Maybe with them being the owners now, they might know the secret to getting back there. Oh, who was she trying to kid. Of course, it was David she was trying to impress. After the way he kissed her after their date in Aberdeen, she had dreamt about it all night.

The digital alarm clock on the bedside chest read two-oh-five. If she was to be ready by three o'clock, she would have to get her skates on and fast. She had time for a quick shower but the hot spray enticed her to spend longer under it.

Sitting at the dressing table to apply her makeup, Robert's face appeared in the mirror. He shook his head. He didn't approve of her use of cosmetics and had made his feelings known. Right now, she wasn't in the past with him. She was in the present with David. Hypnotized by the image in the mirror, Sarah opened the top right drawer of the dressing table. She fumbled for the package of pre-moistened makeup remover cloths. Before she could grab them, Jenny's reflection materialized as well. Not believing her eyes, Sarah blinked but when she opened her eyes again they were still there. Robert stood off to the right behind her and Jenny beside her. While Sarah's reflection was solid, the others were transparent. She spun around hoping they were in the room with her. The only things behind her were the quilt rack and the closed bathroom door. Sarah touched her fingertips to their reflections in the mirror. When she did, Robert and Jenny faded more and disappeared, leaving Sarah alone.

David would be here anytime. Sarah didn't want to keep him waiting, but wanted to do something with her hair. There wasn't time to blow dry it now. She took the towel off her head, bent over and ran her fingers through her hair. Sarah whipped her head back letting her tresses fall around her shoulders. Working in a dollop of mousse, she arranged and scrunched her hair styling it. She finished it with a light spray.

Gravel crunched under tires indicating someone had pulled in or out of the driveway. After casting a critical glance in the full-length mirror, Sarah stepped into the hall.

"You look great, sis. Told you that jumper would look fab with my leather trousers."

There was a time not so long ago wearing Rachel's clothes would have been impossible. Sarah used to weigh almost a stone more than her younger sister.

"Come on in, David," Mrs. Shand called, making her way to the front door.

"Wow, you look amazing, Sarah," he said. "Don't worry, my parents will love you."

"I hope so."

David helped Sarah into her coat, grabbed her crutches and guided her to the car. "Glad you were ready. I left it running because it's so cold out today."

After settling her into the front seat, David climbed in behind the wheel. Before buckling his seatbelt, he leaned towards Sarah and put his hand behind her head. He kissed her like he had the night before.

When he didn't turn left towards Largie Road, Sarah looked at him. "Didn't you miss the turning?"

"No. It might be shorter mileage going that way but it takes longer. I always go this way. Takes less time and the roads are better."

At Duninsch, David turned left onto Commerce Street. He followed it through the village and countryside until he reached the A96. Less than twenty minutes later, he pulled his car into his parent's driveway. "We're here."

The house looked much like Gordonsfield but the dormers in the upper level were a different shape. Where her parents had one added for the upstairs bathroom, the Robb's house only had a roof window.

A net curtain moved in one of the downstairs windows. Sarah eased herself out of the car, not waiting for David's help. She reached into the back seat and retrieved her crutches and handbag.

Mrs. Robb met them on the front step. "Come in. Come in," she greeted ushering them into the lounge. "Art, put that newspaper down. We've got company."

Antique furniture filled the room. Matching curio cabinets on both sides of the fireplace housed a display of figurines. Sarah thought they were Royal Doulton.

"Mum, Dad, I'd like you to meet Sarah Shand."

"This is the young lady you met at the hospital?" she asked.

"Yes."

"Sarah, these are my parents, Isabella and George Robb. He's actually Arthur George but prefers to go by George. The only person who calls him Art or Arthur is my mum."

Mr. Robb stood towering over everyone in the room. He had to be well over six feet tall. Shaking David's hand he leaned down and praised, "Most presentable." He turned to Sarah. "Pleasure to meet you. It's about time this lad found himself a woman. Too damn busy working at the hospital, he is."

"Come on, I'll give you the grand tour of Chez Robb – well at least the ground floor." David extended his arm to Sarah. "We'll start in the study."

When he opened the door for her, the hinges creaked. An old, oak desk, reminiscent of the head teacher's at The Gordon Schools faced the wall to the left. A matching banker's desk chair with a green corduroy seat cushion sat behind it. A four-drawer, black legal size filing cabinet stood next to the window on the far side of the room. To the right, there was a futon with a small coffee table in front of it. What appeared to be a large map hung on the wall above the desk. Closer inspection revealed it was the original floor plans of Weetshill mansion.

Photographs adorned almost every free space on the walls and tables. This room was unlike the lounge where Sarah met David's parents. One picture showed a little boy in tartan overalls with long blonde curls sitting on an end table. Embossed in the lower right corner were the name of the photographer and studio. "Is this you?" she asked.

David turned to her. "Yes. I *hate* that picture. I wish she would put it away."

"What's wrong with it? You look so cute."

David pulled her into his arms but instead of hugging Sarah, he tickled her making her jump and squeal.

"Dinner's ready," Mrs. Robb called from the kitchen.

"Come on. Let's go."

"You sit here," Mrs. Robb pointed to a chair to the left of her husband at the head of the table. "I'll bring in the meat."

"Can I help you with anything?"

"No dear. You're fine."

A few minutes later, the woman reappeared with a huge platter of sliced lamb. She placed it in the center of the table before she returned to the kitchen.

"You sure you don't want a hand?" Sarah called after her rising to go assist.

Before the opportunity arose, David's mother returned with a bowl of steaming, boiled potatoes in one hand and carrots in the other. Once they were on the table, she sat in the chair at the opposite end of the table from her husband.

China, crystal and real sterling silver lay at each place setting. The pattern on the dishes and the engraving on the cutlery were familiar. Sarah couldn't place where she had seen it before.

The clicking of forks against knives and crystal glassware returned to the table were the only sounds in the room. Sarah couldn't stand the silence any longer and spoke up. "This is delicious, Mrs. Robb.

"Thank you, dear."

"So what is it you do at the hospital, Sarah?" Mr. Robb asked.

"I don't work at the hospital."

"But David told us that's where he met you."

"He did but I don't work there," Sarah replied.

The Robbs looked puzzled.

"I told you I met Sarah at the hospital. You *assumed* she worked there," David interjected.

Sarah inhaled then began. "Do you remember reading about a young girl who'd got hit by a car on the Kendonald Road back in August? I'm her."

"You're that girl. The girl David asked me to gather all the family history information for."

"Yes."

"I'm sorry, dear. With the tragedy at the big house and the one little'un in hospital, my mind has been on other things. We could end up facing a lawsuit because of it."

"It's all right, Mrs. Robb. You've got more important things to worry about." There was an urgency to seeing this material but Sarah understood why the woman hadn't looked it up for her.

"Look behind you, dear."

Sarah turned. A huge charcoal drawing of Weetshill hung on the wall. "It's beautiful," she murmured. "When was it done?"

"The date is in the bottom right corner with the artist's signature. Unfortunately, we can't read it."

Sarah stood and inspected the artwork. The year and signature of the artist were unreadable like Mrs. Robb mentioned. Both incorporated into the piece in such a way it looked like part of the foreground. "It was such a beautiful place. It's so sad to see it now. It's visible from our road but the best view is from the stone circle."

"You know we've got planning permission to restore the place and convert it to flats," Mr. Robb declared.

The idea of converting the grand mansion to flats sickened Sarah. "You will keep the fireplaces, won't you?"

"Those drafty old things? They're a drain on the pocket book and a nuisance. Birds getting down the chimneys, having to get them cleaned. No, I don't want them," Mr. Robb replied.

"But you can't get rid of them. They have to stay. They're gorgeous and an integral part of the design of the house," Sarah blurted out.

"I'd like to keep them but ... you heard my father."

"Weetshill would make a wonderful country hotel. Couldn't you go back to the council and get the planning permission changed? Derelict properties get converted to hotels all the time. That way, the fireplaces could stay. Change the ones in the bedrooms to gas. Leave the ones in the common rooms downstairs wood burning."

"Converting all the fireplaces to gas would cost a fortune," Mr. Robb conceded.

"So will rebuilding Weetshill. Okay, so don't convert *all* of them. Maybe a few and make those rooms into luxury en-suites. Leave the mantels and hearths in the other rooms for decoration."

"I told you, she was passionate about the place," David said, breaking into the conversation.

"But there's the Castle Hotel at Huntly and Pittodrie House at Pitcaple. There wouldn't be a need for another in such a short span,"

Mrs. Robb said.

"Yes, but if you were to offer something there neither one of the others does." Sarah stopped talking long enough to take a drink.

"How do you know all this?"

"I was doing my Higher National Diploma qualifications so I could enter Uni in year three in Hospitality Management before my accident. I can tell you *one* thing Weetshill has the other two don't – a chapel. The others are available for weddings but think of the intimacy of the Weetshill chapel. If restored it would be perfect. That's where I'd want to hold my wedding."

Wrapped up in the excitement of the restoration of Weetshill, Sarah had no intention of giving up her idea. The Robbs had to go back to the council and get the planning permission changed. She had to convince them it was the right thing to do.

The grandfather clock in the lounge chimed midnight. David looked at his watch. "We've got to go. I didn't realize the time. I've got to get you back to Gordonsfield before your parents start to worry."

"Well, young people, it's long past my bed time. It's been a pleasure to meet you, Sarah. We'll talk more about your ideas again, I'm sure," Mr. Robb concluded.

Sarah settled into David's car while he scraped the frost off the windscreen. Meeting his parents went better than she expected even if they disagreed on the purpose of Weetshill's reincarnation. It had been fun. The photo of David when he was a little boy was priceless.

On the first corner after leaving the house, the car fishtailed. Sarah grabbed the armrest. She thought for sure they'd be off the road in seconds, but David regained control and continued.

"Black ice," he stated.

She nodded.

The light over the front door was on when David pulled into the driveway at Gordonsfield. He brought the car to a stop and Sarah's parents appeared in the open front door. "Sorry I'm so late getting her back. Lost track of time," he apologized climbing out of the car. By the time he got round to the passenger side, Sarah was already out and had the door closed.

"Thanks for a lovely night. I enjoyed meeting your parents, but you must convince them a conversion to flats is wrong. Try to convince them a hotel is a much better option for Weetshill."

David escorted Sarah to the front door, kissed her cheek and turned to leave.

"I hope you're not driving back to Aberdeen at this hour," Mrs. Shand stated.

"No. I'm going to go back to Williamsmuir for the night. I'll make an early start for there in the morning."

"Well drive safely, and we hope we'll see you again soon."

The car door closed. Seconds later the taillights disappeared around the corner of the house.

37

"Get your breakfast before it gets cold," Mrs. Robb instructed. She placed a heated plate of bacon, eggs, mushrooms, haggis and fried bread on the table in front of him.

Her husband folded his newspaper and placed it on the table. "Thank you, Belle."

She returned with her own meal and the coffee pot. Rather than sit in her usual chair at the opposite end of the table, she chose the one on his right. "What do you think of Davey's lady friend?"

"She's an attractive young woman. Most presentable."

"That's not what I meant," she replied pouring them each a steaming cup of their preferred roast.

"What are you getting at?" he asked. "It wouldn't matter who she was, no one is good enough for your son," he added. Mr. Robb cut a rasher of bacon and put a piece in his mouth.

Belle lifted her cup but sat it down without taking a drink. "It's this obsession she has with Weetshill."

"She said, herself, she can see it from their farm. The girl has seen it almost every day of her life. Let her be. Didn't you dream of marrying a prince and living in a grand palace when you were a girl, Belle?" he stated, arching an eyebrow.

Mrs. Robb didn't reply. She did have dreams but a ruined mansion and a man who worked in a factory weren't them. But she loved her husband and that was what mattered.

"Sarah's an enthusiastic young woman and I applaud her. We decided on converting to flats because we would make back our original investment much faster. But maybe there's something in what she has to say. Maybe a hotel isn't such a bad idea after all. If she marries David …"

His wife scowled at him.

"Let me finish, woman, then you can have your say. You heard her say she was studying Hospitality Management. If she were to marry David, we would have a family member capable of running the place. We could work as much or as little as we wanted."

"Your breakfast has gone cold," Belle scolded standing and reaching for his plate. "I'll warm it up in the microwave for you."

Mrs. Robb paused in the doorway. "We agreed on flats. We got the planning permission for flats. With the price we could fetch on the sale of even two of them within the mansion, any money afterwards would be profit. Why? Are you thinking of throwing good money after bad with Sarah's hotel scheme? There are hotels going into administration left and right. Can you or she guarantee it wouldn't happen to us?"

"It might end up being a moot point, my dear. That Canadian family could file a lawsuit against us. If the courts find in their favor, we could end up selling Weetshill to even begin to afford the settlement."

"Oh, Art, I hope it doesn't come to that," she moaned slumping against the doorframe.

"So do I, Belle. So do I."

Sarah picked up a spoonful of oatmeal, turned it over and let the hot cereal fall back into her bowl. It had never been her favorite. After her hospital stay, it dropped down the 'things I like to eat' list to the bottom. The stuff they graduated her to was lumpy and warm rather than hot by the time it got to her.

But that wasn't the only thing bothering her this morning. Laying her spoon on the placemat beside her bowl, Sarah cleared her throat.

"What's wrong"? Mrs. Shand asked.

"Besides I don't like oatmeal?"

"You always used to."

"That was before the hospital. The stuff they passed off as oatmeal was gross."

"Well at least have some toast," her mother replied, passing the filled toast rack to her.

Sarah took a piece, ripped it in two and took a bite.

"Coffee left?" her father asked entering the family dining room.

"In the pot, Jimmy."

Mr. Shand went into the kitchen stopping to kiss his wife on the way by. Watching her parents, Sarah wondered if she would ever find the right guy. She thought Blair was the one but that fell apart. Robert was perfect but he lived in 1886 and it was now 2010. And now there was David whom she liked a great deal but did she love him? If so, was it a rebound relationship which wouldn't last – at least according to any magazine articles she'd read? She worried about Jenny, too, and what her absence was doing to the little girl.

Christmas was Sarah's favorite holiday and she had looked forward to her first one with Robert and Jenny. She felt certain the asylum didn't celebrate the holiday so 25th December, 1886 would be Jenny's first real Christmas.

A few seasonal cards held pride of place on the buffet but they were the only sign of the upcoming holiday.

"How come you've not got any decorations up yet, Mum? Any other year, you've got your poinsettias on the stairs and a wreath on the door as soon as Halloween is over."

"It didn't seem very Christmassy without you home."

"Can we go to Huntly to pick out our Christmas tree tonight?"

"We'll go tree shopping after supper. I've got work to do. I best get back at it." Mr. Shand put his coffee cup on the table, kissed Sarah on the cheek and headed for the back door.

Rachel dragged herself into the family dining room at the same time her father exited.

"We're going into Huntly tonight to get our Christmas tree. This is going to be the best Christmas ever." Sarah hadn't been this excited about Christmas since she was a little girl.

"I'm glad you think so," Rachel mumbled.

By six o'clock, Mr. Shand had finished in the barn and showered and changed. The table had been set and everyone was ready to sit town to their evening meal.

"It's starting to snow. You best leave these dishes until after we get back, Moira. No telling how bad it will get. I won't have my wee girl, who's spent the last four months in hospital, not have a tree now she's home."

"Will there be any good trees left? We've always got ours sooner than this."

"We won't know until we get there."

Mrs. Shand had made one of Sarah's favorite meals – beef olive with dough balls and steamed broccoli.

"This is wonderful, Mum," Sarah acknowledged and tucked into her meal.

"I have a special sweet for afters but I think we'll wait and have it when we get back from Huntly."

"Right-e-o. Eat up girls. It is snowing a lot harder than it was when I came in."

"I can't eat anymore, Mum. It's way too much."

"That's fine. You start getting ready to go."

Sarah picked her crutches up off the floor from behind her chair. She wished she'd finished with them, too.

It took almost an hour to get from their farm near Kendonald to Huntly. That same trip took fifteen minutes in good conditions. It snowed harder the further they drove. The snowflakes reflecting in the headlights hypnotized Sarah. The road was white, but she felt safe knowing her father was behind the wheel.

Once they reached the car park at the Market Muir, Mr. Shand brought the family's Vauxhall Astra to a stop. He parked near the playing fields where the tree vendor was set up so Sarah wouldn't have far to walk. Christmas music blared from speakers mounted in the branches overhead. Fairy lights twinkled at the various displays.

The family browsed through the trees for a long time before they came to a mutual decision.

When they got home, Sarah waited for her sister and mother to go inside. "Thanks for taking us, Dad."

"You're welcome. I'll get the tree down and let it stand here outside the door overnight. That way the branches will have a chance to drop. I'll put it in the stand in the morning, then you, your mum and Rachel can decorate it. You go on in now."

Mrs. Shand appeared at the door. "I've got the kettle on for tea and I'm warming the sweet in the oven."

"Sarah, you go with your mother. I'll be right along."

"Okay."

Sarah took her mother's arm and they walked inside. "We'll have Christmas dinner in the guest dining room, won't we?" she asked walking by the closed door.

"Yes, don't we always."

"Are Grannie and Grandpa Shand and Grannie and Grandpa Duncan coming?"

"Yes, weather permitting. There's still plenty of time. Don't fret."

"I can't help it, Mum. I miss them … especially Grannie Shand. I need to talk to her about the stone circle and I'm excited about being home and getting back to normal."

"Sit yourself down and I'll tend to things in the kitchen."

"So what's this special sweet you have for us tonight?"

Mrs. Shand stuck her head back in from the kitchen. "Warm Dundee cake with clotted cream."

"Sounds fabulous."

After she finished, Sarah excused herself and went to her room. She leaned back against her door and sighed. It felt great to be home and away from the hospital, but she felt like she was under a microscope lest she overdo it or get hurt. She locked the door and fell onto the bed.

Sarah woke up freezing about three o'clock. Her room felt like an icebox. She pulled back the covers and crawled under. It took a long time for her to get warm and fall back to sleep.

When Sarah finally got up the next morning the tree, already in the stand, stood in the middle of the lounge. "Let's put it here in front of the window so the cars coming down the road will be able to see it," she suggested.

"But there's a radiator there. What about in the corner by the fireplace?" her father offered.

"There's an outlet by the end of the sofa. Let me empty the closet and move the stuff to the airing cupboard."

Mrs. Shand and Rachel transferred the contents to the family dining room. After they returned, Mr. Shand moved the tree into position. He rotated it a quarter of a turn many times until everyone agreed which side needed to face into the room.

"You will have to make sure the tree gets plenty of water over these next few days. I don't want it drying out and burning the house down."

"Yes, Dad."

"I best get back to work and leave you three to it. I put the decorations in the hall outside my office."

"And I have work to do, too," Mrs. Shand added. "I'll fill the watering can so you girls can look after the tree."

Rachel followed her mother and returned a few minutes later. She crawled under the tree to give it a drink.

The phone rang. Sarah heard the Hoover running in the back of the house, and her sister was still watering the tree. She picked up her crutches and started out of the lounge but by then it stopped. When she got to the family dining room, the red light flashed on the answerphone. Sarah retrieved the message, disappointed she missed David's call.

Dropping into the armchair near the door, she decided to wait there so when he called again, she could grab it on the first ring. But would she appear too eager?

The phone chirped again. Sarah jumped. "Hello," she answered.

"Hi, Sarah. It's David. You all right? You sound out of breath."

"Yeah. Phone startled me is all."

"Okay."

"I didn't think I'd be hearing from you this soon. I mean, you took me to the Christmas lights switch-on last Sunday and to meet your parents the next day."

"What have you got on for today?"

"Rugby shirt and jeans," Sarah joked.

"No, seriously."

"We're putting up the Christmas tree and getting some of the other decorations out."

"I was going to come over but if you're busy ..."

"No, please do."

"How about after lunch?"

"Sounds good."

"All right. Mum has all the documents gathered together."

"Brilliant, I'll show you the stuff Rachel got for me at the Family History place, too."

"I'll see you later."

"Okay. Bye."

"Who was on the phone, Sarah?" Mrs. Shand asked.

"David. You know the doctor from the hospital."

"He's a lovely young man."

"He's coming over after lunch. He has some documents his mum has collected during her research of their family tree. He thinks I'll find them interesting."

"Hmm ... it sounds very intriguing."

Mrs. Shand dusted the lounge. "We'll have an early lunch so you and your young man can have a nice visit." She went out to the hallway to Hoover the floor.

"Mother." Sarah knew she had feelings for him but she didn't think the entire family knew. If she could never get back to the year 1886 and Robert, David would make an excellent substitute. He was kind and generous but he would never be the man she had married in the past. Despite those qualities, David would be her second choice.

Rachel brought in the other boxes of decorations. The girls searched through them until they found the lights. It took a long time but they got them onto the tree and plugged into the outlet.

Sarah closed the heavy winter curtains on the windows, blocking out the sunlight.

"Here goes." Rachel flipped the switch. The warm white LED

fairy lights illuminated the room. "I think it looks great like this."

"We need more than lights on it. Where's the star?"

"Likely still in the box. I didn't take it out."

Sarah turned on the ceiling light and rummaged through the boxes until she found it. She handed it to her sister who needed to climb onto a footstool to place the accessory on the treetop.

It took forever for the girls to make any kind of progress. Sarah had to cluck over every object they took out of the box. When she dropped one of the delicate glass ornaments, it hit the coffee table's tile inlay and smashed into tiny pieces. Sarah burst into tears.

"It's a ball. No need to fall apart."

Her sister's comment didn't help. Sarah cried more which brought her mother into the lounge. "I'm so sorry. I didn't mean to break it. I don't know what happened. One minute I had a hold of it, and the next thing I knew I saw it falling – like in slow motion but I couldn't move. I tried, Mum, honest."

"It's fine, dear. Don't worry about it. We'll pick up the bigger pieces and I'll Hoover up the rest."

In no time, they cleaned the shattered bauble up and Rachel and Sarah were alone in the lounge again. "Come on already. I want to get this done."

"Look Rachel, I could still be in hospital, or worse, spending Christmas dead."

"I suppose you're right."

Mrs. Shand interrupted their bickering by calling them to lunch. "Tomato soup with croutons and cream. Dig in girls." She looked at Sarah. "We've got to get some meat on you. You're way too thin."

"I like the way I am right now. It feels good."

"So what time is your young man coming?"

"I don't know. He said after lunch. Maybe around one." Sarah paused then continued, "And he's not my young man."

"Will you be finished in the lounge by then?"

"The way Sarah's going, it'll be next Christmas before we're done."

"Rachel, enough," their mother snapped.

"I hope so. I don't ever remember it taking this long before," Sarah answered working her way back into the conversation.

"Because you have to give a history of every ornament we put on the tree."

"I warned you once already, young lady. We're lucky to have

Sarah home. Things could have been very different this year."

"I know," she mumbled.

"Then show some consideration. Now eat up both of you before it gets cold."

The girls ate the rest of their meal in silence. Before they finished, the doorbell rang.

"You finish your lunch. I'll go," Mrs. Shand instructed.

38

Sarah got to her feet and followed her mother into the hallway. "Hi David. Let's go in the lounge. It will be quiet in there." Sarah turned into the room, walked towards the sofa and sat down. David placed the box on the coffee table and ensconced himself beside her.

"You have to see this, Sarah. I couldn't believe it when mum first showed it to me," David babbled. He reached into the box and pulled out a descendant chart of John William Robertson. "She's researched the family tree going back further but only printed this much of it."

Sarah stared at it dumbfounded. David was a direct descendant of Robert's grandfather.

"See, I'm descended from Robert's sister." David pointed to the chart.

"Margaret. I met her at Weetshill. She was matron of honor when Robert and I got married."

David ignored Sarah's comment and continued, "Anyway, it's through her I tie in. The family disowned her because she ran off to Aberdeen to escape an arranged marriage to a wealthy suitor picked out for her years before.

"I know. Kenneth McIntosh helped out by finding her a place to live and got her a position in Edinburgh as a nanny for a banker and his wife. She also told me both her grandfather and her mother held her responsible for her father's death. She didn't return to Weetshill until after the old man died. She came home for the funeral."

David took the family Bible out of the box and extracted a brittle page of writing paper from it. He read the first few paragraphs of the faded writing.

"Sarah, how did you know that? There's no way you could have seen this letter before."

"I tell you, I met Margaret when I stayed at Weetshill." Sarah traced her finger down the chart through the generations to David. She couldn't believe what she held before her. David and her beloved Robert related. Reality and fantasy were still jumbled in her mind. She couldn't tell where one left off and the other began and this complicated matters further.

"Margaret's husband George brought John Bryce and Mary Elizabeth to Weetshill for Robert's and my wedding."

Still absorbed in the chart, she paused over Margaret's information. "She never mentioned having another son."

"I imagine it was too upsetting for her. That baby was stillborn,"

"She was pregnant again when I met her and wanted to go to the city for the birth because she knew something was wrong. I see that baby was born in Glass, too, so George got his way. I wonder how that made him feel?"

"She lost that son within a year of his birth. Her only daughter wasn't quite fourteen when she died of complications from measles."

"Mary Elizabeth," Sarah whispered. She looked closer at the chart. "The poor woman. Four children and only one survived to adulthood. What did the last baby die from?"

"I'm not sure what they called it back then, but now we call it cot death."

Tears welled up in Sarah's eyes. "Your grandparents died so close together. How sad."

"Granda died of cancer and they claim Gran died of a broken heart."

"And your great-grandparents – they died on the same day."

"Yes. Head-on car accident on the A96 between Williamsmuir and Huntly."

"That stretch of road hasn't got any better over the years."

"You're right. The creeper lane hasn't seemed to help much. I'm glad when I'm going home to my mum's, I get off the road before I reach that section."

"I am, too. I wouldn't want anything to happen to you." Sarah couldn't believe she'd said it out loud. Up until now, she'd managed to keep her feelings for David in check when she was with him – at least she hoped she had. Much as she wanted him to like her, she didn't want to appear easy or forward.

David took the chart away from Sarah and handed her the letter penned by Robert's sister, Margaret.

Sarah began to read. After a few moments, she looked up at David. "That's me," Sarah insisted turning her attention back to the letter. "The fire. I read about it in the newspaper article when I was in hospital. It said the same thing. The young bride disappeared. David, Jean MacDonald accused me of being a witch. She babbled I killed old John, put everyone in the house under a spell and would kill them, too. This is getting creepy."

"I can put it back in the Bible if you like. You don't have to read anymore."

"I don't think so," Sarah responded. "I want to read every word of it," she continued.

I found myself happy here at Weetshill, despite my bitter memories. Our son John met a lovely girl, Susan, and when they married, they lived here with us. About two years after their marriage, they blessed George and me with our first grandchild. Margaret Isabella. Such a delight to us. So full of energy.

Diagnosed with the consumption, my George moved heaven and earth to find treatment for me. He managed to get me admitted to the Sanatoria at Bridge of Weir. Whilst their methods were most different from all other places, I did get better for a time. My George died 29 January, 1927 (three years ago this very day) and I thought my world had ended. I missed him so. He'd been my tower of strength all those years. He was my husband, my lover, my friend and to go on without him was too much to bear. Many times I thought of ending it all so I could be reunited with him, but I didn't. Margaret and Susan kept me going.

Now I have rediscovered my will to live. I'm told my consumption is back worse than before. There is nothing left they can do for me but make me comfortable until the end. How ironic. When I wanted to die, I couldn't and now when I want to live, I won't.

I write this for my wee Margaret, so she knows her family's history. And so she knows how much she means to me. This house should be filled with lots of love and laughter. And because of that, I leave Weetshill to her.

Margaret Elizabeth Robertson Esslemont

"So this Margaret she mentions in her letter, she's your ..."

"Great-grandmother."

"Did she and her husband move into Weetshill and raise their family there?"

"Yes. The family lived there in the wing not damaged in the fire until the taxes got to be too much for them to afford. Not long afterwards, they pulled the roof off and left the place to ruin."

"That's so sad. The house is beautiful."

"Someday, Sarah, it will be again."

Sarah took a tissue from the box on the coffee table and wiped her eyes. The letter had affected her more than she'd expected. She handed it back to him and he placed it in the Bible and returned it to the box.

David took her hand in his. "Once you get rid of your friends," he said pointing to her crutches, "I'm going to take you over to the mansion so you can have a proper look, if you'll come with me."

Sarah thought for a moment. While she lay unconscious in hospital much had happened in her mind at Weetshill. Was she ready to go back there? What if it all happened again? She looked at David and knew he would keep her safe from harm. "Yes, I will go with you. But do we have to wait? I'm afraid the longer it takes for me to get over there, the harder it will be for me. Or ...," she continued, looking down at her lap, "you will have forgotten all about me by then." If he didn't feel the same way about her, it would devastate her.

David looked her straight in the eye and took both of her hands in his. "You will never be just one of my patients. You're special and I care about you a great deal. Don't you ever forget it." He leaned over and kissed her on the lips.

Sarah looked at him, her eyes moist with tears. "Do you really mean it? I mean about caring about me?"

"Yes, I mean it. I wouldn't tell you if I didn't." David put his arm around her and cuddled her close to him. "I think I've fallen in love with you."

Sarah couldn't believe her ears. He did have feelings for her. She was so happy. She snuggled closer to him and closed her eyes, but was unable to say *I love you, too.*

The afternoon spent with David poring over the documents passed faster than Sarah wished. She didn't want him to leave. "You could stay and have your supper with us. I'm sure my mum wouldn't mind."

"Tempting as that is, I have to get this lot back to my mum's house and then get to Aberdeen. I'm back on duty at eight o'clock." David picked up the box and paused by the lounge door. "See you again soon, Sarah."

She reached down to pick up her crutches.

"Don't get up. I can see myself out."

The door closed behind him. A few minutes later, Sarah heard his car start. She walked to the window by the fireplace and got there as his Renault Clio passed by.

39

The following morning, Sarah got up before everyone else. After seeing the documents David had brought over, she was more determined than ever to get back to Weetshill. She bundled up and slipped undetected out the front door. Walking up the hill was more difficult than she had imagined. Much to her chagrin, she had to admit her mother was right. Still, she persevered. When the tops of the stones came into view, Sarah sighed with relief. She was almost there. The worst part of her trek was over. Within a few minutes, she sat atop the fallen boulder.

The farmhouse and barn stood in the same places. The trees obscured the remains of a cottage further down the road. To her right, Weetshill mansion was the ruin she'd always known it to be. A tear escaped and dripped down her cheek.

"You will find the way," a male voice comforted.

She jumped off the rock and twisted around to see who spoke. There was no one there.

The voice spoke again. "You know what to do."

It was Robert's voice. "No, I don't. How can I find the way if I don't know?" she cried out.

He didn't answer. The only sounds audible were the bleating of sheep and mooing of cows coming from below the hill.

More confused than ever, Sarah sat back down on the chunk of granite. Many times at this spot, she had seen Robert and his sister as children playing at the stone circle. Did this place hold the key to getting back to the past? The conversation she had at Weetshill with the archaeology professor about ley lines resonated in her mind. Maybe they were the key?

Sarah followed the path through the field to where it ended at the road. Unable to climb over the five-bar gate, she fumbled with the chain until she got it off. The cold metal made her fingers numb. She stepped through then secured the opening to the field so the animals couldn't get out.

She followed the path she took on the night of her accident until she reached the Kendonald Road. Standing well back from the tarmac surface, she looked both ways. The tree with the scarred trunk was about fifty to a hundred feet off to her left. She was never good at gauging distances. The track to Weetshill was almost straight across from her. If it was the magic of ley lines then something should be happening but there wasn't.

Sarah stood there for a long time wishing and hoping Robert and Jenny would come for her but they didn't. A cold, damp east wind blew up and she shivered. A few flakes of snow swirled around before becoming a blizzard. With reluctance, she started back towards Gordonsfield but instead went to see her grandmother.

40

"Hi Gran," Sarah called as she pushed the side door of the end-terraced cottage open and stepped into the warmth. Her grandmother's back was to her so she spoke out again so as not to frighten the woman.

The elder Mrs. Shand turned wiping her hands on her apron. "Sarah, my word child, what are you doing out in this weather?" she scolded then pulled her granddaughter into her arms and hugged her. "Does your mother know you're here?"

"Yes," Sarah lied, hating doing it. She knew if she didn't, her grandmother would be straight on the phone to her parents who would be down to take her home.

"Dougie, come here. Sarah has come for a visit." When he didn't respond right away, she shouted to him again – this time louder.

Sarah's grandfather shuffled into the kitchen. "It's good to see you up and about, my girl." Supporting his weight with his cane, he embraced her with his free arm. "This cold, damp weather is making my arthritis play up something wicked. You'll excuse me if I go back to my chair and heating pad?"

"Of course, Grandpa. It's good to see you." Sarah hugged the man one more time before he hobbled back to the lounge.

"Sit yourself down at the table and I'll fix us a nice cup of tea."

"Thanks Gran," Sarah said. She took her mitts off and shoved them into her pockets. Removing her winter jacket, she draped it over the back of the chair and sat down.

It didn't take long before a steaming Brown Betty teapot along with mugs and plates were on the table. Mrs. Shand placed a platter of her homemade shortbread biscuits with the other things. "I'll fix a tray for Dougie then we can have a chat," she commented. Before taking the refreshments to her husband, she placed the quilted tea cozy over the pot.

Sarah couldn't wait until she was alone with her grandmother. She needed to speak to the woman about the stone circle. What had she seen when they went there together years ago.

Everything remained untouched when Mrs. Shand returned to the kitchen. "You didn't have to wait for me. You could have helped yourself. You know that," she stated sitting down in her usual place at the table.

"I know, Gran. I wanted to wait for you. I need to talk to you. Nobody else believes me but I know you will." Sarah fidgeted with her rings.

"Heavens, what is it?" she asked pouring them each a cup.

"It's about the stone circle. I loved it when you took me there when I was a wee girl. I loved your stories about the place. But sometimes I saw a boy and a girl dressed in Victorian clothes there. I'm pretty sure you saw them, too, the way you always hugged me and smiled right after I mentioned them. Please, Gran, it's important. I need to know," Sarah implored.

"I didn't see things, dear. At least not as much as I felt them."

"What do you mean?"

"Drink your tea before it gets cold," Mrs. Shand said, passing the platter of shortbread to Sarah. "It's hard to describe. It was like when you think someone is watching you. That's the only way I can relate it."

Sarah thought about her grandmother's portrayal of the sensations she experienced at the stone circle. Those same feelings, like the children Sarah saw had been watching her. It felt creepy. "Is the stone circle a portal to the past?"

"My, but you do ask some difficult questions." The woman avoided eye contact and added more tea to her mug.

Unsure if she would extract anything further from her grandmother, Sarah didn't know what to do. She had to get the answers. Taking a deep breath, she started. "Everyone says I was in a coma from mid-August until November. If that's true, then how come I lived at Weetshill mansion in 1886? How come I got dragged off to an insane asylum, but had my happy ending when I married the Laird? How could I be in two places at once?"

"Sarah, dear, I'm sure you only think you were there back then," she soothed patting the back of her granddaughter's hand.

"Explain where I got these then if it didn't happen." Sarah thrust her left hand in her grandmother's face.

The woman's complexion paled. "Wh-where did you get these?"

It was obvious she recognized them. "Robert gave them to me. Robert, the Laird I married in 1886. You're starting to scare me, Gran. Why did you react that way when you saw them?"

"Those are my mother's rings. Did you take them from here?" she accused.

"No. I didn't take your mother's rings. Robert bought me this one from a jewelry shop in Aberdeen. Two people's names. One of them started with Z."

Mrs. Shand glared at Sarah then stood and left the room. She returned a few minutes later with an ornate, silver ring box on legs and placed it in the middle of the table. "Open it."

Her hands shaking, Sarah reached for the chest. She hoped her great-grandmother's rings were in it. She couldn't bear her gran accusing her of stealing them when she knew she hadn't. Taking a deep breath, she lifted the lid and sighed with relief when two rings sat side by side in the slot.

"Oh Sarah, I am so, *so* sorry to accuse you. I should have known you would never do such a thing." A tear ran down her cheek. Mrs. Shand picked up the jewelry box and clutched it to her chest before putting it back on the table.

Sarah slid the box over to take a closer look. The rings were almost identical. No wonder her grandmother reacted that way. She wanted to take the ruby and diamond ring out of the box but was afraid to even touch it. When Mrs. Shand nodded her approval, Sarah lifted the ring and held it in her palm. "Gran, when you told me the stories of how your parent's met and your father staying at Weetshill after the war ..." She started then stopped. The idea was beyond ludicrous but it could be possible. "Do you think your father saw these rings in a portrait or photograph at Weetshill? Surely, there was still evidence of the family having lived there at the time. When Robert and I married, he had a photographer come and take pictures. I remember trying to make sure my rings were always visible."

"Go on."

"Because the couple in the picture looked so happy on their wedding day. Maybe he wanted to make his wife ... your mother ... as happy as I looked? Finding a similar ring was how he could do it?"

"But how would he have known the stone was a ruby if he only had an old black and white photograph to go by."

"Maybe after I came back here, Robert commissioned someone to paint one of our wedding photographs. He of all people would know what stone was in my ring and would be able to describe it in detail to the artist."

Sarah's grandmother sank into her chair. "Sarah, I am sorry."

"It's okay Gran. It's okay," she reassured and took the elderly woman's hand in hers. "Now if we could just come up with the proof," she mused. "If only we had pictures from when your father stayed there."

Her grandmother's eyes lit up. "There is an old box of photographs that belonged to my parents. I remember looking at the snapshots for hours upon hours. I asked about the people in them and the locations. Now, I wonder where it's got to. It's here somewhere. I'll have to look for it."

"Thanks, Gran."

"You should make a start for home. Your mother will be going out of her head with worry. Do you want me to ring her to come get you?"

"No. You're fine. I don't mind walking. It's only just up the road." Sarah put her coat on and before she had a chance to zip it, her grandmother had already done it for her.

"We'll figure this out between us. I love you, Sarah." Mrs. Shand bundled her granddaughter into her arms and hugged her.

"I love you, too, Gran," she replied and embraced the elderly woman. "Call me when you find those photos."

"I will. Bye now."

"Bye Grandpa," Sarah called. "Bye Gran."

Outside the door, she pondered the exchange between herself and her grandmother. It hurt that the woman would think Sarah would take her things. When she saw how much the two sets of rings resembled one another, she understood the confusion. She hoped that her Great-grandfather took pictures at Weetshill mansion when he was there. If such things existed, they could be the evidence she needed to prove that she did travel back into the past.

When Sarah closed the front door behind her, her mother scolded, "Where have you been? I've been worried sick."

"I went to the stone circle. You knew it was only a matter of time before I did. I've wanted to go right from the time I got home from hospital."

"You daft thing. Sitting on cold rocks, you'll catch your death. Get in the lounge in front of the fire and get yourself warmed up. I'll bring you a hot mug of Horlicks."

"Thanks Mum," Sarah answered shaking the snow off her coat. She hung it on the banister at the foot of the stairs, kicked off her Uggs and entered the lounge. "I stopped to see Grannie Shand when

I was out," she called.

Even though it was still light out, she reached down and flipped the Christmas tree lights on. They sparkled making the room cheery.

Her mother brought the hot drink and turned up the electric fire. "Sit down here and get this into you," she emphasized pointing to the chair next to the fireplace. "How was your Gran? I hope she gave you trouble for being out and about by yourself," Mrs. Shand concluded still hovering.

"It's okay, Mum. You can leave me on my own. And no, she didn't give me a hard time. She was happy to see me."

Relieved to be alone and out from under the microscope when the lounge door closed, Sarah sighed. She sipped her hot chocolate. The flavor triggered recollections of sledging down the hill from the stone circle with Rachel. Her mum always made it when they came in afterwards. While those were happy memories, she cherished the ones she had at Weetshill with Robert more. And if she could never get back to him, all she'd have were her memories and the rings. She held her hand out in front of her. Since the swelling had gone down enough to get them on, Sarah hadn't taken them off. She had no intention of ever taking them off again.

"Dougie, do you remember where I put the box of old pictures? The one with the snapshots my Da took during and after the war?" Mrs. Shand asked standing beside his chair with her arms folded across her chest.

He scratched his earlobe and furrowed his brow. "I've not given that lot much thought over the years, Effie. I know they're here somewhere. Why the sudden interest?"

"Something Sarah said," she answered.

Supporting himself with his cane, and his other hand on the arm of the chair, he stood up. "Let's go see what we can find, shall we?"

Mrs. Shand followed him out of the small lounge. She stopped at the airing cupboard, opened the door and peered in. She didn't remember seeing the cardboard box tied with a piece of string to keep it from falling apart in here. Sarah's grandmother was always in and out of here on rainy laundry days. Today was one of the rare occasions that there wasn't something drying in the closet. She was able to see all the way to the top shelf and the bottom and all the deep recesses between.

The racket of door and drawers opening and closing in their bedroom snapped her out of her thoughts. She went to see what her husband was doing. When she reached their room, it looked like a bomb had gone off. Clothes were flung on the bed and hanging out of the dresser drawers. Drawers pulled out to the point of falling off the tracks.

"Nothing in here, Eff," he stated.

Dismayed, she slumped onto the cedar-lined blanket box at the foot of their bed and rubbed the back of her neck.

"Didn't go through your dressing table or your other personal places, though." He sat down beside her and patted her leg. "It'll turn up. Don't fret."

"I know it will." She wanted to say something about the destruction he'd left in his wake. She was thankful he hadn't rifled through the rest of the room.

"I'm going back to my telly and heating pad." He kissed her on the cheek, stood and shuffled out of the room.

Despite her husband's good intentions, the mess he left behind was hers to clean up. Mrs. Shand heaved herself up from the blanket box. She began the arduous task of folding clothes and putting them back in their proper places.

Task completed, she paused at the door to turn the light switch off. While standing there, she turned and took one last look around the room. Her eyes fixed on the blanket box. It was the only place they hadn't looked.

Unlike her husband, Effie was slow, neat and methodical. She got down on her knees, removed the large, crocheted doily and folded it. She placed it on the stool in front of her dressing table.

When she opened the lid, the only objects visible were blankets. She lifted them out along with numerous sets of sheets with matching pillowcases. On the bottom, tucked in the back corner lay the box of pictures. Her father's camera, and a packet of letters tied in a faded purple, satin ribbon sat beside it. She wiped her brow with the back of her right hand and pushed her hair back into place. Effie extracted the items from their resting place. She made a mental note to find a more accessible location when it came time to put them away again.

Once things were back in their place and the room tidied, Mrs. Shand placed the camera, letters and photos on the blanket box. She sat down beside them. She was too old to be on her knees like that. Bending over hauling everything out and putting it back again wreaked havoc on her back.

Holding the camera, she remembered her father's stories about being the first person between St. Mary's and Kirkwall to own such a thing. He took great pride in it and took it with him everywhere he went. Thinking of him and her birthplace brought on a feeling of homesickness for Orkney. She wondered if she would ever go back again. Her mother had returned not long after her father's death. Mrs. Shand had only been once and that was for her mother's funeral.

"I found them," she announced walking past her husband's chair on her way to the kitchen.

Steam rose from the kettle on the Aga. Mrs. Shand dumped the cold tea from the pot, rinsed it and made fresh.

Sitting down at the table, she slid the string along the box until it came off. Inside, the pictures were in no semblance of order.

Dougie shuffled into the room and sat at the table. "What have we got here, Effie?" he asked reaching for the packet of letters.

"Never you mind," she replied slapping his hand.

Most of the photographs were black and white. Those ones were scattered loose in the box. Envelopes from the chemist's held faded color ones.

"Can I help you look?"

She didn't answer but handed him a stack of photographs.

"What am I supposed to be looking for?"

"Anything taken at Weetshill during the war." Mrs. Shand continued through the handful she had.

It seemed their search would be fruitless until Mrs. Shand removed the last of the snapshots from the box. At least this last bunch had a picture of Weetshill mansion near the top of the pile. Effie pored through them searching for anything that would mesh with what Sarah had told her. She didn't know if her father would or could have taken pictures inside the house during his stay there.

Her fears were soon put to rest when a black and white image of a framed portrait of a couple came to the top. Sitting the rest of the photos on the table, Mrs. Shand examined this one in detail. It looked like a special occasion, like a wedding. Looking at it closer, the woman in it was the image of Sarah. It couldn't be. It wasn't possible, was it? She'd never known her granddaughter to lie to her but the resemblance had to be a coincidence.

Looking at the rings, she couldn't make them out in enough detail to confirm they were the ones Sarah wore when she visited. Mrs. Shand set that picture aside and continued. Further down in the stack, she found a faded, color photo of an oil painting. It depicted the same couple and in the same pose. The woman seated sideways wore an ivory gown with off-the-shoulder sleeves. Her hands folded in her lap – left over right – and her jewelry visible. The shape and color of the stone in the ring looked like the ruby and diamond ring Sarah had on earlier. The woman's eyes were bright emerald green like her granddaughter's. The artist included the mole on the left side of her neck below her ear. The black and white photograph of the couple stood on the hall table beneath the portrait.

It must have cost her father a fortune to buy a spool of color film let alone have it processed. Except for the pictures of the couple and the mansion when it was a grand house, everything else went back in the box.

She reached for the packet of letters and untied the ribbon holding them together. Some of the writing was in her mother's hand. The other had to be her father's. It seemed each one had a reply, all except for the one on top. It had to be the last one her mother received. She removed it from the envelope and read.

15 May, 1945

My dearest Susan,

VE Day has come and gone. There was much celebrating here at the front when it became official that the war was over in Europe. It won't be much longer now before I'm back in your arms again, my darling. They say we're to be demobbed at the end of next month. Time will tell if they're right.

Some of the lads are talking of re-enlisting for another term of military life. You can rest assured I won't be one of them. I won't be sorry to leave but my heart goes out to the millions of people here on the continent affected by this atrocity of war. They have no choice but to remain here and rebuild their shattered lives. In some ways, I wish I could stay longer and help them with this process but every day I'm away from you seems like a lifetime. I've already been away from you for far too long.

I remain faithful to you always.

All my love,

Dermid xoxo

A lump formed in Mrs. Shand's throat. Her eyes filled with tears reading her father's words pouring his heart out to her mother. She swiped a tear away and put the letter back in the envelope.

Whether she should read more or not, this letter piqued her curiosity. She checked the postmarks on all the envelopes. They were in reverse chronological order. She took the earliest one which was in her mother's writing and pulled it out.

3 April 1943

My dear, sweet Dermid,

> *Since that night we first met at the ceilidh at Weetshill mansion, I knew you were the only man I would truly ever love. It's because of my undying love for you and my fear that I would never see you again I gave myself to you freely the night before you left to go to war.*
>
> *I have some news for you and I don't know how to say it. Please don't think badly of me. Father has insisted I write to you and tell you of my predicament. You see, after our one night together I've found myself with child. I have no doubt that you are the father since I've never been, nor ever will be, with a man other than you. Please believe me.*
>
> *When I told my parents, they insisted I come back to Kirkwall at once. They said the other women at the factory led me down this path of ill repute. You being almost ten years older than me took advantage of my naivety.*
>
> *They also insist that you get leave at once and come here and do the right thing by me and take me as your wife. If you are agreeable, please let me know soonest when you can come.*
>
> *I do hope you don't feel as if I've trapped you but if you want nothing to do with me knowing what you now do, I'll understand.*

I love you with all my heart and soul.

Susan xxoo

Effie dropped the letter dumfounded by its contents. Conceived before her parents' marriage? All she knew was her mother had fallen head over heels in love with a soldier from the Gordon Highlanders while they were both in Aberdeenshire.

She had dealt with the reason behind finding the box of photographs. Still, she had to read more of these love letters and took the next one out of the envelope.

18 April 1943

Dearest Susan,

I am most honored to be your husband. Had we more time together before my battalion mobilized, I would have asked you then. I only wish I had a proper engagement ring to give you but I promise that one day you will have one.

I have arranged leave beginning 3 June. Unfortunately, it's only for a few days. I will be with you in Kirkwall standing proudly at the altar beside you. I must report back for duty on 7 June. However, we will have a proper wedding night together in each other's arms before I leave. I only wish it could be sooner.

Don't worry yourself about the other news. If you could see how puffed out my chest is with pride, you would know you have nothing to fear. In a few short months, I'll have my best girl and our child with me.

You've made me a very happy man. I can only hope that my news pleases your mother and father when you share it with them.

I'll be counting the days until I've made you my wife.

I remain faithful to you always.

All my love,

Dermid xoxo

At least her father seemed thrilled at the prospect of a rushed wedding and impending birth. That was something. There were too many men even now who shirked their responsibilities.

The cuckoo clock in the lounge chirped four times. Mrs. Shand put the letters in the box with the photographs. She would read the rest another time. Her husband snored from his place at the end of the table having dozed off earlier. The pictures she'd set aside to show Sarah remained on the table. It was too late to go to the farm now before supper but maybe in the evening, she and Dougie could go for a short visit.

Once she tidied the table, Mrs. Shand began supper preparations. She peeled potatoes and carrots to go with the gammon steak she'd taken out of the freezer that morning. The pot of tea she made earlier remained untouched and cold. She poured some of it on her geraniums in the kitchen window and the rest down the sink.

When she heard tires crunching on the gravel driveway, Sarah walked to the dining room window. A few seconds later, her grandparents' purple Vauxhall Corsa drove by. "Grannie and Grandpa Shand are here," she announced. She continued to the kitchen and returned with the bottle of ketchup.

"Sarah, I could have got that for you," her mother scolded.

"It's okay, Mum. I'm not an invalid. I can do things for myself." She squirted a dollop of the red sauce onto her plate then picked up a chip and dipped it in.

"I hope we're not disturbing anything," Sarah's grandmother called from the back hall.

"Come in, Mum. We're having our tea," Jimmy answered.

"Sorry son. We should have waited a while before coming but your mother insisted we come straight away. I know you eat later than us because of the farm chores but would she listen?"

"It's okay, Dad. At least sit down and have a cup of tea with us."

While they removed their coats, Moira pulled one of the small nesting tables over in front of the sofa. When her in-laws were comfortable, she disappeared into the kitchen. She returned with two steaming mugs prepared to their liking.

"After you left, Sarah, Dougie and I went on a hunt for the box of pictures that belonged to my da. How did you know about the photograph and the painting?"

"I told you earlier Gran, the day I married Robert he hired a photographer to come to the mansion."

"Oh yes, that's right. You did. But the painting? How did you know about it?"

"That was just a guess. It seemed like something Robert might do."

The elder Mrs. Shand produced the two pictures she'd set aside earlier. "I think everyone should look at these," she said holding them out to Sarah.

She took them. The picture of the black and white photograph was dark. The frame surrounding it made it look like a daguerreotype. The paper was stiff like card stock. Sarah turned it over. The back looked like a postcard. The washed out color picture of the painting hinted at the color of the stone in the bride's ring. It was about the same size as the first one but not printed on heavy card stock. "I'm going to scan these and see if they look any better printed on A4 paper."

Before anyone had a chance to view the images, Sarah clutched them in her hand and escaped from the room.

Once in her father's office, she turned on the computer. While she waited on it to boot up, she placed the two photos side by side on the desk. The portrait artist did a remarkable job given what he had to work with. As it was, she hadn't seen the wedding photographs until seeing this one now. Fate intervened and sent her back to her own time.

By now, the computer was ready. Sarah selected the scanner program and placed the photo of the picture in the scanner. In order to enlarge it to fit on a sheet of paper, she'd need to select a high resolution. The default in the software was 100 dpi. She changed it to 500 and started. The scanner whirred into life. She watched the light make its way along the bed in steps. When it reached the other end, it came back in one smooth pass.

Assured the ink jet printer had plenty of paper in it Sarah selected print followed by fit to page.

While it printed, she scanned the color photograph of the painting. She repeated the process with printing. After printing it in its faded out state, she clicked on the color restore option. Immediately, the picture came to life. The hues weren't exactly the same as Sarah remembered but they were much closer than before. She printed this version, too.

Photographs and printouts in hand, Sarah shut down the computer and returned to the family dining room. "Here you go," she said handing the items to her grandmother. "They can go back into Great-Grandad's things."

Thrusting the printouts at her parents, she cried, "Believe me now?" She took a deep breath and continued. "Look at my rings." She held her left hand out and pointed to the jewelry in the color pictures she'd printed.

"Sarah, this isn't funny. You've taken that ring and the other one from down at your grandmother's. Why on earth would you do such a thing?" her father yelled.

"She didn't, Jimmy. That's what I thought at first but no." Mrs. Shand extracted the silver ring chest from her purse and lifted the lid. "My mum's rings are right here." She took Sarah's hand and squeezed it.

Jimmy and Moira looked at the pictures and their daughter. They looked at Sarah's hand wearing the jewelry and the box holding his grandmother's wedding and engagement rings.

Sarah felt vindicated. Her parents appeared ready to accept what she'd told them since waking up in Aberdeen Royal Infirmary.

Rachel got up and peered at the papers in her parents' hands. "OMG! It *is* real. You *did* travel through time."

Early the next morning, Sarah returned to the stone circle. The fallen boulder she'd sat on from the time she was a wee girl was a welcome resting place. Catching her breath, she hoped for a clue that would lead her back to Robert and Jenny and the others. Everyone there, even the servants, felt like family to her. Weetshill mansion remained a ruin. The family farm stood at the bottom of the hill. Everything was as it should be in the present. But where was the scene from the past? Robert had spoken to her telling her to come back and she knew the way. She needed his help. His cryptic message meant nothing to her.

The cows in the fields walked to the drystane dykes as she passed on her way to the Kendonald Road. Since nothing happened at the stone circle, then the clue to get her back in time had to be there. She approached the scarred tree, expecting something to happen. Again there was no magic to propel her back to 1886 and Robert and Jenny. "Please tell me what to do? You need to be more clear. I don't understand your instructions. Please Robert. You say I know how to get back to you, but I don't. I need your help. I love you and Jenny and want to get back to you but I need you to tell me," she begged into the empty air.

Sarah's days followed the same routine. After she'd eaten and dressed, she went to the stone circle. If nothing happened there, Sarah ventured to the Kendonald Road. She stood on the grass verge hoping for something to transport her back to 1886. Trying to summon the magic, she walked to the tree where the Ford Ka came to rest and touched the scar on the trunk.

Each day she pleaded for Robert's help, but if he spoke to her, it was always the same. Those cryptic messages confused her. If she couldn't figure out what he meant, she would never get back to him. The shadows from her past loomed larger with each day. She wanted to dispel them and return to the time where she could live without the hassles of modern-day life.

She thought of David. He was such a nice bloke, so much like Robert and so unlike Blair. She would miss him a great deal. During her hospitalization, he'd been there almost every day. He came to see her on his rounds and even when he was off duty. It was down to him, too, that she didn't get transferred to Woodend.

41

Sarah woke well before daylight on the morning of the winter solstice. Her restlessness the past few days had become worse. She didn't know why and hoped it would pass. The lack of sleep was taking its toll on her. Padding to the en-suite's bathroom, she noticed the moon turning red. Sarah remembered reading this was the morning of the lunar eclipse. She slipped on a pair of jeans, a t-shirt, and a turquoise roll neck sweater. Her down-filled, winter coat hung in the wardrobe so she grabbed it and a toque, scarf and pair of mitts.

No one else in the house stirred. With the time, her father was apt to be out working in the barn or would soon be getting ready to go tend to his livestock. He did keep long hours. He worked hard, too hard she thought.

Slipping her feet into her Uggs, she closed the front door behind her. Sarah stood on the front step and watched the eclipse's progress in the star-studded sky. The urge to be at the stone circle during the event became overwhelming. She struggled into her coat as she picked her way across the frozen, snow covered field.

From the top of the hill, the view of the eclipse unfolding before her was spectacular. Was this the day she would get back to Robert and Jenny? Would the combination of the two events provide the much needed magic?

Cold from sitting on the fallen boulder, Sarah crept to the track leading to the Kendonald Road. The frozen ground was slippery and she had to be careful. The last thing she wanted was to fall and end up back in hospital. She'd seen enough of that place since emerging from the coma to last her a lifetime.

The eclipse progressed, darkening the sky even more making it difficult to see. A light skiff of snow covered the road running by the farm. It had drifted from the stone fences and the plastic-wrapped hay bales alongside.

When she came out at the main road, Sarah ensured she checked for traffic. The tree, where the car came to rest after striking her still bore the scar from the impact. She still had no memory of the actual accident. All she knew was what her parents told her.

Sarah removed a mitt and touched the imperfection on the trunk with her bare hand. Something strange happened. A buzzing sound began, softly at first, then growing louder, until it was unbearable. Despite clapping her hands over her ears, she could not silence the painful, droning noise.

Mrs. Shand poked her head around the edge of Sarah's door to see if she needed anything. The bed wasn't made but her daughter wasn't in it. No beam of light streamed out from under the bathroom door either, suggesting Sarah was in there.

Checking all the rooms downstairs she became more worried when Sarah wasn't found in any of them. Frantic, she ran upstairs and checked that level of the house, too. No trace of her daughter anywhere in the house.

A sound emanated from the back hallway and she hurried downstairs to see if it was Sarah. Nothing or no one was there.

Plunging her feet one at a time into her wellies, Mrs. Shand yanked a jacket off one of the hooks. She wrapped it around her shoulders and scampered towards the barn. A solitary light shone through one of the windows.

"Jimmy," she cried out. "I can't find Sarah anywhere. I've searched the house from bottom to top and back again. She's not there."

"Calm down. We'll find her. She's probably gone to that blasted stone circle again."

The air shimmered. Sarah's clothes transformed into a paisley pattern Victorian gown, and a heavy, long, black woolen cloak. Her forearm crutches and leg brace disappeared. Was it possible? Was she going back to Robert, Jenny and the others at Weetshill?

When the shimmering stopped, Sarah looked around. Things were the way she remembered them in the past. The tree trunk, albeit not as big around, was pristine with no sign of scarring. She looked at her clothing again to ensure it wasn't her imagination, and ran to Weetshill mansion.

Racing toward the house, Sarah worried about how, or if she should warn Robert about the impending fire that would take his life. Would he believe her? What would her returning to the past do to the course of history? Had she already altered the future by her original trip back to 1886?

What about her parents and sister? Could she leave them forever? Maybe it wouldn't be forever. Maybe there would be a way she could travel back and forth between now and then. Too many painful memories existed in the present.

Mr. and Mrs. Shand followed Sarah's footprints in the snow to the stone circle. She wasn't there either. More marks in the snow from her Uggs led across the hill to the gate and they followed them.

"What is she playing at?" Moira asked gripping her husband's arm tighter.

"I don't know, luv, but she deserves a good swift kick up the backside for putting us through this."

They followed the tracks to the Kendonald Road. At the scarred tree the footprints seemed to walk in circles. Since the surface of the road was free from snow any trace disappeared.

"Sarah," Mrs. Shand called out. "Sarah, where are you?"

Jimmy's voice echoed hers but it didn't make any difference. There was no reply.

"You don't suppose …," Mrs. Shand started.

"Nothing that girl does surprises me anymore. Come on, Moira." Jimmy took his wife's hand. When it was safe to cross he led her to the other side.

They picked up the impressions from Sarah's boots on the lane to Weetshill. Mr. and Mrs. Shand followed them until they grew faint and vanished.

Standing hand in hand, they gazed at the mansion in the distance. Moira blubbered, "She's where she needs to be, Jimmy."

"I know, luv. I know." He put his arms around his wife and held her close.

Mrs. Shand sobbed into her husband's chest. Her wee girl, her first born was gone. Lost to them like she would be if she had died in the accident. The more she thought about it, the harder she cried. "What are we going to do, Jimmy?" she wailed looking up at her husband's face. His eyes were wet with tears, too.

"Robert, Jenny," she yelled drawing near the front of the house. "It's Sarah. I'm back."

A curtain twitched in the library window. Sarah waved her arms over her head continuing toward the building.

When she reached for the knob, the front door flew open. She stumbled over the threshold into Robert's arms. "I'm home, Robert. I finally made it back home," she exclaimed.

"Sarah, I've been so worried about you. I thought I would never see you again," he replied pulling her to him. He held her close and brushed his lips against hers before kissing her.

Sarah wrapped her arms around him and returned the kiss happy to be back at Weetshill with him. For so long she had tried to find her way back but had been unsuccessful. Now, she was afraid that if she let go of Robert time would separate them yet again.

Feeling a tug on her skirt, Sarah looked down and saw Jenny looking up at her, eyes sparkling. "S-Sarah h-home," the little girl stammered.

"Yes, I'm home sweetie." Sarah knelt and hugged the child as tight as she could.

Robert scooped Jenny up in one arm and pulled Sarah back to him. The three embraced; their family complete once more.

Also by Melanie Robertson-King

A Shadow in the Past
(4RV Publishing)

The Consequences Collection
Tim's Magic Christmas
The Secret of Hillcrest House
(King Park Press)

Cole's Notes (A Short Story)
EFD1: Starship Goodwords – a cross genre anthology
(CARRICK PUBLISHING, 2012)

MELANIE ROBERTSON-KING

http://www.melanierobertson-king.com

Melanie Robertson-King has always been a fan of the written word. Growing up as an only child, her face was almost always buried in a book from the time she could read. Her father was one of the thousands of Home Children sent to Canada through the auspices of The Orphan Homes of Scotland, and she has been fortunate to be able to visit her father's homeland many times. She even met the Princess Royal (Princess Anne) at the orphanage where he was raised.

www.ingramcontent.com/pod-product-compliance
Lightning Source LLC
Chambersburg PA
CBHW050508260626
47157CB00004B/1236